Escape from Nowhere

Stacey Womack

Published by Stacey Womack, 2020.

I'm dedicating this book to M. Chris Johnson, who was the first to read this book in it's rawest form. Her belief in the story and encouragement to me are the only reasons this story isn't still sitting in my computer unseen. Thank you for the many, hours, weeks, and months you helped me add flesh to this idea.

This book is also dedicted to Abuse Recovery Ministry Services because it contains the message they teach, that we all need to believe. You are chosen, valued, and loved. If you struggle with believing this or found fear holding you back because of life's heartaches, this message is for you. www.abuserecovery.org

A portion of all proceeds is being given to help victims/survivor of domestic violence through Abuse Recovery Ministry Services.

Prologue

Timorous forced herself to run as fast as she could; her heart pounded against her chest and sweat ran down her back. The muscles in her legs burned, and she pumped her arms wildly. Dried dirt matted the thick strands of hair that hung around her bug-bitten face. She glanced over her shoulder. The large thing chasing her seemed somehow familiar. An Obliterist. She'd been warned they would be here in Obscurity, where no one traveled.

The twisted trees of the dense jungle-like forest took on an almost monster-like appearance. The thorns in the underbrush cut her clothes and skin. She'd lost a shoe and now her foot bled where it wasn't caked in mud.

She'd only come because she'd been told it was a matter of life and death, but the protection she'd been promised had not appeared.

This Obliterist was at least thirteen feet tall. His dark leathery skin bore an almost orange sheen. Large claw-like hands and feet made it easy for him to thrash his way through the thick forest. Something like hair hung from the top of his large, oddly shaped head to his muscular shoulders. A scar ran down his face, right through one dead eye.

Timorous darted back and forth in an irregular pattern to confuse her foe, but it didn't seem to work. She ran down a small hill, finally gaining a bit of distance, but then tripped on a rock. Timorous slammed to the ground hard, with a loud *oomph*. It took her a moment to realize what had happened. She lay there breathing heavily and spitting out the dirt now crusted to her lips. *What's the use? There's no way to outrun this thing.* Hadn't her life been simpler before she began this journey, this quest? Before she met *him*? Were all the promises just lies? What a fool she'd been to believe the mystery man.

The creature charged down the hill and slid to a halt. His one black, deep-set eye widened with triumph, and an evil grin slowly pulled at the corners of his scarred mouth.

Chapter 1

Two weeks earlier and deep in thought . . .

Timorous's small hand was tucked into her father's warm grasp as they stood before a black casket.

"Say good-bye to your mother, Timorous."

At five years old, she was confused by what had happened to her mother. One day she was there, the next, gone. Timorous stood shaking slightly—whether from the cold or the fear of the unknown, she wasn't sure.

Timorous looked up at her father's stoic face. The only sign of grief was a hint of red around the rims of his eyes. "Where did she go, Daddy?"

Without looking at her, "Where people go when they die." His tone held no emotion. The discussion had ended.

That night and many to follow, Timorous wondered about the mysterious death of her mother. They'd been close. They often took walks in the park, her mother pointing out the different flowers. They'd talked about whatever came to mind, even things that were forbidden. Her mother warned her not to speak of such things with anyone else. Kneeling and holding Timorous' small hands, her mother's voice was gentle but serious, "Promise me you won't tell anyone about our secret talks."

Timorous jumped when a customer thumped a fishing vest and several boxes of ammunition down on her counter. Startled out of the memory, she scanned the items.

She worked at Outfit Outlet, the local retail store that boasted green and black throughout its decor. Clothing for sports, everyday wear, and sports equipment hung neatly on racks in their designated areas. This average kind of job fit her, someone who didn't like taking risks.

Timorous worked at the second checkout stand in a row of eight. Being able to see who entered the store gave her a feeling of security. She rarely spoke to customers except to say, "Did you find everything you needed?" which her boss required of her. She almost never made eye contact: one of her perfectly honed avoidance tactics.

Timorous tucked a loose stand of brown shoulder-length hair behind her ear—a nervous habit she hadn't been able to break. As she finished with the customer, the familiar ding-dong announced another guest. Timorous peeked up but looked again when a wave of energy swirled around her. Several others in the checkout line glanced toward the door as well. Mesmerized, she stared as the man walked around the line of registers toward the camping section. Was it possible to feel someone's presence?

Timorous hadn't gotten a good look at his face, just the back of his blue jeans and leather jacket. Feeling drawn to him, she twisted around, concentrating her attention in his direction. Her foot caught on the back of her ankle as she turned to get a good look at his face. This precarious position caused her to lose her balance and she fell to the floor.

Heat rushed to her face as she jumped to her feet. The next woman in line rolled her eyes.

"I'm sorry." Timorous avoided the woman's disapproving gaze, pulling her hair behind both ears. As she scanned the items, she took one last quick peek toward the man. Just before disappearing into the camping section, he briefly gazed her way.

Was he smiling at me? No, more like he was laughing at me. How embarrassing. I just made a fool of myself.

She struggled through the next twenty minutes of work, making mistakes as she wondered who he was.

Her supervisor scowled at her. By the time Timorous made her fifth mistake, her supervisor arrived at her counter. "Timorous, why don't you take your break early?" The woman crossed her arms and lifted her chin. "You don't seem very focused right now."

"Um, sorry. I promise I'll do better." Her shoulders slumped.

"Flip your light off after the next customer."

"Yes, ma'am." She couldn't afford to lose this job.

She silently berated herself for acting so foolishly without noticing her last customer. There, right in front of her stood the mystery man. Again, she felt a strange sense of energy. He laid a plaid shirt and socks on the counter. Timorous quickly looked down as her heart raced.

He cleared his throat. When she glanced his way, she noticed his unusual golden eyes. They were so intensely extraordinary. He smiled, and Timorous embarrassed herself by staring at him.

He quietly laughed and she quickly diverted her gaze with an "I'm sorry." Her face grew warm. "I'll just run this transaction for you."

"No problem." He continued smiling.

Timorous struggled to find the price tag on the shirt, let alone run the machine. After several failed attempts at folding the shirt the way she'd been taught, she broke into a sweat. She finally gave up and reached for a plastic bag. In the process, she knocked his socks to the floor. With a nervous giggle, she picked them up and stuffed everything into the bag with as much grace as a gorilla.

"My name is Radimar. What's yours?"

Her head snapped up to face him. She again found herself lost in those wonderful pools of gold. *Did he just introduce himself and ask my name? He's probably going to report what a horrible job I'm doing.* Timorous usually picked up on other people's intentions fairly quickly, but at this point, she was so beside herself she couldn't think clearly.

She finished the transaction and handed him his bag. Radimar looked at her name badge, then leaned forward and said in a voice she could only describe as kind, yet commanding, "Thank you, Timorous. I hope we meet again soon." Then he left.

Timorous stood motionless, still sensing his presence even though he was no longer there. *What just happened?*

"Tims, who was that?" Hearsay, her best friend, hurried over from station three. Hearsay always used her nickname, complaining "Timorous" was too many syllables to bother with.

"Come on. I'm taking my break with you." Hearsay wrapped her arm around Tims and began moving toward the break room.

The moment they were out of earshot of others, Hearsay began her inquisition. "Who was that? He was cute." She sighed dreamily. "What did he say to you? Was it inappropriate? Are you in shock? Tims. Hello, can you hear me?" She shook Tims' arm gently. "Why are you acting so strangely?"

"His eyes were so amazing and his smile . . ." Timorous sighed.

"Who was he? What did he say? What about his eyes?"

When Tims remained mute, Hearsay move to stand right in front of her. "Snap out of it. I've never seen you so interested in a man before. You've got to give me some details. I'm dying here."

"He said his name was Radimar."

Hearsay's eyes widened to the size of miniature saucers. "Radimar. You mean the guy the whole town's been talking about?"

"You know I don't really watch much news."

Hearsay groaned. "Radimar has been the talk of the cluster of Nowhere for the last couple weeks. He just seems to appear and strange things happen when people are around him. No one knows where he came from." Hearsay waved a hand in the air. "Some say he came from a cluster outside of Nowhere, which is ridiculous because we know no one travels between clusters. Rumors about him have been spreading all over Uncertainty."

Hearsay clutched both of Tims' upper arms. "Details, girl, I need details. No one is going to believe we just met

Radimar." Hearsay practically salivated over the juicy information.

Timorous considered pointing out that *we* didn't meet him, *she* did, and he said her name with that amazing voice of his. She kept her thoughts to herself about how she felt when he was near her.

Hearsay leaned closer. "You looked so stunned. Did he ask you out?"

Tims hadn't been on a date in years, nor had she even considered dating now. "No, that's ridiculous. You know I don't date. And why would anyone like that ever choose me? He asked my name, and like a dummy I just stood there gawking at him. I'm totally embarrassed. Hopefully, I won't ever see him again." She wished Hearsay would just drop the subject.

"What are you talking about? He wouldn't have asked your name if he wasn't interested," Hearsay gushed.

"He just tried to make polite conversation. Can we drop it? It was just a chance meeting. He could have ended up at anyone's station." Tims glanced around. "People are looking at us." Tims avoided drawing attention to herself at all costs. "Look, I'll tell you more when we get off our shift."

Hearsay's shoulders dropped as she dragged herself away from Tims. But Hearsay hadn't gone fifty feet before telling another employee about her and Tims' meeting Radimar. Timorous shook her head and walked back to her station.

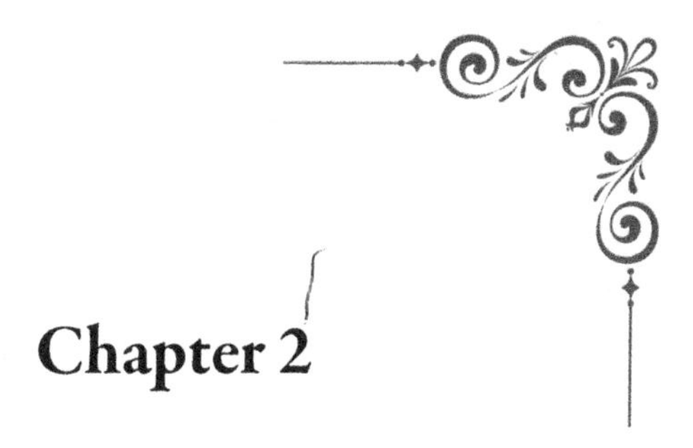

Chapter 2

When her mother died, Timorous was left her with a distant father and, soon after, an abusive stepmother and older brother.

"You worthless piece of dung," her stepmother told her often. The verbal assaults took a toll on her fragile self-esteem.

Her stepbrother often flicked her hair in her face and called her, "Ugly plain cow." After she turned ten, he began sneaking into her room at night to do unthinkable things. His threats, along with the constant spoken and emotional abuse by her stepmother, left her feeling worthless and powerless. She left home as soon as she had saved enough money but was never able to outrun the nightmares that plagued her.

Timorous turned to shut her apartment door and caught sight of herself in the mirror next to it. She felt rather average at five-feet-five with blue eyes and light brown, wavy hair that hung just past her shoulders.

To create a sense of safety, Tims practiced regular routines. She perfected many skills to protect herself from this dangerous world—skills like how to stay in the background and avoid eye contact, therefore skirting conversations.

Hearsay, her only friend, was sure to arrive in a few minutes for more juicy details that she would probably embellish when telling others, making it sound more glamorous than it was. Tims flipped on the TV and went to the kitchen to make a salad for two. She glanced into her living room when she heard the newscaster reporting on Radimar. She hurried to the living room, carrot in hand, and parked herself on the ottoman in front of the TV.

"Who is this unusual man called Radimar? Is he a doctor? Is he a magician? Some amazing things seem to happen when he's around. Mr. and Mrs. Resident reported Radimar stopped to talk to them while they were on their way to the doctor with their daughter who was ill with a fever. Once he left them, their daughter seemed completely fine."

Newscaster Corra held her mic out to Query Mole, owner of a local diner, "How did Radimar answer when you asked him where he came from?"

Query, a short heavyset fellow, grumbled, "He gave me some kind of cryptic nonsense saying, 'Where everyone comes from.'"

"KILZ News is looking into the possible meaning of this. We've been unable to locate Radimar for an interview. Questions need answering, but why is it so difficult to find him? Yet the good citizens of Nowhere agree that whoever he is, you can't deny his impact on our cluster."

They went on to interview other people. Some had spoken with him; some were speculating. Some praised him; some were suspicious.

Timorous sat leaning forward, intently focused on the TV. She'd hoped they had interviewed Radimar. Timorous wondered if anyone else had felt his presence like she did. Secretly she hoped not—that somehow, she was special. Even thinking about his eyes, she felt his presence near her and sighed.

A knock on the door startled Tims. Hearsay rushed into the room. Normally, Timorous always locked the door and the two interior locks the moment she arrived home. Only when she expected Hearsay to visit did she refrain from this cautious behavior. Hearsay thought it silly and had teased her about it in the past.

Tims barely finished saying hello when Hearsay darted past her and squealed. "Here it comes." She took Tims' place on the ottoman and turned up the volume.

"What?"

There, in living color stood her friend, being interviewed by KILZ News. Stunned, Tims slowly lowered herself down on the couch.

"We have Hearsay Blather here. When did you meet Radimar?" the newscaster asked.

"I . . . I mean, my friend Timorous and I met him today at our store, Outfit Outlet." Hearsay gushed, flashing her best movie-star smile and batting her pretty eyes.

Timorous gasped. "You gave them my name?"

"Shh. There's more." Hearsay bubbled and bounced on the ottoman, flapping her hands toward Tims to keep her quiet.

"And what was your impression of him?"

"He is really amazing and so polite. He asked us our names. Oh, his eyes were golden." The Hearsay on the screen clasped her hands together and looked up in a dream-like state.

The news reporter went on to other people who said they'd had contact with Radimar. The report ended with, "So there you have it. Radimar is causing quite a stir in Uncertainty. The governor of the cluster of Nowhere would like to give him a proper welcome. Radimar, if you are watching, please contact us. I'm Corra Spondance and this is KILZ News."

Timorous turned the TV off.

"Wait," Hearsay jumped up. "They might show my interview again."

Frowning, Timorous clutched the remote and planted herself in front of the TV.

Hearsay rushed on. "I heard they were recording around the corner from our store, so I ran there right after we got off work. Didn't I look great? I mean, I could have looked even better if I hadn't worked all day, but didn't my hair look shiny? I made sure I stood with my shoulders back like a model. I thought I saw the camera guy wink at me. I'm sure someone is going to discover me and my talent."

Rare anger filled Timorous. "How could you? You lied and . . . and you told everyone my name for the whole world to hear."

"I didn't lie. I just included myself. I couldn't just say my friend met him. They might not have interviewed me at all. Didn't I look great? I think the camera likes me. Maybe I'll start taking acting lessons. What do you think?"

"What kind of creeps are going to start coming around to find me now?" *What if my stepbrother comes to find me?* Tims' heart raced.

"Oh, let it go, Tims. Aren't you exaggerating a little? The whole world isn't going to see it. You know the news in each cluster is separate from the rest."

Many years ago, Prince Peccadillo slowly worked to take control of the world. His lies infiltrated the media, commercials, movies, and television shows. Once he had succeeded, a strange forest-like jungle, now called Obscurity, grew around each cluster. Within a month, the vegetation became impassable.

"You know each cluster is a world unto itself and that travel from one cluster to another is forbidden ever since Prince Peccadillo took charge."

Peccadillo controlled the airwaves. Wi-Fi was a thing of the past. Computers, phones, and TVs all used cables and were limited to each specific cluster. Each cluster knew very little about the other clusters these days. In school, the teachers spoke of the other clusters only in history class. They were taught the clusters were created for their safety. Only a few old-timers remembered what life was like before Prince Peccadillo took over, and no one listened to the elderly anymore.

Radimar's appearance created many questions for Timorous and everyone. How could he just appear in a cluster when travel was no longer possible? Had he stayed in the background until now? And what about the whisperings about him coming from Bliss, which was thought to be a myth. Talking about Bliss wasn't only discouraged but considered risky.

"I can't believe you said my name on television. Did you even think about me?" Tims whispered to Hearsay. In truth, the strength of her anger shocked her. She had so carefully buried her emotions and the many memories of her ugly past.

"I was thinking about you." Hearsay stuck out her lower lip and batted the lashes of her sappy eyes. "This is the most exciting thing that's happened to you. Knowing you, you wouldn't tell anyone. Where's the fun in that? Come on, Tims; live a little. Enjoy your moment of stardom. I know I am." She hugged Tims, then stood back. With a smug smile, she folded her arms across her chest.

"I can't believe you." Avoiding further conflict, Tims returned to the kitchen to finish the salad.

Hearsay followed her and leaned against the counter. As she watched Tims aggressively chop the carrot, Hearsay mischievously smiled. "Tims, I know you're upset, but you don't have to take it out on that carrot."

Tims looked up. She never could resist Hearsay's grin. They both giggled. Maybe she was making too big a deal out of this. By tomorrow it would be old news. Probably no one even paid attention to Hearsay's little stunt—she hoped.

There was a knock at the door and Timorous went rigid. No one other than Hearsay visited her. Had someone come looking for her already?

"Relax." Hearsay walked toward the door. "I ordered pizza for us to celebrate." She turned the knob and in walked Meddling.

She'd lived above Timorous for the last year and dropped by only when she wanted something or wanted to know something that was none of her business. Timorous decided early on that Meddling couldn't be trusted. Hearsay disagreed. In fact, they seemed to connect almost immediately.

"Hearsay, I didn't expect to see you here."

She's lying. Timorous frowned.

"I just saw the evening news and, wow, there you were." Meddling's tone dripped with honey. Obviously, she'd seen Hearsay enter the building.

Hearsay clapped her hands together. "I know. Wasn't it amazing? Who would have thought we'd be celebrities in our own town?"

"Tell me more." Meddling planted herself on the couch as if she came over regularly. She hadn't even said hello to Timorous.

Hearsay jabbered on about her fictitious encounter with Radimar. Somehow the story morphed to Radimar taking Hearsay's hand and kissing it.

Excited, Meddling added, "A friend of my best friend's daughter headed out to the doctor for some kind of treatment. I think for cancer. Anyway, Radimar stopped and talked with them, and when they got to the hospital, the tests came back normal. They had no explanation. They're calling him some kind of miracle healer."

"Really? That's amazing. And I got to hold his hand." Hearsay giggled, bringing the attention back to herself.

"You're so lucky. Maybe he gave you some kind of power when he touched you?" Meddling looked hopeful. "I have this growth on my foot that just won't go away."

"I don't think it works like that." Hearsay rushed on to cover up her embellished story.

Tims stifled a laugh, knowing Hearsay really didn't want to touch Meddling's foot.

The pizza delivery person arrived and the three young women finished off the pizza and salad quickly, Meddling and Hearsay chattering away.

Listening until well past dinner, Tims was amazed how they analyzed Radimar from so many different angles, especially since they had never met him and knew so little about him.

Finally, Timorous couldn't take it anymore. She gave a big yawn and stretched like she was seriously tired. They didn't take the hint. In fact, they barely noticed her. She walked around the couch to stand behind Meddling, out of her view and tried again.

This time Hearsay caught the gesture. Standing abruptly, "Well, I think it's time for me to head home. It's been quite a day." She looked at Tims sympathetically.

Meddling had no choice but to follow. Timorous opened the door, Hearsay mouthed, "Sorry" to her and gave a sheepish grin.

Timorous headed to bed early and laid there a long time thinking about how she'd felt when she met Radimar. She wondered if he really was a good guy, what with the reports of healing and how peaceful she had felt around him, or if he had ulterior motives in stirring up the town. She hoped he was good. It felt good to be near him. When sleep finally came that night, she slept better than she ever remembered and without a single nightmare from her past.

Chapter 3

Prince Peccadillo who ruled over the Netherworld and all the clusters, paced back and forth, arms flailing. He muttered angrily and screamed an occasional obscenity.

Usher, Prince Peccadillo's attendant, stood nervously off to the side. He both feared and admired his master. Being the Prince's attendant came with its perks. He held one of the highest ranks in the Netherworld. While only five feet tall, his cunning nature had served him well. His red hair spiked out in all directions. Some thought he worked to look taller since he sometimes wore thick platform shoes. The red hair complemented his ruddy, scaly skin. He always wore a suit, as did most of the high-ranking officials who lived in the Netherworld. His broken lizard-like tail hung out of the back of his coat but dragged crookedly along the ground. He had a straight, broad nose and beady eyes.

The Prince stood six-feet-six-inches tall and had broad shoulders and a slim waistline. His face could make anyone swoon. His high cheekbones and mesmerizing gray eyes drew the humans to him. His jet-black hair was trimmed to perfection. His full lips, when pulled back, revealed a set of perfect white teeth.

Peccadillo chose black for all his suits because it was void of light. He rarely wore any other colored shirts unless making an appearance for the media and, on rare occasions, meeting with cluster officials. He was both beautiful and terrifying to behold. His pleasant looks were only a façade he used to hide the truth about the curse he incurred by choosing to commit treason against King Iam.

Only when he became enraged did his true form present itself—that of a terrifying dragon. Nowadays his human form worked better to persuade the people of the clusters. It took many years, but he finally succeeded in his evil plan to control the humans.

The Netherworld monitored all the happenings in the clusters but could not be reached by mere humans, at least not while they were alive. Its surface resembled the forest-like jungle called Obscurity, as a ruse, a trick to hide the evil underground activity.

The Prince had sculpted the Netherworld by carving caves into rooms and hallways that twisted and turned into smaller rooms. The inside was only dimly lit. Construction was constantly underway to add more space for those who arrived daily to be held hostage in the dark emptiness until the coming Great War.

The vast army who worked for Prince Peccadillo all had the same black hearts and desire for evil. They'd chosen to follow him in his treason against King Iam.

Usher had seen his master in a foul mood before, but today seemed especially bad as the Prince's fierce gray eyes sought him out.

Under his angry steady gaze, Usher began to sweat. Breaking the silence, Prince Peccadillo growled. "How did we miss this? Where were the guards?"

Usher knew exactly what he meant. It had been all over the news in the metropolis of Nowhere. Here in his capital city, the Prince observed all within his control. Each cluster had no knowledge of their neighboring clusters, but the Netherworld saw it all.

Radimar not only made it to Nowhere but was stirring up trouble. The lack of travel between the clusters kept everyone ignorant, just the way Prince Peccadillo wanted it. It allowed him more control. But Radimar's appearance caused people to question his system.

"How could the Guard allow this to happen? Our lines were secure. He has no right to interfere with my possessions," the Prince bellowed.

Usher stood completely still, waiting for Peccadillo's command.

"Usher, call the Commander of Obscurity."

When Usher hesitated, Prince Peccadillo screamed, "Now!"

Usher ran out the door, but he hesitated for good reason. Commander Deamon, the commander of the entire borderland known as Obscurity, was not the type of character anyone wanted to have contact with.

Three times larger than any human, his size alone frightened the bravest servant. While his structure looked similar to a human, his dark leathery skin had a red sheen to it when the light hit it just right. His hands hung like a large gorilla's but each long finger boasted a six-inch claw. His nose was large, wide, and slightly crooked, as were his yellowed teeth. His hollow eyes seemed empty of life.

Darkness clung to the Commander, and those within a five-mile radius felt his evil presence. Commander Deamon led the Obliterist Guard and all others in Obscurity, second in command only to the Prince himself. Usher had met him only once before, but that was enough.

He took pride in being the Prince's assistant. Others bowed slightly as he walked by. Many worked their way up the ladder by their connections with those higher up, not to mention lying, cheating, or even destroying those ahead of them. And Usher had toiled hard for this position. A lot of relationships and lives had been destroyed on his way here. He wasn't about to risk losing it now by not completing this unpleasant task.

He walked briskly, feigning confidence but worried those he passed could see the concern on his face. His mind filled with strategies on how he might best handle this predicament. There must be someone else he could send in his place. Going into Obscurity alarmed him. While he outranked most in that miserable area, they didn't care and would treat him as if he were a mere human to be toyed with. It was insulting, not to mention terrifying. They might destroy him without even knowing who his orders came from.

Deep in thought, he turned a corner and ran straight into Deceit. Usher hated him. He always appeared at the worst times. It wouldn't have surprised Usher if he'd listened in and was just waiting for him to come this way.

"What's your hurry, my friend? You look concerned. How can I be of help?"

Usher caught himself before responding with a snarky comment. Instead he smiled politely. "I'm just in the middle of an important task." Usher immediately realized he'd said too much even with his short answer.

"Really," Deceit purred. "Tell me about it. I'm sure I can help."

Deceit could never be trusted. With him, what was up was down, yes was no. Working with him would be absolutely impossible. He'd weaseled his way into many situations to better himself while undercutting those who were given orders.

Usher knew if he didn't watch himself, Deceit would take everything he had worked hard for. Just looking at his thin wiry frame with his pointed fingernails and crooked smile made Usher angry. "I appreciate your offer, but this matter requires someone, let's say, of a higher stature." Usher watched to see Deceit's reaction as he let his meaning sink in—and he wasn't disappointed.

Red crept up Deceit's dark neck, and his mocking smile turned flat. "Well, I have pressing matters of my own. You should watch yourself, my friend. Not everyone is as willing to help you as I am, if you know what I mean." He walked away.

Usher smiled to himself.

As much as he did not want to be the one seeking out Deamon, if he sent someone else and they failed, it would be his life. He stood taller and decided to take the risk to personally seek out Deamon. Usher hurried down the hall to his personal suite, another perk of working for the Prince. The door swung open before he placed his bony fingers on the doorknob.

"Welcome home, great Usher."

Usher too, had his own helper. Aide was a short, rather round fellow with bulbous green eyes. His scaly skin had a pale green sheen to it. Each of his flat feet had only three toes. His hands were similar, with two-inch black claws at the ends of his six fingers. He stood only three feet tall and was hunched over. Aide lacked in brains and didn't have much skill, making him a perfect helper. Usher never worried about Aide scheming against him. He had it too good right here.

"You're back early. Is anything wrong?"

Usher threw his cloak at Aide, landing it on his head. "Yes, I've been ordered to seek out Commander Deamon," Usher whined.

As Aide hung up the cloak, he tensed with the mention of Deamon's name. "That . . . that's terrifying. What will you do?" His hands shook.

Usher pretended to show no fear. "I will go, of course, you fool."

Aide averted his eyes.

Usher plopped down in his favorite chair. "The worst part is I have to go to Obscurity to find him. From my previous experience with the filthy inhabitants of the place, they aren't going to treat me respectfully. They are likely to undermine my efforts."

"You'll show them your strength," Aide reassured him. "They just need to see who they're dealing with." He ran to the wardrobe and fetched Usher's black cape and the official crest that proved he worked for Prince Peccadillo's high court. "Is there anything else you need, Great Usher?"

Usher scowled at Aide, annoyed by his minion's apparent eagerness to see him on his way. He walked to his wall of knives. Collecting them was his hobby. They had all been used in battle and each still held the dried blood of his enemies. He picked up a large machete, put his nose to the blade, and inhaled deeply. "Ahh, the smell of death. I will need this as well." He swung it through the air, missing Aide by only an inch.

Aide stood wide-eyed with his back flattened against the wall.

Usher laughed wickedly.

Aide gulped and slid along the wall. "Will there be anything else I can assist you with?" He kept eyeing the exit, clearly wanting to leave.

"You may go." Usher waved a hand carelessly to dismiss him. Aide ran out the door.

Usher eyed his machete and practiced a few slices through the air. "I just need to show them who they're dealing with. I will not show fear, and with my head held high, I will put them in their place."

LOOKING BACK AT USHER'S door, Aide ran down the hallway and encountered Deceit.

"Hold up, my friend," Deceit said slyly. "You seem to be upset. What seems to be the matter?" He stroked Aide's head.

"Ush—Usher almost cut my head off in there." Aide pointed his chubby thumb back toward the door he'd just exited and placed his other hand on his thick neck, somewhere under his layers of skin.

"Oh my. What the Abyss is he so upset about? What did you do?" Deceit asked innocently.

"No, no, it's nothing like that. The Great Usher has an important command to fulfill and happened to be practicing with one of his swords."

Deceit chuckled. "Well, it must be very important for him to need his sword."

"And his crest and cape, as well," Aide announced with pride.

Deceit rubbed his chin and furrowed his brows. "Do tell." He moved closer, as if he were Aide's best friend with whom he often shared secrets.

"Oh, I couldn't do that." Aide leaned toward Deceit, placing his hand to the side of his mouth while still looking back at the door.

Deceit bent down to listen.

"The orders are always top secret," Aide whispered.

"Aide, you and I go back a long way. You can trust me." Deceit flashed a crooked, yellow-toothed smile.

Aide eyed him suspiciously.

"Come on, my friend. What fun is it to have a secret if you can't share it?"

Just as Aide opened his mouth, Usher rushed out of his suite but stopped cold, eyeing Deceit and Aide.

Usher's body stiffened. "What the Abyss are you doing, Aide? Have you been sharing top-secret information with him?"

"N—no, your greatness. I would never share your orders." Aide cowered, bowing down to the ground.

Usher shook with anger as he glared at Deceit, who now leaned against the wall, arms crossed, as if nothing had happened.

Usher stomped in Deceit's direction with his machete raised high in the air. "I know what you're up to, Deceit, you slimy swindler."

"Calm yourself, Usher. Your little helper and I were just passing the time of day. Nothing of importance passed his lips." Deceit gave a disappointed smile.

Usher swung the machete at Deceit, who moved quickly out of the way and down the hall. A loud clang came as the blade struck the wall next to Aide, who still bowed low. "Don't you ever talk to him," Usher hissed at Aide. "Do you hear me? He can't be trusted."

"Yes, my Great Usher," Aide whimpered and crawled to his living quarters.

Chapter 4

Timorous woke the next morning with a full-body, arms-spread-out stretch. She laid there wondering what had changed. *Why do I feel lighter? Is this happiness?* She lingered in bed a little longer, hoping not to lose this newfound feeling, as if it might disappear the moment she put her feet on the floor. To her surprise, the feeling remained.

While absentmindedly brushing her teeth, she imagined Radimar's eyes looking back at her in the mirror, searching the depths of her soul. She shook her head in disgust at her silliness.

As she dressed for work, she scolded herself. *This is crazy. I have responsibilities. Come on, Tims, pull it together.* Her sense of reason and fear, which seemed to be her constant companion, quickly crowded out her happiness.

She lived less than a mile from work, so she usually walked, except in the winter when the days were shorter. She felt it safest not to walk home in the dark. As she approached Outfit Outlet, she noticed a small crowd standing outside the main entrance.

That's strange. People don't line up to shop at Outfit Outlet even on sale days. She checked her watch. Still ten minutes before they opened. *Was there something special happening today I've forgotten?* She checked her uniform—black pants, green shirt, green and black visor—to make sure she hadn't forgotten anything.

The crowd parted to let her through. People cupped their hands on the window, trying to see in. As she neared the door, an old woman, who stood at eye level with her name badge and yelled, "Hey, everyone, I think she's one of them."

Timorous started fumbling with her keys, but just as the crowd moved to converge on her, the door opened. Someone grabbed her arm and quickly pulled her in before shutting the door again. She stood stunned, looking out at the people who were now banging on the door, but it was nothing compared to the scene behind her.

Timorous turned around to find every employee, from the shelf stockers to the cashiers, staring at her. Right in front of the group stood her boss, Officious, and her best friend, Hearsay, with a big movie star smile across her face.

"Here's our other celebrity," bellowed Officious.

Tims never really cared for him. Not that he was a bad person, but because he was lazy. He liked to bark orders at everyone but rarely offered to help, even when they were short-staffed.

Officious wore a clean Outfit Outlet shirt spread across his large belly and tucked into his black trousers. This was the first time Tims had seen him in a shirt that didn't have some kind of food stain down the front. Her eyes went back to Hearsay, who was still smiling.

"I have an announcement to make." Officious pulled up on his black belt. "Today Hearsay and Timorous are being given the honor of sharing Employee of the Month for putting Outfit Outlet on the map.

"Thanks to them, we're going to have a great month. Since Hearsay and Timorous met this mysterious Radimar fellow, everyone is talking about the fact that he shopped here. And, well, the phone hasn't stopped ringing. I even got a call from the local news. Do you see those people just waiting to come in?" He pointed at the door as he made eye contact with each employee.

"And we expect more. We are advertising to the whole community. 'Outfit Outlet, Where Important People Shop.'

"Now, for a few ground rules. No customers are allowed to talk to our Employees of the Month unless they come to the checkout stand to purchase an item. Got that, everyone? You need to protect our local celebrities."

Everyone nodded in excited agreement.

They've all gone mad. Tims felt the heat rise to her face and her stomach tighten.

She knew this had nothing to do with protecting her or Hearsay. This was all about the sales.

"Okay, everyone, to your stations," Officious said. "Two minutes and counting until opening. You girls take the two front registers. I want people to see you as they walk in. Armor will guard you against non-paying customers. Remember, they need to purchase items before asking about your meeting with this Ramerd guy."

"Radimar," Hearsay quickly corrected.

Officious ignored her.

Hearsay and Timorous gathered their tills and prepared for the day's work.

"Isn't this great, Tims?"

Timorous said nothing but gave her an "I can't believe you" look.

"Oh, come on. This will be a new adventure for you. It'll be fun, you'll see." With that, Hearsay flipped her blond ponytail around and marched to her post.

Tims watched her leave. Cute and spunky Hearsay looked like she'd been a gymnast and always dressed in the latest fashion. Tims wished she had her confidence.

The moment the doors were unlocked, the crowd pushed their way and headed straight for the two of them. Thankfully, Armor blocked their way by spreading his arms and giving everyone a warning glare. Officious made his announcement to the group about the rules. The crowd grumbled, their disappointment and frustration obvious.

To Tims' amazement, they didn't leave like she secretly hoped they would. The day wasn't as bad as she thought it might be, at least not after the first couple of hours. The first group was the worst. They found small items to purchase and rushed to her and Hearsay's registers. Some of the people were really annoying, asking ridiculous questions like, "Where does he live?" or, "Is he coming to see you again?" What bothered Timorous even more were the people who wanted to touch her. "Why do they want to touch me?" she asked Hearsay.

"They think his magic or power rubbed off on you, like Meddling thought last night."

People poured in all day. Tims thought it the way people acted was crazy. A few people tried to sneak past the "buying first rule," but Armor did a good job of moving them along.

Formerly in the military, Armor struck an imposing stance, his large muscular arms crossed over his broad chest and feet planted firmly apart, looking fiercely at anyone who dared to return his watchful gaze. Tims had grown to trust him even if they didn't speak often. Armor always treated others respectfully but used his stance to intimidate. He rarely had to intervene. Tims felt thankful for his presence today, especially when she had a hard time getting customers to leave her station.

Two of the earlier customers were an elderly couple. Tims hoped they'd be easy ones to deal with.

"Miss, Miss," they repeated when she didn't look up.

She could see from under her lashes they were leaning toward her. She looked up and did a double take.

Their faces were etched with concern.

"Did you find everything you needed?" she asked dutifully. For the life of her, she couldn't think of anything else to say.

The couple blinked at her and took one quick look at each other.

"Well," the woman said, "we were, um, wondering if you, um, were one of the young ladies who met Radimar?" Timorous gave a quick nod. The woman rushed on: "You see, we have a sweet grandson, Jed. He's only four years old." Her eyes welled up with tears. "He was diagnosed with incurable cancer last week." A tear rolled down her face. Her husband appeared to be on the brink of tears as well.

Tims quickly looked down at the items they planned to purchase: an action hero coloring book and crayons. She didn't even know Outfit Outlet carried these items. She felt her own emotions stirring but kept them in check. "I'm sorry to hear that."

They leaned over the counter clutching the edges with their aging, arthritic hands. The woman said, "We were hoping you could talk to Radimar about paying him a visit. We've heard he has some kind of healing power." Hope glinted in her eyes.

What did they expect of her? She didn't know where to find him or if he really did have healing abilities. "I . . . I'm sorry. I don't know where he lives or how to get a hold of him."

"But he was here yesterday, right?"

"Yes, but he didn't give me an address or his number." She blushed at the thought of him doing that.

"Please, Miss, we're desperate for our sweet Jed. You've got to help us." The elderly man wrapped his arm around his crying wife.

"I'm sorry. Really, I am. But if I see him again, I'll tell him about your grandson." Tims hoped this would help ease their pain.

They stared at her, and she stared back at them awkwardly for several moments. When she handed them their bag, they both latched on to her arm.

"Do you feel that, honey? Radimar's power is still in her. Maybe we can transfer it to Jed." They smiled broadly.

Tims tried pulling her arm back, but they hung onto her until Armor stepped up and gently put his large hands over theirs.

"That's enough. You need to move on so our employee can continue her work."

They looked stunned and a little afraid. Armor stood much taller and more powerful than they. The couple let go and mumbled their apologies. As they walked out, they glanced back one last time with a look of awe.

"Thank you, Armor. I think everyone's gone mad."

Armor just dipped his head to her and walked back to his position by the door.

A couple of male shoppers came to her counter several times wanting to know what Radimar purchased. Confused, she tried to describe his purchases but really couldn't remember all the details.

They brought up multiple plaid shirts. "Which one did he purchase? Do you remember what size he wore?"

Tims tried not to scowl at the ridiculousness of their questions. Officious watched with pleasure a short distance away. She smiled and did her best to answer them.

Hearsay received the same sort of questions. Several times she leaned over to ask Tims for the answers she didn't have, but Tims wasn't much help.

Tims especially struggled to remember which socks he had bought. After a man came to her station a fifth time with more socks, Officious pulled her aside and frowned. He raised a brow. "What seems to be the problem?"

"He wants to know which socks Radimar purchased and I can't remember."

Officious huffed, annoyed at her inability to handle the situation. He walked past her to the counter and looked down at the pile of socks the young man brought. He quickly picked through the pile to find the most expensive pair. "These are the socks our famous guest purchased," he announced loudly, making sure others heard him.

The young man eyed him suspiciously. "With all due respect, I'd like to know from the person who ran his transaction." The young man smiled at Tims and waited for her answer.

Officious stood frowning at her. She felt caught between her lack of memory and the possibility of losing her job. "Um, I think he's right. I mean, I know he's right. These socks were purchased by Radimar."

The young man smiled and purchased the socks and shirt. Tims found out later the store sold out of their entire stock of those expensive socks. Officious was notably happy.

The last few customers asked simpler questions. Tims relaxed a little. She didn't think she had talked that much in one day in her entire life. She yawned.

The final customer of the day came to her counter, a distinguished man in a business suit with a serious face. Tims glanced at him only once. His presence made her feel uncomfortable. Her heart beat a little faster, and her body went tense. She became almost robotic in her movements.

"So, you spoke with this mystery man?"

She nodded. Out of the corner of her eye, she realized Armor wasn't at his usual position by the door. Where had he gone? This guy intimidated her. If she could just make eye contact with Armor, he'd come intervene.

"Cat got your tongue or something," the man said condescendingly. "Did you speak to him or just ignore him like you're doing to me?"

She swallowed hard. "I spoke with him briefly." Tims kept looking down, chiding herself for her lack of confidence.

"You should be careful about who you talk to, especially when it comes to someone who is not from 'round here and no one can find." He held out his money for his purchase. When she reached to take it, he didn't let go, causing a small tug-of-war until Tims slowly looked up into his arrogant face.

His lips were a thin, tight line. His almost-black eyes bored into her. Clearly, he was warning her. He let go of the money, put on his dark sunglasses and left.

Chapter 5

The only way to reach Deamon was to venture into the borderland of Obscurity. The foliage was so dense it almost looked like the dead of night during the middle of the day. All who lived in this foul place were evil and bent on causing as much distress and pain as possible to anyone who entered. These creatures ranged from one-inch tall Sprites to very tall Obliterists. Deamon, the largest of all, served as their commander.

Usher disliked traveling through this dreaded place. The evil didn't bother him, but he felt Obscurity was below his station as Prince Peccadillo's royal assistant. He outranked most of the beings, yet they still treated him with disrespect.

He cloaked himself in a hooded black cape and now made his way out of the underground tunnel, exiting directly into Obscurity, a space of the unnatural, where even technology could find no airwave to travel through. This was not a well-traveled path. If not for his wearing the royal seal, he wouldn't survive more than an hour. Swinging his machete, he made his way through the overgrowth. At first, he swung with vigor, pretending to swing at Deceit.

Soon the local inhabitants of Obscurity took notice of him. He heard their excited whispers. The little pests probably didn't see much action here. They might try to make his travels difficult just for the fun of it. Sure enough, one dashed under Usher's feet, causing him to trip and fall.

"You vile creature. Leave me alone."

Another pushed him from behind while others bit at his ankles. Usher spewed curses on them all. "Don't you fools know who I am?"

The path grew more and more difficult. Almost everything had thorns or were poisonous to the touch. While none could cause his death, they still could be painful and extremely annoying to deal with.

After two exhausting hours of swinging his machete, Usher felt like he had made little progress. Eerie sounds caused the hairs on his back to rise. They were playing on his fears. This was the way of the Obliterists. The more fear they could cause, the stronger they became. It was a vicious cycle.

Deamon was the most terrifying. He never hid his hideous dark face or arrogant scowl. His body was covered in the blackest leathery skin Usher had seen on any Obliterist. Usher shuddered at the thought of meeting him. Trying not to think about it, he decided to focus his hopes on possibly seeing Miss Enchantress.

Miss Enchantress was Deamon's personal secretary of sorts. With her high cheekbones and full red lips, her beauty was beyond compare. Over her perfectly sculpted curves, she usually wore a long flowing white gown, as gorgeous as it was seductive. When one looked at her, it became almost impossible to look away.

Just then, a gigantic tree fell in front of him, snapping Usher's mind back to attention. Even the vegetation had an evil mind of its own.

"What the Abyss?"

He heard snickering in the underbrush.

"You will not keep me from completing my order from Prince Peccadillo!"

The snickers faded away.

"That's better," Usher huffed.

He surveyed the enormous huge tree trunk. "Great, just great. This is sure to double my time to get to my destination."

As he made his way around the tree, his anger smoldered. "I'm here on Prince Peccadillo's orders, so you can leave your games for another."

Just then a large Obliterist named Warpt appeared, leaning against a twisted tree trunk. Arms crossed, Warpt gave Usher a nasty smile. He wasn't the largest Obliterist Usher had seen, but his appearance was still quite imposing.

"So, you're not afraid, aye?"

Usher worked to stand a little taller. "You're quite good at your job, I admit. But I am here on official business. I must see Miss Enchantress at once."

Warpt, his hands locked behind his back, paced around Usher and glared down at him. "Ahh, you wish to gaze on Miss Enchantress' beauty. I see." Warpt gave him a wicked grin.

"No, I'm not here for—"

"Many have tried to make such a trip . . . and failed," Warpt growled.

Usher took a step back.

Warpt smiled wickedly. "You shouldn't feel so bad you cannot fulfill your lust. You've made it farther than most."

Usher took a step toward Warpt, even though the creature towered over him. He threw his shoulders back, tossing back the edge of his cape to reveal the Prince's seal. "You will take me to Miss Enchantress at once. As Prince Peccadillo's personal assistant, I demand it." Usher pressed on the crest and a blood-red, 3-D image of Prince Peccadillo shot from it.

"All praise to the Prince," the seal announced.

"All praise to the Prince," Usher shouted, as he fell to one knee with a fist to his chest.

Warpt's eyes opened wide and he took a step back. Along with all the other underlings, he took a knee and proclaimed, "All praise to the Prince." Everyone knew the seal went both ways. Once someone activated it, the Prince saw the response of those within its hearing until all complied.

His impatience growing, Usher glared at Warpt. "You will take me to Miss Enchantress immediately."

Warpt stubbornly stood still and stared back at Usher.

"If you must know, I have been sent to give Commander Deamon some very important information."

Warpt took a step back and looked around nervously.

Usher smirked at him, "An enemy breached your lines."

"What? This can't be." Warpt's face twisted with fury. "Our lines cannot be penetrated." He stomped about, screaming, and swinging his sword at some nearby branches.

Usher darted out of reach. "Obviously, that's not true. Now, please escort me to Miss Enchantress or at least move out of my way, so I can continue on my mission."

Clenching his jaw, Warpt stared darkly at Usher. He gripped and loosened his hand around the hilt of his sword. Without warning, he abruptly turned and moved quickly through the underbrush. Usher assumed this meant *yes* and tried his best to keep up with him. At least Warpt made a path for him. Moving angrily, he swatted branches out of the way, breaking many of them, and uprooted bushes, which greatly sped up Usher's journey. He felt relieved to be back on track to carrying out his orders.

RADIMAR MADE HIS WAY to the outskirts of Uncertainty to meet with one of his dearest friends. He approached a cabin that looked as ancient and resolute as its owner. The home stood so near to the boundary it almost looked as if it were part of Obscurity. The overgrowth of borderland hung over his cabin like a canopy yet didn't quite touch it. Normal trees and a small, well-manicured lawn surrounded the cabin.

Heavy moss weighed down the roof, causing it to sag slightly. A curving stone pathway led up to the door. The path was bordered by beautiful rosebushes, originally planted by his friend Warder's wife who had died a few years back. Now only Warder and Cozy, his cat, lived here. Radimar smiled to himself as he walked to the door. He loved this place but loved its owner even more.

WARDER HEARD THE KNOCK on the door and immediately knew who it was. His body moved slowly, yet his mind was quick. Whenever he received this visitor, something important was sure to happen. His excitement mounted.

He heard Radimar's muffled chuckle though the door as he neared the threshold. Warmth filled not only Warder's heart but the whole cabin when he opened the door.

"What took you so long, my old friend?" Radimar laughed as he carried in several bags of groceries.

"It's taken quite some time for you to find your way back to this small town. What's a few more moments for me to get to the door?" Warder pretended to be gruff, but it wasn't enough to hide his pleasure at having his Prince in his home.

Warder looked outside the door, this way and that. "Where is your sister? Didn't she journey with you?"

"Essince is here but has other work to attend to tonight." Radimar put away the groceries he had purchased, all of Warder's favorites in abundance. "How does it go for you, my friend? Have the Messengers been treating you well?"

Warder waved his hand in the air. "They come and go so quickly they are no company at all." He watched Radimar, amazed at the thoughtfulness and kindness he always showed him.

He noticed his favorite dessert among the foodstuffs. "If I knew this work you called me to would be so tediously slow, I might never have agreed to it." He frowned. "The time grows long, and I sometimes feel discouraged."

"Patience, my friend, patience. I know for you it seems like forever, but we are right on schedule. All things must be in place for the Gathering and the end of Peccadillo's regime."

Warder was one of the few still around who had seen firsthand the power that Prince Radimar and King Iam possessed. He'd also seen the destruction Peccadillo brought to the people. To let such suffering and evil continue seemed unreasonable. Not to mention he grew old and wanted so much to be a part of the coming victory.

There were others who felt this way because in each city, in each cluster, there were ancient ones like him. These men and women had been tasked with preserving the *Book of Actualities*, which held the Truth about all things from the beginning to the end and the end to the beginning.

The book held the true history of the world and the rightful King. When Prince Peccadillo took over, he ordered all copies of this book destroyed. Anyone found with this powerful book, or even portions of one, would be put to death. Even speaking of King Iam, Bliss, or the book was dangerous. And most people didn't remember much about any of it now. But the evil Prince didn't know King Iam hid a *Book of Actualities* with his trusted servant in each cluster.

Radimar put his hand on Warder's shoulder. "Don't worry, my friend. The end draws nearer than you realize. I have specific work here in Uncertainty, but it will take some time to strengthen my new chosen one."

"I heard the talk around town. The news seems to constantly talk about you. You are putting yourself at unnecessary risk. The young woman, Hearsay, also spoke of you, but I do not think that's a wise choice. Her mouth runs wild."

"No, Hearsay is not the one, though there is still hope for her." Radimar sighed and sank into the nearest chair.

Warder shook his head in dismay. The choosing process always confused him. Often, they seemed the most unlikely sort.

Chapter 6

Timorous spent the next three days at work answering questions about her chance meeting with Radimar. Little by little life returned to normal. Yet talk of Radimar continued. He seemed to appear quickly, then be gone just as fast. The media hounded anyone who'd talked with or seen him. No pictures of him existed but people gossiped non-stop about him. Most of it sounded ridiculously made up.

Two prominent themes kept surfacing. Some claimed he was a con artist while others said he was a miracle worker. Amazing things always seemed to happen when he showed up and not just healings but also acts of kindness. Since meeting him, Timorous knew there had to be some truth to what people were saying. Sometimes she thought she felt him, even when she knew she was alone. It seemed so strange. She didn't mentioned it to Hearsay.

Tims' days off were Sunday and Monday. On this beautiful Sunday, Tims decided to take a walk through the park. She called Hearsay, but no one answered. Her anxiety heightened. Being a woman walking alone in the park might be unsafe, even though it was open and well-traveled. She rarely went out by herself.

Timorous decided to push past her fears and enjoy the nice weather. She put on her favorite white organza summer dress. Sleeveless and fitted at the waist, it hung nicely on her.

She cautiously stepped outside her apartment complex and looked around to make sure plenty of people were out and about. The park was only a short walk away. Anxiety lingered, but to calm herself she took a couple of deep breaths. The sun warmed her face, lifting her spirits as she walked along the path that wove in and out of the trees and shrubs around the park's wide-open grassy area. Tims looked up into the trees, enjoying the way the sun shone through the leaves.

Families picnicked, couples held hands, and an occasional dog chased a ball. She decided it would be safe to continue on the path even though the path ducked behind more bushes, making it a little more secluded. Putting her hands in her pockets she continued on. Walks like these always reminded her of her mother and the way she pointed out different flowers and plants while telling stories of the time before Obscurity divided the clusters. She talked about a peaceful and harmonious life.

Timorous vaguely remembered asking her mother why things changed. She'd said, "Things always change when people are selfish and prideful."

Most of Tims' early memories were muddled together. There was something about a king and how he wanted people to choose to thrive rather than be controlled by selfishness. But she couldn't remember the rest of it.

Looking down she noticed a patch of flowers. She bent down to take a closer look at some unusual white ones with red centers and a splash of red on each of their four petals. They were beautiful. She had never seen anything like them before. She gently touched them. Tims caught sight of a pair of tennis shoes about a foot away. Frightened, she lost her balance and fell backward, catching herself with her elbows. How had this intruder been able to come so near without her noticing? Tims' heart raced as she slowly looked up.

With a gentle laugh, a man reached down to help her up. She recognized the laugh immediately. Radimar.

"I'm sorry I startled you. Timorous, right?"

Her eyes widened as she looked up at him, her mouth hanging open like some kind of guppy.

"Here, let me at least help you up. I hope I didn't ruin your pretty white dress." He gave her that same sunshine smile he'd given her at the store.

The moment his hand touched hers, warmth flooded her whole body. He pulled her up easily, and she now found herself standing much closer to him than she'd expected. Her eyes locked on his. Power seemed to emanate from him and increased to the point where she began to slightly sway.

Radimar let go of her hand and took a step back.

This is ridiculous. Embarrassed over the situation, she averted her eyes and brushed nonexistent debris off the back of her dress.

"I'm sorry. It *is* Timorous, isn't it?"

She stared at him again, her mouth still hanging open.

"You know, I've heard that's a good way to catch flies." He laughed softly as he put his finger under her chin to help close her mouth.

His power overwhelmed her again. Why had she even allowed him to touch her? She willed herself to say something.

"Um . . . thank you. I'm . . . I mean, I'm fine. My dress is fine. Thank you." Totally embarrassed, she turned to walk away.

"Beautiful day for a walk, isn't it?"

Timorous nodded but didn't look back.

"Did you know these are called Promise Flowers?"

She stopped and turned around.

Radimar knelt beside the flowers she'd just been looking at. She took a step toward him but didn't get too close.

"When I was small," he said, "my father took my sister and me for walks and pointed out all the different plants."

"My mother used to do the same with me. I don't remember seeing these flowers before though."

"Promise Flowers don't bloom often. When they do, there is always a promise of something good to come. How fortunate for us to have found them today."

Timorous noticed how gently he touched the flowers. They almost glowed in his hands. He seemed deep in thought.

She moved closer. "Promise of what good things?"

When he stood, she took a step back.

"There are good promises around us all the time, but we rarely recognize them."

Feeling bolder than usual, she asked again, "Promises of what good things?"

"The good things that were before Prince Peccadillo and the good things to come after he is no longer in power." Radimar spoke with confidence.

Tims tensed. "I'd be careful talking like that. The Prince seems to hear and see things everywhere. You might get in a lot of trouble." She looked around, looking for someone who might be watching and listening to them. Not sure how the government seemed to know everyone's secrets, she didn't want to take any chances. She'd always wondered if that kind of talk caused the sad fate of her mother.

"I only speak the truth. Do you believe it?" Radimar didn't seem the least bit concerned.

Tims creased her brows. "I'm not sure what I believe."

Compassion softened his face.

Why is he looking at me like that?

"I'm sorry, but I need to be on my way." She spun around and began walking as fast as possible without running. *I should never have come out today. Something bad always happens when I don't just stay home.*

But the warmth of his presence still coursed through her. Hadn't she wanted to see him again? What drew her to him? She'd never felt this way before. She took one last look back. Seeing he still watched her, she quickened her pace.

ESSINCE APPEARED OUT of nowhere with her pretend-to-scold look on her face. "You know you really shouldn't do that to her."

"Do what?" Radimar crossed his arms over his chest and continued to gaze in Tims' direction.

Essince smiled. "You know exactly what I'm talking about. Another moment so close to you and she'd would have been overcome by the power of King Iam. I saw the way she looked at you. You are confusing her before you've even been properly introduced."

Radimar looked at his sister. "I introduced myself to her at the store."

"Right, like that's what I meant." She shook her head.

They both looked back in Tims' direction, even though she was gone from their view.

"Look brother, she dropped her wallet. Father is making a way. You plant the seeds, and I will help to water them."

Radimar hugged Essince's shoulder. Essince, stunning in every way, had the same golden eyes, but they seemed to change with specks of blue, green, and brown. She had the ability to change her form from tall to short, blond hair to black, young to old. Most importantly she carried the Power of Sagacity, wisdom beyond the wisest of the wise, a gift from King Iam.

Radimar sighed. "You are right, Essince. All in due time. Are the plans in place?"

"Yes, which reminds me. I need to get going. I have work to do." They hugged again, then both disappeared in the blink of an eye.

Chapter 7

T*his is crazy.* Timorous picked up her pace as she walked toward home. *How could I have seen Radimar twice when almost no one seems to be able to find him? Maybe he planned it. But that's ridiculous. There's nothing special about me. I'm, just another blade of grass in a whole lawn.*

She looked at the hand Radimar had taken to help her up. It still felt warm. Tims held it up to her face, but she pulled it away quickly when she felt faint. *That's so strange. I'm just embarrassed.*

She made her way back to her apartment, determined to spend the rest of the day inside. As she rounded the corner, she saw a moving truck being unloaded outside the front door of her building. Two men carried items into the apartment complex, while another man stacked additional boxes beside the truck. Thankfully, they ignored her and focused on their job.

Slowly, she squeezed through the door and slid sideways along the hallway, then bumped right into the new tenant.

"Oh, I'm sorry, I didn't see you." She ducked her head and edged around a pile of boxes.

"No worries."

At the sound of the young woman's sweet, melodious voice, Timorous looked up and stared at the prettiest woman she'd ever seen.

"Hi, I'm Essince, and I'm just moving into apartment 1C." She extended her hand in greeting.

Timorous cautiously shook it. The same warm sensation she'd felt earlier swept through her.

I must be going crazy or something. "Hi. I'm Timorous. Most of my friends call me Tims. I live in 1B." *What am I thinking?* She didn't really have friends other than Hearsay, and she never shared personal information.

While Essince stood calmly, Timorous assessed her and decided Essince seemed safe. Her eyes radiated genuine care in what seemed like a pool of golden blue, like the sun setting on a clear blue lake.

"Wow, I guess we're neighbors. I'm so happy to meet someone on my first day here."

One of the movers interrupted her to ask her where to put an item.

Timorous loved how Essince's golden brown hair seemed to bounce when she turned her head. Suddenly aware of her staring, Tims turned away before she embarrassed herself further.

"Hey, Tims, is it okay if I call you that?"

Tims gave a quick nod.

"It's really nice to meet you. I hope we can become friends. I'm new to this area, so I could use some help getting to know my way around." Essince smiled and turned away. Timorous felt like the noonday sun had just shown on her as her heart picked up its pace.

She entered her apartment and locked all three locks, as she always did, and sat on her couch. Out of habit, she dialed Hearsay's number to tell her about her walk, but there was no answer. *Probably better that way. Hearsay would have grilled me for every last detail. What is going on with me? Maybe I'm just making all this up in my head? First, I feel strange around Radimar, and now around this new neighbor, Essince. This is crazy.*

Absorbed in her thoughts, she jolted when the phone rang. Tims didn't get many calls, so she assumed Hearsay to be her caller. Hearsay had been constantly bugging her to join her in seeking Radimar the last few days, like some kind of a treasure hunt. She picked up the phone and spoke with a bit of an edge. "Hearsay, I've already told you I'm not interested in hunting down Radimar."

A silent pause and then a chuckle. "Then lucky for me I found you first." Radimar.

Heat rushed up Tims' neck and into her face. She threw her hand over her eyes as if to hide, "Uh, how, um, what? Why? How did you get this number?" She wasn't sure whether she should be happy or feel afraid. She felt flustered but thankful he couldn't see her.

"You dropped your wallet when you fell. I didn't notice it until after you left. I assumed you'd want it back. You're quite organized. I found your note inside. 'If found, please call 232-8775.' I thought it best to get ahold of you right away so as not to worry you."

Shocked, Timorous quickly checked her dress pockets. "Uh, I guess it must have fallen out of my pocket." Several seconds of uncomfortable silence passed, but what should she say?

"Would you like me to bring it to you? Your address on your license shows you're right around the corner from the—."

"No. Um, I mean, thank you, but I'm, uh, busy right now."

"I can drop it off at another time if that works better for you."

Oh my. What do I do, what do I do?

"If you are uncomfortable with me coming over, we could meet somewhere, like the small coffee shop on the corner of First Avenue and Sunset Street."

Not wanting to endure any more awkwardness, Timorous rushed ahead. "Sure, that would be fine."

"Great. How about eight o'clock this evening? Does that work for you?"

"Okay. Bye." As she started to hang up, she quickly put the phone back to her ear. "Will you be alone?" Embarrassment swept through her. "I really don't want to be on the news or anything." She hoped it explained things.

He laughed softly. "I know I'm rather popular right now. I'm pretty good at keeping a low profile. See you at eight."

She hung up. *What in the world have I just done?* She needed her wallet back, but courage had never been her strength. *Oh, why didn't I ask him to mail it to me or something?*

Chapter 8

Warpt came to an abrupt stop.

Usher panted as sweat dripped down his face. He wondered if Warpt even remembered that he followed behind. Or maybe he just didn't care.

"Out of shape, are we, Usher? I'm surprised Prince Peccadillo doesn't require his personal assistant to be fit. But I do know how he loves to use weaknesses to his advantage."

Usher ignored the insult, which he'd expected. He knew the Obliterists felt no regard for him.

When he finally caught his breath, he realized they stood at the entrance of Commander Deamon's lair. The opening was set back into a cave, and the underbrush hung down in a tangled mess of twigs and half-dead leaves from above. Usher knew that somewhere in that cave he'd find a hidden door. Had Warpt not led him here, though, he might never have found the cave. The air surrounding it felt odd, as if death wrapped around the entrance. Yes, it definitely smelled of death. Usher knew the scent well.

Warpt conveniently disappeared. This left Usher in an awkward situation. Should he enter, or should he wait? Just as he decided to move forward, the air immediately changed. Usher fell to his knees and bowed low, knowing he was no longer alone. He felt the presence of Miss Enchantress. He longed to gaze at her beauty but feared her wrath.

In an almost angelic singsong voice, she asked, "To what do we owe this irritating interruption?"

Usher trembled and bowed low. "Miss Enchantress, Prince Peccadillo sent me for Commander Deamon."

"Why?" She no longer sounded angelic.

In his fear, Usher lost his voice.

"Why" she demanded again. "Stand up and face me like the head servant of Prince Peccadillo."

Usher managed to get his shaking legs underneath him but still stood bent over, keeping his eyes to the ground.

"You coward, look me in the eyes when I speak to you."

A small crowd of creatures who lived in Obscurity began to gather . . . and laughed.

Usher stood up straight, slowly lifting his head, taking in every perfect part of her body until he met her eyes. Because of her height, not to mention the way his eyes lingered as he took in her beauty, this took several moments. He lingered a little too long on certain areas, but she actually looked pleased.

"That's better," she cooed. "Now tell me why you are here."

"I'm here to speak with Commander Deamon, as the Prince commanded me." He bowed slightly, never taking his eyes off her.

She raised one perfect eyebrow. "And what is it you want to speak to my Lord about?" She crossed her arms in front of her, methodically tapping her long fingers on her bare arms. Each finger sported a six-inch-long claw-like fingernail painted black with a red serpent design on it.

Usher swallowed hard. "I mean no disrespect, but the message is for Commander Deamon."

As soon as the words were out of his mouth, Miss Enchantress swung her face down toward him as she turned into death itself. Her appealing appearance was a façade to the true dark evil that all Prince Peccadillo's realm held. She turned black and her beauty disappeared, revealing her true self, a skeleton with pieces of flesh hanging from her body. Her ugly skull swung down. Baring her teeth, she screamed into his face, knocking him down by its sheer force.

"You dare to treat me like your servant? I will chew you up and spit you out into a million pieces."

Usher fell to the ground certain this would be his end and shook from the force of her rant.

"Precious," Deamon spoke in a syrupy voice. "Is this how we treat our guests, especially when they are sent by our Prince with important information?" The Commander stood enormous and terrifying, just the way Usher remembered him.

Quickly she transformed back into her beautiful façade, which she preferred, using it to her advantage regularly. Many thought her and Deamon's relationship more than just business, but no one dared mention it.

Miss Enchantress sauntered over to him, leaned in close, and spoke with a sweet voice. "I suppose not, but those like Usher always need to be reminded of their proper place."

Usher didn't mind the constant insults. He felt relieved to have survived her attack.

"Agreed. But let us hear him out. Come this way." Deamon whipped his hand in the air in a commanding gesture, then turned abruptly and entered the dark cave.

Usher got to his feet quickly and hustled to fall in behind the Toadies, creatures of lesser status in the hierarchy of Peccadillo's realm, just beneath Obliterists.

Deamon led him through the cave and into a hexagon-shaped room with high ceilings and dark gray walls with very little light. Other Obliterists milling about the meeting hall stopped to see what all the commotion was about.

"So, what is this important information you came to give me?" Deamon's voice boomed and echoed throughout the room.

Usher moved to stand directly in front of the Commander but avoided making eye contact with his piercing gaze. He gave him a slight bow. "It's an honor to see you again, my Lord. I've been commanded by Prince Peccadillo to inform you that your presence is requested immediately."

"And why is the Prince requesting my presence?" The commander didn't look especially pleased when Usher peeked up. Deamon pulled back his broad shoulders and puffed out his muscular chest, looking even larger and more terrifying than usual.

Usher shot a glance around the room, then turned back at Deamon. "The Prince did not give me permission to divulge that information, your Lordship."

Usher saw Deamon's rage building. The commander took two big steps in his direction and Usher's blood went cold before he quickly proceeded. "But I am sure the Prince wouldn't mind me telling you, his most powerful leader, that this is in regard to—" He hesitated. "—Radimar . . . who has crossed the lines into the cluster of Nowhere."

In response to the enemy's name, everyone spat on the floor. Usher cowered and covered his head to avoid the certainty of physical blows.

Deamon, his face marked by rage, moved closer and hovered over Usher.

"What?!" Deamon screamed and flexed his fists. "How can this be? Our lines are secure!"

Usher wanted to point out his error but decided against it.

Deamon paced the room. Everyone moved out of his way. "Someone, many someones, will die because of this." His bellowing was deafening.

Usher clamped his hands over his ears.

Deamon stood, chest rising and falling with every angry breath. Everyone was silent in anxious anticipation.

"We leave at once." With that, Deamon grabbed Usher by the hair and marched out, dragging him toward the Netherworld to meet with his Prince.

Chapter 9

Timorous fretted all day. *Why, oh, why did I agree to meet Radimar? I didn't even get his number to call him and cancel.*

She considered all her options, ending back where she'd started. She needed to get ready for this unavoidable meeting.

She rifled through her limited wardrobe, trying to decide what to wear. All her shirts were displayed on the bed. She worked herself into a frenzy trying to decide. Then she heard a quiet knock on her door. Who could that be? Not Hearsay or Meddling. They knocked loudly.

The light knock came again. She quietly stepped toward her door and looked through the peephole. Essince, her new neighbor stood there smiling. Tims immediately felt something. Peace?

"Timorous, this is Essince. Are you there?"

Timorous took a deep breath and, as quietly as possible, unlocked all three locks. She didn't want her neighbor to think poorly of her. The moment she opened the door, an overwhelming peace—like a gentle breeze—came rushing toward her.

Essince smiled warmly, though she looked a bit messy from the move.

"Uh, hi, Essince. What can I do for you?"

"The movers just left." She gestured behind her. "But I can't seem to find my tea in all my boxes. I really need a cup of tea. Moving is really stressful." She brushed a loose strand of hair from her face. "I hoped you might have some I can borrow. I'll replace it." Her smile never wavered.

Timorous related to feeling stressed. "Sure. Come on in. What kind of tea do you like? I have lots of varieties, especially for stress." Oops, maybe she shouldn't have shared that.

"I like them all, so just pick the one you like best."

Timorous anxiously rifled through her cupboard.

"Is everything all right?" Essince moved closer.

Tims froze and tried to slow her heartbeat down. "No . . . yes . . . no, I'm just in a hurry." She handed Essince several kinds of tea bags that overflowed her petite hands. "Don't worry about replacing it. I have plenty." Tims bent down to pick one up that fallen from her shaking hands.

Essince thanked her and turned to leave. She reached the door and turned around, both hands still cupped together with multiple tea bags. "Could I borrow a teacup and maybe a spoon, too? I promise to return them."

"Oh, my gosh, where are my manners?" Again, Tims felt heat rush to her cheeks. "Please stay, and I'll make the tea for you right here."

"You don't have to do that. I can make do."

Now horrified for not being truthful, she stammered on. "I . . . uh . . . I don't have to leave for a little while, and—. Tea sounds like a good idea to me too. Please stay."

Tims led her guest to the kitchen table and retrieved two of the tea bags from her hands. Her hand brushed against Essince's, sending a little jolt through her and causing her to drop the tea bags. She froze and stared at Essince.

"Is everything okay?" Essince asked.

Had she felt it, too? No, it's just a figment of my overactive imagination. "Y—yes," Tims stammered, making her way to the kitchen to put the kettle on.

Essince sat down at Tims' small table. "You have a really nice place here. I like all the calming colors you decorated with, and everything is so neat and tidy."

"I like things to be in order. It helps me feel calm. I'm sure your place will be beautiful once you're all settled in."

"The whole unpacking thing is my least favorite. It will be nice when it's done, but it will probably take forever."

Tims smiled at the way Essince put the emphasis on the word *forever*. She poured a cup for her guest and herself. They sat at her table, quietly sipping. How strange that she didn't feel the need to make conversation. Instead, it felt peaceful. Everything about Essince made her feel that way.

They did eventually quietly chat about nothing important, which suited Tims just fine. The evening sun shone across the table right onto Essince. She almost appeared to be glowing. Tims couldn't take her eyes off her. Why did Essince's presence feel so similar to being near Radimar? However, Tims was more comfortable with Essince.

"I don't mean to pry," said Essince, "but you did seem really nervous when I first came in. If you ever need a friend to talk to, I'll always be here for you. You can trust me. I'm really good at keeping things confidential."

In a moment of courage, Tims dared to ask, "Have you heard about Radimar?"

Just then Hearsay knocked and quickly barged in since Tims hadn't relocked the door after inviting Essince in. "Tims, I'm glad you're here. I just heard—" As she spoke, she realized Tims had a guest. Hearsay slid to a halt.

She looked back and forth between the two. She broke into a big smile and sauntered over to the table. Tims knew she probably hoped this would be a new groupie for their fan club. "Who do we have here?"

"Hearsay, this is Essince, my new neighbor. Essince, this is Hearsay, my best friend."

Essince rose. "It's nice to meet you Hearsay. Tims, thanks for the tea and the talk. Maybe we can do this again soon." Essince left quickly, shutting the door quietly behind her.

"New friend? Did she come because of us meeting Radimar?" Hearsay sounded hopeful and a little suspicious. "I've never known you to entertain people."

"No and we met earlier when her movers were here. She needed a cup of tea after they left. All her things are boxed up."

A big grin spread across Hearsay's face. "Well, look at you. See, this whole experience is bringing you out of your cocoon." She crossed her arms with satisfaction, giving herself all the credit. "I knew all you needed was a little push to get you going."

Tims didn't appreciate her comment but said nothing as she took the dishes to the kitchen.

"I found out some more about our dream man, Radimar."

Tims rolled her eyes.

"I guess someone saw him in the park, and I hoped you'd seen him. I got your message about wanting to go to the park but you probably didn't go by yourself," Hearsay rambled on.

For some reason this really irritated Tims. "I do a lot of things by myself. I go to work and back, I grocery shop and . . . and I actually did walk in the park by myself today." She surprised herself by her quick comeback.

Hearsay plopped down on the couch. "Wow, I'm impressed. But mostly about the walk in the park. So?"

"So, what?"

"What do you mean, so what? Did you see Radimar?" Hearsay's voice edged with impatience.

Uh, oh. Now what should I do? How can I tell the truth but omit any other information? Hearsay's inquisitions were often very thorough.

Hearsay stood up, her hands on her hips, waiting, and eyebrows raised.

"I thought I might have seen him for a moment, but I'm not sure, I barely got a glance." Heat rose to her face, remembering him standing so close. She hoped Hearsay didn't notice.

"What? You saw *him,* and you didn't even call me?"

Tims turned back to the kitchen, trying to calm herself.

"You didn't answer your phone. Plus, there's nothing to tell." Well, there was, but she had no intention of sharing more.

"If I didn't know you better, I'd think you were lying to me."

Tims gave her a blank look and stood still.

"Anyway, it means he's still around," Hearsay continued on. "Do you want to go see if we can find him? Maybe he's still in the park."

"No. I have things to do." Tims busied herself in the kitchen, wiping counters that had already been wiped. She really needed this conversation to end. If Hearsay found out she was about to meet Radimar, she would demand to go with her. Going with Hearsay would be even more embarrassing.

"What things?"

"Um . . . well, I need to do the wash, cleaning . . . you know how I am. Sunday is my cleaning day."

Hearsay huffed. "Whatever. You're no fun." Hearsay stiffened before she hurried to Tims' side. "Sorry. That didn't come out like I meant it to."

"It's okay. I don't like adventure like you do. Tea with a neighbor is enough adventure for me today. Go have fun chasing Radimar down, but I bet you won't find him."

Hearsay grinned mischievously. "Oh, a dare. Now I have to try. Do you know if Meddling is in? Maybe she'll go with me." Without waiting for an answer, Hearsay ran out the door.

Tims heard her pounding up the stairs.

She worried about her friend becoming close to Meddling, but at least she didn't have to tell Hearsay the rest of the story. Really, there wasn't much to share. She'd lost her wallet. She needed to pick it up. She swallowed hard at the thought of who she was picking it up from.

Chapter 10

Prince Peccadillo paced the floor. "What is taking that moron so long?"

Just then, in marched Commander Deamon, ducking to clear the archway entrance. Deamon unceremoniously dumped Usher to the ground, then bowed. "My Lord and Prince, I came as soon as I received your message." Anger resonated in his deep rumbling voice.

The Prince eyed Usher, who sat crumpled on the floor rubbing his head. "Maybe I need a new assistant who can do his job more efficiently."

Usher glared at Deamon for accusing him of being the cause of their lateness. He knew it would do no good trying to put the blame back on those in Obscurity. Usher groveled on his hands and knees toward Prince Peccadillo. "No, my Lord and Prince. I moved as quickly as possible. The undergrowth has grown quite thick. Please, my Lord, I will do better next time."

The Prince kicked Usher twenty feet across the rocky floor. Usher held his side and, limped slightly, before collapsing at the wall nearest him.

Prince Peccadillo paced around Deamon. "We had a breach in security." He scowled at Deamon, piercing him with his eyes.

The Toadies watched with anticipation but stepped to the edge of the room. The Throne Room had six sides and a sixteen-foot ceiling that vaulted to a point in a glass steeple several feet higher.

Deamon stood almost to the very height of the ceiling. "I have heard, my Prince, but have not yet had the opportunity to conduct a proper investigation."

"Why would there need to be an investigation at all?" He pointed an accusing finger at Deamon. "Are you admitting you had no knowledge of this breach?"

The Commander stood at attention, mute before his Prince.

"You gave your word nothing could pass through the barrier. You assured me every inch of Obscurity was heavily guarded and incapable of being breached." Prince Peccadillo's voice grew louder and louder with each statement. "You claimed you had it under control. Yet, here we are with not only a breach but Radimar, our sworn enemy, expanding his influence into Uncertainty." He spat on the ground. Everyone in the room did the same. "You failed me and all of my kingdom. What shall we do with you? Hmm?"

Rage shone in Deamon's eyes. "My Lord and Prince, may I ask what you know of his plan?"

"You know well enough he is out to destroy my kingdom. To take what is rightfully ours. He never fights fair, the weakling. He and his stupid king think they can win this war through the weakest of them all, the simpleminded humans.

But he will not win since we control the humans he so dearly loves." Prince Peccadillo spat on the ground again. Again, everyone followed suit.

Deamon confidently continued. "We must do a proper investigation of the cluster of Nowhere. We will find our enemy's weakness and forge a plan to stop him. We will punish those who did not report this infraction immediately."

"What makes you think it is only the cluster of Nowhere our enemy has breached?" Prince Peccadillo stated a little too calmly, setting everyone on edge.

Deamon remained calm. "I have not heard otherwise, my Prince. "We will increase the Toadies in every cluster. They can at least stir things up and provide extra security in the towns while we shore up the breach."

Most Toadies were about the height of a human but much heavier. Their slimy green skin, covered with brown spots, varied in tone and darkness. Their bellies had several rolls and, while they only had three fingers and toes on their hands and feet, they sported the same dangerous claws as the other creatures of Peccadillo's kingdom.

They were not only powerful but carried a menacing six-foot stick with a point at the bottom and a ball on the top, called an Amplifier. It was far from a walking stick since they could use it to increase their destructive power. The slime on their bodies allowed for quick movement, and they sometimes slithered on their bellies because it enabled them to move faster than running.

"I just don't want Radimar out in the clusters. I want him stopped for good. I don't want him traveling from Bliss to our domain *ever*," Peccadillo fumed. "It is time for us to destroy him once and for all. Failure is not an option."

Deamon and all the Toadies raised a cheer in agreement.

Their cheers died down as they saw their Prince shake with indignation. Deamon and the others backed away slowly. The fury to come created the greatest of fear in them. They knew they should run, but they rarely had the opportunity to witness their Prince in his true powerful form.

Peccadillo's eyes turned blood-red, and his skin turned to black scaly leather, blacker than the darkest cave. He increased in size. Once the Toadies saw him reach halfway to the steeple and his wings begin to form, they scattered. Pushing, shoving, and even trampling others to get out of the room, they ran. Within a few short moments, he rose to his twenty-five-foot height, crushing the rock ceiling and cracking the glass steeple in the middle of the room. Rock and glass fell to the floor. One unfortunate Toady left with a piece of glass sticking out of his arm.

Prince Peccadillo's leathery wings spread out, rising and falling, filling the entire width of the room. His shiny, razor-sharp claws dug holes in the rock floor. No creature looked fiercer or more dangerous. Even Deamon fell to his knees in fear. When Peccadillo roared in rage, fire bellowed from his mouth. With a loud hiss and the stench of burnt flesh, he screamed obscenities. Scorched underlings lay scattered on the ground and against the walls as blackened statues.

Chapter 11

Tims' unseen companions, Anxiety and Fright, watched as she changed her clothes repeatedly. After Hearsay's inquisition, they were able to gain access to her, making their way up her body and now hung, one on each shoulder.

There was a light knock on the door. Tims looked out the peephole and then glanced at the clock. Almost time to go.

She opened the door and the presence of King Iam swept through the room.

"No!" Anxiety and Fear hissed.

"Hi Tims, I thought I'd take a break and head down to the store to get some groceries. Then I realized I don't know where the nearest store is." Essince laughed, which sounded like a choir of fairies. "Can you help?"

Tims fidgeted with her hands. "Um, GoGo Groceries. It's just down the street and to your right." She hastily pointed in that direction.

Anxiety and Fright, clung to her shoulders and dipped their ugly heads down, trying to hide from Essince.

"Tims, would you mind walking me there? I'm not so good with directions." While she waited for a response, the two little underlings made their way down Tims' leg, peeking around it and glaring at Essince.

Tims blinked a couple times, unaware her two companions were losing their hold on her. "Well . . . um, I guess. I planned to go out myself. I can show you the way. It's in the same direction I'm heading."

"Oh, thank you. That would great. By the way, I really love your pants." Essince squatted down and lightly tugged on the hem. In the process, she brushed the two small annoyances off Tims. Trembling, they let go and ran to the other side of the room. As Essince stood back up, she continued, "What brand are these? I think I'd like a pair."

"Oh." Tims' body relaxed. "I work at Outfit Outlet; they have them there. They're actually on sale right now."

"Well, I just might have to go there and get a pair." Essince smiled as they walked out the door together.

They chatted as they strolled down the block. When they arrived at GoGo Groceries, Tims asked if she needed help getting back home. Essince thanked her and assured her she'd find her way.

"Have a great night." Essince waved as she went in. Anxiety and Fright followed from a distance. Before Essince entered the store, she sent a little of King Iam's power their way as she blew their direction. The two fell backward in shock and confusion, then took off running in the other direction. They'd be back to bother Tims, but not before her meeting with Radimar.

"I'LL JUST GO IN, GET my wallet, thank him, and leave," Tim coached herself. "How hard could that be? I'm here anyway." *Wow, I must really be getting more adventurous.*

She reached the door of the small, rustic coffee shop. The front window proudly boasted Uncertainty Brews and Blends. Timorous still felt a little unsure about meeting Radimar in what seemed an intimate setting. But testing her newly budding confidence, she walked in.

The little bell over the door jingled. She cringed. *Nothing like being announced.* She'd only been in here once before, but it had been in the morning when it seemed brighter and more open. Now, it was dimly lit, and only a few customers sat about the place.

Standing just inside the door, Timorous squinted her eyes. She almost gave up when a man stood in the far corner. *Radimar.* His infectious smile was undeniable. Her heart skipped a beat.

She walked slowly to the table as her stomach twisted, telling herself all the reasons why this wasn't a good idea. She had her little speech ready, but as soon as she stood face to face with him—when she *felt* his presence—all thoughts went out the window.

"Please have a seat." He waved a hand toward a chair.

She sank into the empty chair. She knew she should say something, but she sat staring into his eyes. He chuckled. This brought her out of her trance.

She looked down. "I'm sorry. I really don't behave like this most of the time."

"How do you behave most of the time?"

Tims ventured a quick look at his smiling face, then looked away again. "I don't usually stand around with my mouth hanging open or sitting . . . " She felt lost again, incredibly embarrassed, and wished she'd never left her apartment.

"Well, I think you have a beautiful mouth whether it's open or closed."

What? Did he just say my mouth was beautiful? The twists in her stomach were now full-blown knots as she continued to look down. She decided to risk the question she'd been wondering about all day. "We seem to keep running into each other. Why is that?"

"What do you mean?" He leaned forward.

Tims automatically leaned back, her eyes wide. This conversation required more of her than anticipated. "I . . . um . . . I just mean, everyone seems to be looking for you and haven't been able to find you. Yet this is the third time I've seen you. Don't you think that a little strange?" She blushed. Why was she asking such probing questions of someone she hardly knew? And Radimar no less?

One hand still on his cup, Radimar leaned back. "I believe everything happens for a reason, don't you?"

She waited to see where he was steering the conversation.

"There's always a purpose to be served. For instance, tonight your purpose is to pick up your wallet."

Horrified, Tims stood. "You're right. I came to get my wallet, and then to leave." She spoke robotically, just like she had rehearsed.

Radimar stood and gently touched her arm. A shock of something like electricity ran through her, stopping her in her tracks.

"Hold on. Please sit back down. I only hoped to get to know you a little better in the process. Would that be okay?" He looked at her with pleading eyes.

Tims sat slowly. "Why would you want to get to know me?" Awe and confusion swept through her.

"Why not you?" Radimar gave her an encouraging smile.

His eyes were so beautiful, so inviting.

"Because I'm me, unimportant," Tims squeaked out, then rushed on. "And you're Radimar, someone special. There's a whole cluster of important people out there who want to meet you." She finished breathlessly.

"Timorous—" He reached out to still her shaking hands. "You're someone special, too."

The warmth from his hand radiated into her whole being. She avoided men and now this man's hand held hers. It felt strange to her, yet wonderful at the same time. Her head told her to run, but instead, she stared at their hands trying to discern what she felt.

"Timorous."

She looked up.

"A lot of people seek me for the wrong reasons. I have no interest in them or their agendas for me. There's something very special about you. Do you believe you are special?"

Not used to talking about herself, she pulled her hands away and shook her head. She felt incredibly uncomfortable and glanced toward the door. She was nothing. Used. Dirty. Unlovable. Less than ordinary—invisible. All the feelings about her lack of worth came rushing back to her. She'd worked so hard to push those emotions down. Now it felt like someone opened the release valve, and the emotions flooded from her soul.

"Timorous." He waited for her to look up, then said, "You're not invisible to me."

Oh, my gosh, can he read my mind? She needed to get away. Again, she glanced back at the door. She'd thought she would be safe, but she felt so uncomfortable.

"What's wrong?"

She stood abruptly. "I have to go. This isn't right . . . I mean, it doesn't feel right."

He stood up next to her. "Tell me what you mean. How is this not right? Have I done something wrong?"

She hadn't realized it, but he'd taken her hand. "Have I frightened you? Do you feel unsafe with me?" His piercing eyes looked deep into her soul for an honest answer.

She stared back for a long time. "I don't . . . I'm not sure . . . no, I feel peaceful when I'm with you. I believe you're a safe person." It was a stupid thing to say, but she said it anyway. *If he really saw me, he would never want to take my hand again.*

"And how do you know this? What is it about me that makes you feel safe?"

It took her a moment to find the words. They sat back down. "I don't know. I just have this sense about who I can trust and who I can't." She risked a shy peek at him.

"What do you do when you meet someone who isn't safe?" He still held her hand.

"I usually avoid them like the plague. I don't associate with them more than I have to."

"How do you think you came to have this ability to know who is safe and who isn't?" When she didn't answer, Radimar continued. "Maybe it has a purpose in your life, a wonderful purpose that you don't yet grasp?"

She'd never thought about it that way. No, she just thought she must be a crazy person after so much trauma in her life. Could it be a gift she possessed? Her thoughts spun in her head, making her feel almost dizzy.

When she looked at him again, he continued. "And what do you do when you meet someone you can trust?" The warmth of his touch filled her from head to toe.

"I don't know," she whispered. "I don't know many people I trust. It's less risky not to take chances even if I think someone might be trustworthy."

Radimar let go of her hand, leaving her feeling empty.

After a long pause, she asked, "Who are you?"

"The right question isn't who. It's why?"

Now even more confused, she asked, "Why?"

"I have a purpose for being here with you tonight. I'm here to tell you that you are special and worthy. I have come specifically for you. You have purpose. I've chosen you." He spoke softly but with authority.

Before she could think of a reply, he vanished.

Tims sat there dumbfounded. She blinked several times and looked around the shop. Had she imagined it all? No, she still felt the power of his presence.

A few moments later a waitress approached her. "The gentleman who just left wanted me to give you this." It was her wallet. "He also wanted you to have this gift card for any inconvenience."

Tims stared at her. "Did you . . . I mean did he . . .?"

The waitress sighed impatiently, put the items on the table, and walked away.

Hours later, Tims lay in bed, still feeling exhilarated by her time with Radimar. She kept questioning herself. *Did it really happen? Did I black out and miss his exit? Maybe I should go see a doctor. What did he mean when he said I'm worthy—that he* chose *me? Chose me for what purpose*?

Something deep inside her, something very broken and dark began to change. While not sure why, she just knew she'd never be the same. She had never felt this way before. It felt like . . . hope. Now what? Who could she talk to? Not Hearsay. She'd be over the top with questions.

Essince came to mind. *Maybe. We'll see.*

TIMS' TWO CONSTANT companions, Fright and Anxiety, were in the room but too afraid to come near her. She radiated with the power of King Iam. Even though she couldn't see it, to them her body glowed brightly. She would sleep well tonight, but tomorrow they would find ways to weasel their way back in.

"Should we tell our Master?" Fright asked.

"No. Do you want to be sent to the Abyss?" Anxiety thought for a few moments. "We need to get some local reinforcements to help us."

Chapter 12

The next evening, Warder heard a knock on the door and slowly pulled himself up from his favorite chair.

Essince didn't wait for him but walked through it . . . literally right through the door.

"Dag nab it, Essince, it freaks me out when you do that."

She kissed him on the cheek and quickly skipped passed him. She looked back over her shoulder and winked. "You know you're my favorite."

"Yeah, I know we're all your favorites." He tried to hide a grin.

"I need to talk to my brother."

"He's in the back. He did that poppin' in and out thing. That also gives me the creeps." Warder pretended to shudder. "Sounds like things are heating up again. You know how I love it when the enemy feels discombobulated."

He watched Essince walk through the closed door to join her brother. Warder shuddered again and sunk back into his chair. "I'm glad they're in charge and not me."

ESSINCE WALKED THROUGH the back door and stepped into the Throne Room of Bliss. Neither she, her brother, nor her father were hindered by time or space. The room flooded with the brilliance of King Iam.

"Father," Radimar, stood before the Throne, "the time is right to move forward with our plan."

"I agree with Radimar." Essince stepped up beside him. "The enemy is aware of Radimar's presence. My presence is also known but more on a local level. Your chosen one still needs more time to find the courage to move forward. With our help she will find her way."

"Are there others from this cluster to be sought out at this time?" King Iam inquired.

"There are, and they will come when the time is right. At this point it looks like it will be just Timorous," Radimar explained.

"Continue as planned. Each one who overcomes brings us closer to our ultimate victory. We will celebrate with Timorous in her overcoming."

WHEN TIMOROUS WOKE up, she felt especially refreshed. She often slept poorly, experiencing frequent nightmares. She decided not to leave her apartment today. Yesterday proved to be exhausting and she felt more comfortable in the safety of her own apartment than in the outside world.

"That's our girl." Fright smirked at Anxiety. "Playing it safe."

Timorous' glow had begun to dim. Not able to quite latch onto her yet, they continued yelling from the sidelines, hoping to wear her down.

Timorous thought all morning about her encounter with Radimar. She replayed the meeting over and over in her head—every word, every touch. Each time she could almost sense his presence. While contemplating her confusion at his interest in her, she stared in the mirror, seeing the same ordinary girl she'd always been. She questioned her sanity about his mysterious disappearance. To clear her mind, she decided to busy herself by cleaning, but it didn't work. Thoughts of the night before continued no matter what she did.

The phone rang, and she cautiously answered. "Hello?"

"Hi, Tims," Hearsay said on the other end. "What's wrong? You sounded like you were expecting someone calling for your execution." She laughed.

"Um . . . nothing. I—I just didn't expect any calls today."

"When do you ever expect calls? Who calls besides me?"

Tims felt a twinge of defensiveness. "You're not the only one who calls me."

"Okay, something is up. You either tell me now, or I'm coming over there right this minute to make you spill it," Hearsay ordered. "No one else calls you, and you know it. And what is this, you getting all huffy with me?"

An awkward pause hung between them.

"Tims, I'm your best friend. I've kept all your secrets. We've been through everything together," she whined.

Timorous thought for a moment. Maybe Hearsay was right. Maybe talking to her would help her make sense of what happened. They were friends after all.

"Radimar called me," she blurted out and closed her eyes. She waited to hear her friend's over-the-top reaction.

"Okay," Hearsay said after a prolonged pause, "and why did he call you?"

Encouraged by her friend's calm response, Tims continued. "I guess I dropped my wallet in the park, and he wanted to return it to me. I met him at the coffee shop around the corner last night to pick it up." Tims nibbled a fingernail.

"You went on a date with Radimar?" Her friend sounded shocked. "How did he get your phone number?"

"It not like that. He found my number in my wallet and called. I just went to the shop, got my wallet, and left." Tims' hands shook as her unseen companions, Fear and Anxiety, bit into her. She second-guessed her decision to tell Hearsay and decided not to share any more, at least not now.

"So . . . you didn't even talk to him?"

"Um, briefly, but just small talk. You know, just a 'hi' and a 'thank you.'" Tims felt sure she hadn't fooled her friend. Hearsay knew her too well.

"I can't believe you didn't call me. I would have gone with you," Hearsay groaned. "It sounds like you're holding out on me. I'm coming over."

Tims heard the line click. Hearsay certainly was on her way. Tims wrung her hands and walked in circles around her front room. Hearsay's expert detective skills were sure to dig out every detail. Tims' resolve would collapse and she'd end up telling her everything. She continued to pace. Tims felt almost suffocated.

Maybe she should leave? Hearsay would be mad and even more suspicious, but it might give her time to figure out how to handle this situation. But where to go? Staying home wasn't an option. Hearsay had a key to her apartment for "just in case" moments.

Essince came to mind. It might not be too strange to see how her neighbor was doing. She quickly boiled some water and prepared a small tray with tea bags and cups. In her nervous state, she had difficulty balancing it all. Thankfully, Essince lived just across the hall.

When Essince came to the door, her beautiful blond hair stuck out in all directions, but she still looked adorable. Multiple half-unpacked boxes laid open around the living and dining areas.

"Hi, Tims. It's so nice to see you, and look, you brought us some tea. How thoughtful." She waved Tims into the room.

Tims sighed with relief. A sense of peace filled her as her unknown companions ran away the moment Essince opened the door.

"I hope I'm not inconveniencing you." Tims never visited anyone—ever.

"Of course not. I am so thankful for the break from this mess." Essince motioned with her arms at the chaos around them.

Tims giggled.

"Yeah, I know it's funny. Organizing really isn't my thing. I'm more of a free spirit." Essince moved boxes off her small table and found a couple of mismatched chairs. As before, while she moved about the room, the sun shone directly on her, making her almost glow. Her eyes shone golden brown today.

Tims stared at her. "You have the most unusual eyes. They're so beautiful. They change color. Not the gold but the specks of blue and brown and—" She trailed off, feeling a little silly for bringing it up.

"Thank you. I have my father's eyes. I've always loved how they change with what I wear or how I feel." Essince smiled sweetly at her.

Tims stared down at her tea. She wished there were good things to say about her own father. At least being in Essince's presence made her feel happy. It had been a good decision to visit her neighbor. Feeling a little braver, she continued. "Your eyes remind me of someone else I met recently."

"Oh, yeah, who?" Essince glanced her way knowingly.

"Have you heard of Radimar?" Tims' cheeks grew warm as she said his name.

The corners of Essince's mouth twitched up. "Yes, I know Radimar."

"How? Are you two related? I mean, your eyes are so similar." Tims felt a prick of self-consciousness, as though she were a young teenager with a crush on the most popular boy in school.

"We're actually very close."

"Oh." Tims' heart sank. Radimar said he chose her. Maybe he didn't mean all those things. She looked down at her tea feeling confused. "Well, I need to let you get back to your unpacking. I'm sorry if I imposed on you." She stood to leave.

"Don't be silly, Tims. You are not imposing on me. We're friends now, right?"

"If you say so." *Did having tea make them friends?* "It's just not like me to invite myself over. To be honest, I feel a little embarrassed," Tims shared, feeling a bit confused by her willingness to make this confession.

Essince touched Tims' shoulders. Like a warm drink on a cold day, peace and comfort flowed through her. "Tims, you are not imposing on me. Didn't I invite myself over yesterday?" Her eyes locked on Tims. "You're a beautiful person. Thank you for allowing me into your life."

Tims opened her mouth but nothing came out. She abruptly shut it. She felt Essince looking into her soul, just as Radimar had. Tims swayed. Essince quickly removed her hands and averted her eyes.

"Tims, I could really use your help unpacking. Please stay for a bit and help me?" She gestured to the mess in the room and gave Tims a pleading smile. "What do you say? Do you want to help this free-spirited princess put some order to her domain?" All awkwardness fell away as Essince spread her arms wide and looked from side to side, then back at Tims.

Tims laughed and agreed to stay.

Chapter 13

Fright and Anxiety ran to the other side of the hall and clung to each other. This was the third time Essince had interfered with their plans.

"We need to stop this now, but how?" Fright whined.

The next thing he knew, Anxiety slapped him hard enough to knock him down. Anxiety balled his little fists in anger, his face contorted, and he let out a string of profanities. "We need to get some reinforcements. You go talk to Snoop. Tell her she needs to step up her game with Gossip."

Snoop clung to Meddling as her primary vile companion, just as Gossip clung to Hearsay.

"I have other plans to put our charge in her place. We'll meet back in an hour." Anxiety took off in the opposite direction, moving at an unnatural speed.

Unfortunately for Anxiety, just as he turned the corner, he ran into three of Deamon's Toadies.

"There you are, you little Sprite," the lead Toady announced. "We were just looking for you and your stupid friend. We heard you've grown lazy and opened the door for our enemy."

Anxiety took two steps back. Someone must have told on him. Disgusted by their slime, he tried to muster up some confidence. "Everything is under control." He gave them a slight bow.

"Then why are you not with your charge?" The Toady tapped his foot impatiently. "Did you leave her alone? Have Messengers scared you away?" All the Toadies laughed at this. The leader glared at Anxiety. "Speak up!"

Anxiety jumped back.

The Toadies laughed again.

"I . . . we are stepping up our security. I'm on my way to meet with new additions to our team."

The leader leaned over Anxiety. His threatening glare terrified him.

"And?" he said. "Why is this necessary? If you have things under control, why would you need reinforcements?"

The group of Toadies all took a step closer, towering over Anxiety.

He leaned away from them. "Begging your pardon, great Toadies of the Netherworld." He gave them another low bow. "We are doing our job. It's not uncommon for us to partner with others in dealing with situations before they get out of hand. Our charge in not alone."

It seemed advantageous to remain silent about whose presence Timorous currently was in. "I know we are small, but we are very good at not drawing attention to ourselves. The humans have no idea that we coexist with them. You wouldn't want Lord Deamon to think you exposed yourselves when it was unnecessary, would you?" He hoped to warn them off and smiled at their response.

The Toadies took a step back, each trying to hide his own fear. They'd been brought in to provide support in guarding the town but were specifically told not to draw attention. Worry etched their ugly faces as they conversed. They looked around nervously. Stepping a short distance away, they huddled together and whispered among themselves.

After a few moments of discussion, the leader responded. "Okay, you little Sprite, we will give you a day to prove yourselves, but we'll be watching. If you're withholding any information, don't think you won't be punished for it." The Toady's spit hit Anxiety in the face, insulting him further. "But we will be watching you." He roared and jumped at Anxiety.

Anxiety took off running. The group of Toadies laughed as he ran.

WHEN HEARSAY ARRIVED, she slammed on her brakes, not bothering even to park her car correctly along the curb. She hurried to Tims' apartment, banged on the door, and tried to walk in as she usually did.

When the door didn't budge, she stomped her foot. "What the heck? Tims, you knew I was coming. Why isn't the door already unlocked? Tims, it's me, Hearsay. Let me in." She pounded again. Still no response. "Tims, you know I have a key. If you don't let me in, I'll let myself in."

Worried now, she spent a few minutes rifling through her purse to find the key. She'd never used it before. "This must be serious," she muttered. She walked in, still calling Tims' name. As always, everything was neat and tidy. She checked every room. "Something is terribly wrong. What should I do?"

She'd worked herself into a frenzy. *Gossip whispered into her mind, "Meddling."*

Speaking what the thought put in her head, Hearsay repeated, "Meddling. Meddling would know." Running out the door and taking two steps at a time, she reached Meddling's door on the second floor, out of breath and heart pounding. After she'd knocked loudly multiple times, a scowling Meddling opened the door.

"What is your problem?"

Hearsay leaned over, trying to catch her breath. "I . . . can't . . . find . . . Tims. Have you . . . seen her?" She gulped a few more breaths before straightening up.

The little Sprite Snoop, Meddling's constant unseen companion, hovered on her shoulder. Fright had just paid Snoop a visit, asking for her help. Eager to do her job, Snoop prodded Meddling to dig deeper.

"How should I know? It's not like we really hang out together." Meddling inspected her fingernails, as if she couldn't care less. "She barely leaves her apartment. What's going on?"

"I spoke to Tims on the phone just a little while ago and told her I was coming over, and now she's not home." Hearsay spread her arms out in desperation.

Meddling pursed her lips. "So, what's the big deal? Maybe she just went for a walk or ran to the store?" She turned and walked toward her kitchen.

"You don't get it." Raising her voice, Hearsay followed her. "That's not like Tims. She would never leave her house knowing I was on my way." She grabbed Meddling's sleeve.

Meddling looked down at Hearsay's hands. "Why were you coming over anyway?" She squinted suspiciously. *Snoop threw a thought her way.* "What did you say to her?"

Hearsay quickly let go of Meddling. "What do you mean, 'What did I say?' I didn't say anything to make her leave."

"Well, it just sounded like you must have argued or something."

"I told you, it's not like that." Hearsay stood there wringing her hands. Hearsay finally whispered, "Well, she did tell me something I may have overreacted to."

"Oh really. What was that?" She invited Hearsay to sit down. "I'm sure it's not as bad as you think. It's not your fault if she's choosing to ignore you." She patted her arm to comfort her.

Hearsay's shoulders slumped before she drew in a deep breath. "Please don't tell anyone, but Tims been seeing Radimar . . . secretly."

Meddling immediately stood up and her face went red. "No! That can't be."

Hearsay nodded. "She told me herself. I felt like she withheld information from me, so I told her I was coming right over. I guess that upset her, but still, she'd never leave knowing I was on my way over. We're best friends. She tells me everything." Hearsay dabbed at unshed tears.

"Well, obviously she's not being completely truthful with you or she would have already told you everything. I'll come help you look."

Hearsay sighed with relief.

Snoop and Gossip exchanged evil grins.

"Where's the first place you think we should look? Do you think she's out with Radimar right now?" Meddling quickly grabbed her sweater as if finding Radimar was now an urgent matter.

"I'm not sure. That might explain why she's not home. She did mention she met him at the coffee shop right around the corner. Why don't we start there? Maybe questioning the people who work there will give us a lead."

"Like being private detectives." Meddling shut the door behind her. "Wow, to think she's dating Radimar when he's so elusive. I wonder why he picked *her*," Meddling scowled disdainfully.

Snoop giggled as Meddling repeated aloud the words he'd just whispered into her mind.

"She didn't exactly say they were dating, but wouldn't that be so awesome? We would have exclusive access to him. We'd be famous." Hearsay sighed dreamily.

"Well, what did she tell you?"

Hearsay mentioned the two interactions Tims had had with Radimar.

"So, they aren't secretly dating?" Meddling sounded skeptical.

"Maybe there are other times she hasn't told me about."

Meddling frowned. "I guess we'll ask when we find her."

Hearsay's face was still etched with concern. "This is so not like Timorous. She's afraid of men. She's shown no interest before."

"Then Tims must be hiding something. If she's not dating Radimar, what is she doing with him?"

Jealousy jumped on Meddling's shoulder.

Chapter 14

Prince Peccadillo ordered Deamon to call a meeting in the Netherworld with all the Lead Guards of the Obscurity. Each leader oversaw a place in Obscurity between the clusters. They were dangerous beings, all working within their area to protect the borderland from breaches like this. Deamon was the Commander of the Lead Guard, second only to the Prince himself.

They now awaited the Prince at a large table in the Battle Room. Deamon thought it ridiculous to have a table because someone always destroyed it in a disagreement, usually Peccadillo himself. But he never spoke a word about it to his Lord.

Deamon stood nearest the door, with his arms crossed in military fashion. The Captains of the Guard grunted whispers at one another. This was their first time to meet in person and confer over their notes. The Prince's interrogation would mean a certain end to at least one of them. They searched for ways to protect themselves while finding weaknesses in the others' stories.

Prince Peccadillo strutted into the room dressed in an expensive black suit, his absolute authority evident in his regal bearing. He slowly made his way to the head of the table, casting an arrogant and expectant glance at each Lead Guard.

Commander Deamon took his position next to the Prince. Usher followed closely with his gnarly hand wrapped tightly around his tablet, and stood to the side, just behind the Prince. He appeared small at a foot and a half shorter than the Prince. Deamon caught Usher's pleasure at the Prince's coming inquisition, but the moment Usher looked his way, Deamon growled, baring his teeth. Usher dropped his smile.

"All power and authority to our Lord and Prince Peccadillo," the Lead Guard chanted together in their deep, husky voices. They didn't dare look up until the Prince had acknowledged their greeting.

"Sit," the Prince ordered.

The Guards obeyed immediately.

Lowering himself into his throne chair, the Prince did not look pleased. Anger radiated from him. He took his time to survey the room, staring hard at each Captain. Each one met his gaze, then quickly diverted their eyes.

Prince Peccadillo drew in a long, slow breath and released it just as slowly, filling the room with the stench of death. "We are here today . . ." His voice rose with each word. "To discuss the breach!" he finished with a shout.

They all flinched.

"I'm sure Commander Deamon filled you in on the details. Our enemy, Radimar, made an appearance in the cluster of Nowhere."

With the mention of the enemy's name, every Guard spat and grumbled.

Prince Peccadillo glared at them from under his dark eyebrows and pulled his lips back into a snarl. "Why have you allowed this interference from our enemy?" The Guard shot glances at one another but said nothing.

"Usher." The Prince beckoned his aide to his side.

Head bowed, Usher moved forward quickly.

"How many have we lost to our enemy in the last year?"

"One hundred and forty-four, my Prince."

The prince stood and slammed a heavy fist on the table. The first crack appeared.

Usher rushed on. "But of those attempts to cross through Obscurity only sixty-eight were successful. The others were disposed of."

The prince paced around the table, stopping to slam his fist on the table between two of the Guards.

"And why do you think we are seeing an increase in escapees when there should be none?"

No one dared answer.

"Laziness. You have all grown lazy and lost your focus on our mission to destroy the enemy." Again, his voice rose, this time to a scream. "Answers!" He raised a fist to the ceiling. "Answers!" His nostrils flared, as they always did before he began his hideous transformation.

"My Lord and Prince," Deamon began, seemingly unfazed by the Prince's display of anger. "There seems to be an increase in the Messengers' activity as well."

The Guard growled. A few laughed. Deamon quickly scanned the room to see who'd laughed. Everyone froze.

"You think the Messengers are weak because of their size?" Peccadillo roared.

They all went silent.

"I used to know some of these Messengers personally. They never move without the orders of King Iam."

Everyone spat on the table.

Peccadillo focused on Deamon. "What is the level of increase?"

"My Lord and Prince, from my initial calculations, there is a forty-five percent increase in Messenger activity."

"What?" The Prince, his eyes fiery red, ran to Deamon. "How long have you known this and not reported it?"

Deamon looked straight ahead without flinching. "It has only come to my attention in the last few days. The Guard failed to get their reports to me."

The Guard spoke over one another, casting blame in all directions.

Returning to his place at the head of the table, he enunciated each word with a blow to the table. "This. Is. Not. Acceptable."

With a loud crack, the table split, falling inward on itself.

Prince Peccadillo's blood-red eyes pierced each Guard. "This must be connected to why Radimar himself has entered Nowhere."

The Lead Guard from the cluster of Mystification hesitantly spoke up. "My Lord and Prince, rumored reports are circulating of Radimar being spotted in our cluster as well." He rushed on, "But we were unable to verify this information."

Barely controlling himself, Peccadillo's body shook and shifted. Through clenched teeth he hissed, "How many of our clusters have had sightings?"

The Guard mumbled and looked at one another.

"How many?" he roared.

Deamon stepped forward. "I have completed a thorough investigation of the Lead Guards' reports. It seems all of the clusters have had at least one sighting, but all were unconfirmed, until recently in Nowhere." He hurried on. "They withheld the report only because of the lack of substantial proof."

"Our enemy is up to something, you morons. Why haven't you been talking amongst yourselves and comparing notes? It seems your stupidity is our weak link. You are worthless and shall all be sent to the Abyss."

The Guards drew back, then begged and made promises.

Usher smiled. Deamon took a step toward him with a growl. Usher quickly lost his smirk and stepped back.

The Prince raised a hand, motioning for silence. "This is not a time to argue. This is a time to pull our forces together, tighten up the lines." He eyed Deamon. "Step forward."

Deamon stood to attention. "Yes, my Lord and Prince."

"You will add reinforcements to borderland around each cluster, with a special focus on Nowhere. Apprehend any human directly involved with our enemy and bring them in for questioning. I expect all of the Lead Guard to put their most skilled at the frontlines. Send in the Toadies only when you are narrowing in on the location of our target." He glared at the Guard, then back at Deamon. "I demand daily reports. Have I made myself clear?"

"Yes, my Lord." He gave slight bow.

The Prince gave him a sly smile. "To help you, I will remove any distractions that might keep you from your duties."

With that, the doors opened and Miss Enchantress entered wearing a black full-length dress that hung with an open V-cut down to her navel and all the way down to her lower back. Amazingly, the gown stayed on her shoulders as she glided across the floor and into the arms of Prince Peccadillo. She stood much taller than Peccadillo's human façade. It put him at chest level of her full figure.

He stood there with his arm around her waist, smiling wickedly. "I am sending Usher in her place to assist you, Deamon. I think a little more work and, um, less *play* will help you achieve your goals."

Shamed in front of his Lead Guard, a deep red sheen rose up Deamon's neck and into his face. The Lead Guard let out a few snorts and jeers even as they gawked at Miss Enchantress.

"My Lord and Prince, you know best." Deamon bowed. "However, I must say that Miss Enchantress' abilities are far superior to Usher's. Her help is needed most now."

"Yes, I'm sure her, as you say, her *abilities* are far superior to Usher's. I think those abilities would be best served with me at this time." The Prince emitted another wicked laughed.

Miss Enchantress leaned down to seductively lick Prince Peccadillo's face. The Guard jeered and laughed.

The Prince pulled Miss Enchantress closer, resting his cheek on the side of her chest. "Besides, Usher has his own abilities and uses. Do you question my top assistant would not be equipped to support you?"

Deamon's red face looked close to exploding. He took a measured, condescending look at Usher's small frame but with another bow said, "No, my Lord and Prince, as you wish."

Usher's face fell, and his skin turned gray.

"Come, come now, Usher." The Prince smirked. "Show Deamon why you are my personal assistant. This is a great honor, and if you do your job well, maybe you can receive an even higher position."

Usher's lips curved upward.

"Maybe you could become Deamon's permanent assistant." He chuckled at Usher's horrified expression.

Chapter 15

Accura zipped into Bliss, passing the powerful Legionnaires who guarded each of the four entrance gates. They had eyes on all four sides of their heads, so they could see in all directions at once. They never needed to rest because King Iam's power flowed through them and sustained them. Their bronze skin glistened in the constant light of Bliss. Each Legionnaire was armed with two large, double-edged swords. They wore gold tunics with large leather-like belts. Their feet were strapped in sandals winding halfway up their pillar-like legs. The Legionnaires opened the gates of Bliss for no one unless Radimar gave his approval.

"Welcome back, Accura." The Legionnaire needed only to crack the gate open for his entrance.

He waved as he passed through. Messengers were tiny beings, as small as a firefly, yet proud, loyal servants to King Iam. They were often sent to help the humans. Their little wings fluttered so quickly they could barely be seen while they hung in midair.

From the moment of entering, Accura sighed at the beauty that was both seen and felt through the unconditional love of King Iam, where everyone felt fully accepted and at peace. The colors were so vibrant in Bliss, the plant life so beautiful, and the smells so delicious. Nothing compared to the music. No human words could describe its majesty and beauty.

Bliss wasn't a cluster nor under the control of Prince Peccadillo. It could not be reached simply by slashing through the overgrowth in Obscurity. As it had always been since before the rebellion of Peccadillo, the only way to enter Bliss was with the help of Prince Radimar.

From the seen world, Bliss appeared like a high cloud at day and a bright star at night, otherwise invisible except for those who called it home. Outside of the clusters, yet connected in a mysterious way, it slowly roamed over them.

Accura made his way to the circular throne room at the center of Bliss. In the center of the large room sat King Iam's throne. Circling it were smaller thrones where the King's twelve advisors sat. The floors were made of crystal-clear diamonds, polished and without blemish.

King Iam laughed as he often did, and Accura felt pure joy. The sound of his laughter carried throughout Bliss, bringing joy to everyone. King Iam welcomed everyone in Bliss to approach his throne, and they frequently did since they all loved to be in his presence. For Bliss held light and beauty, peace and harmony. Children's laughter and songs rose as Bliss inhabitants went about their work.

Messengers came and went more frequently than normal these days. Even more noticeable was the number of Legionnaires visiting King Iam. This did not cause concern to those living in Bliss. Their full trust rested in King Iam.

Accura approached the throne and bowed.

King Iam called, "Speak, Accura. What news do you bring me from the clusters?"

Accura had short dark hair, and his skin reflected the light of King Iam, as all Messengers did. He bowed. "Most High King, Peccadillo and his forces have become aware of our increased activity in the clusters. In response, reinforcements have been deployed."

"With the Gathering drawing nearer, this is not unexpected." King Iam gave further directions to Accura before he moved to the side to let others make their reports.

Digits, the King's Director of Messengers, moved forward next. Digits was a bubbly, curly headed creature whose wings made small tinkling sounds whenever she took flight or landed. "At your service, my King." She curtsied and stood in midair, showing her dimpled smile.

"Digits, how are the Messengers doing with delivering their services to the humans?"

"Many of them are doing very well." She looked through her notes. "Others are being blocked by the underlings, who are quick to cover their charges' ears or confuse them into believing the messages are false."

"Peccadillo is a master deceiver. The humans have forgotten their power to overcome the enemy and believe his lies. But no fear, my little one, the *Book of Actualities* is still in the hands of the faithful ones. Essince will help lead those chosen back to their rightful place." Extending his finger, and with a mischievous grin, he lightly tapped her on the nose. "We will help them see the Truth that is right in front of their noses."

Digits spun head over heels giggling.

King Iam's laugh boomed throughout Bliss. Everyone joined in. "Radimar has a special interest in Timorous. What is your report on her progress?"

"I see there has been an increase in underling activity around Timorous, but Essince is creating some interference without bringing too much notice to Peccadillo's forces. I believe they are right on schedule."

"My King," Advisor Seaman spoke. "I don't recommend we send more Legionnaires to this cluster at this time. A greater presence would be perceived by Peccadillo as an act of war."

Accura appreciated King Iam's desire to include all those he loved in the work at hand. "Advisor Financer, what do you think is best here?"

After a moment of thoughtful consideration, Financer said, "I believe we can find a healthy balance here. If we send only two Legionnaires at a time, and gradually, the action may remain unnoticed."

"Call in our Captain of the Legionnaires." King Iam's voice thundered throughout the room.

Chapter 16

In the late afternoon, Timorous left Essince's apartment feeling lighter and happier than she had ever felt. They accomplished a lot in the hours they'd spent together. Tims' organizational skills kicked in as she made sure the kitchen and bathroom items were well arranged. Essince's free spirit, as she called it, brought creative personality to the décor in each room. They teased and laughed most of the time away. Tims wished every day could be like this.

When she came back to her apartment door, she reached for her key. That's when she noticed the door hung slightly open. She froze.

Anxiety and Fright watched from a distance. They would have leaped on her, but she still glowed from being in Essince's presence. They yelled from the sidelines, "Not safe. Not safe. Don't go in."

Tims felt cautious but not as fearful as she usually felt. Maybe she left it this way. She had been rather upset when she left. Remembering Hearsay's plan to come over, Tims decided it had to be Hearsay's doing.

Tims slowly opened the door and looked around. Everything looked normal. She stepped in and shut the door behind her, forgetting to lock it. Before she reached her kitchen, Hearsay came bursting into her apartment with Meddling right on her heels.

Hearsay ran to Tims and hugged her. "Are you okay?"

Tims stood wide-eyed, her arms limp at her sides, not knowing how to answer.

"I was so worried about you. You never just disappear. Where have you been?" Hearsay was clearly concerned, yet the more she spoke, the more upset she became. She didn't even wait for Tims' answers.

Tims noticed the way Meddling stared at her with silent accusations and wondered why Meddling was in her apartment.

After she ran out of questions, Hearsay put her fists on her hips and tapped one foot. "Well?"

Seated on her shoulder, Gossip's face held a similar expression. The glow coming from Tims both angered and frightened him. He cut an angry glare at Fright and Anxiety. They both cringed. They hadn't been entirely truthful about whom they were dealing with.

Tims looked away from Hearsay. "Well . . . um, my new neighbor . . . well, she asked me if I would come over and help her unpack." The last part sounded more like a question than a statement. "I didn't realize what time—"

"What? And you went?" Hearsay fumed. "And you didn't think to call me and tell me that?" She looked up and flung her hands up in the air as if Tims were out of her mind.

"You hung up on me and left." Tims motioned to the phone.

"You knew I was coming," Hearsay huffed. "You could have left a note."

Tims stood speechless. She could have left a note, but then Hearsay would have come to get her. She would have missed out on her wonderful time with Essince. She looked back and forth between Hearsay and Meddling.

Meddling leaned in. "So, Tims, let's lay it out in plain English. Hearsay said you are secretly dating Radimar." She crossed her arms and raised an eyebrow.

"What? No. What?" Timorous took a step back and glanced back and forth between the two women. "Hearsay, why would you ever say something like that?" Now she felt annoyed. "I told you I just went to pick up my wallet."

Hearsay cringed, looking only slightly guilty. "This isn't like you. You don't go out and meet men alone or at all. You don't just leave your apartment when you know I'm coming over. What's going on?"

A sudden flash of light passed the little underlings. They knew right away a Messenger had entered and left in a blink.

"What's going on?" Snoop yelled to the other underlings. "Get busy and stop them."

Something changed inside Timorous. She straightened and crossed her arms. "I don't have to tell you everything I do and everyone I see." Her response surprised even her.

Hearsay stood massaging her jaw, as if trying to figure out how to respond to this new Tims.

Tims softened her tone. "I appreciate your concern, but right now, I'm really tired. I worked hard today, and I want to rest before I have to go back to work tomorrow." She walked to the door and opened it. "So, if you don't mind, I'll see you tomorrow." She hardly believed what she was doing.

Hearsay's mouth hung open with that same guppy-like look Timorous often had.

She really needed to stop doing that around Radimar. It's very unattractive. Tims almost giggled out loud at her silly thought.

Hearsay finally stomped to the door and bent close to Tims' face. Through gritted teeth, she said, "We'll talk about this later when you come to your senses." With her chin up, she marched out as if a great injustice had been committed against her.

Meddling followed her but stopped in front of Tims. She looked her up and down, with one eyebrow raised and a smirk on her face. She swaggered out the door, never breaking eye contact until Tims closed the door.

Had she just lost her best friend? Tims slumped onto her couch, unable to believe what she'd just done. But in the midst of her guilt and sadness, something new ebbed into her . . . encouragement, comfort, and strength.

Messengers dusted her with a fine gold powder that held the power of King Iam, filling her very soul.

GOSSIP, SNOOP, ANXIETY, and Fright, all yelled at once as they made their way up the stairs with Hearsay and Meddling,

"Quiet," Anxiety shouted. "Do you want the Toadies to know what just happened? It will be the end of us."

"Who said the Toadies were involved in this?" Snoop asked. "This isn't their area."

"I ran into a group of them on my way to get reinforcements," Anxiety said. "They know we are having difficulties with our assignment. They said they'd been called in to increase the Guard in our cluster."

"And you brought us into this mess?" Snoop screamed.

"We only asked you because we knew you were the best." Anxiety hoped to flatter Snoop. "Just think how this could promote your position. We'll show those Toadies they don't have anything on us. The Prince will probably give us a reward." At least Anxiety hoped so.

His words seemed to cheer the others too.

"Anxiety, what kind of reinforcements did you get?" Snoop asked.

"I found a few friends. Jealousy joined us last night at Meddling's apartment. I also found Duplicity to help with Hearsay." Anxiety rattled on. "I even talked Lust into helping, although he seemed disinterested. I think he only agreed out of boredom."

"Hopefully, that's enough." Gossip scowled.

"I'M SORRY ABOUT THAT," Meddling said to Hearsay. "You never really know who your friends are until times like these. I'm going to be right here to help you figure out what's going on."

"She never behaves this way. What just happened in there?" Hearsay ran her fingers through her hair in confusion. Tims just blew her off for the first time ever.

"Obviously, she's keeping something from you. How do we even know if she helped the neighbor? Maybe she's been out with Radimar this whole time?" Meddling shook her head. "I've seen people do crazy things for love . . . if you can call a crush on him love."

"She did seem especially happy when we first walked in, didn't she?"

Gossip laughed. Things were looking up.

Meddling gave Hearsay an encouraging smile. "Yes, and I'll bet she just doesn't want to share him with you. Has she even offered to introduce you to him?"

"No." Hearsay shook her head. "No, this isn't like Tims. We tell each other everything."

"Look at the evidence." Meddling rubbed Hearsay's shoulders. "She's met with Radimar more than once. People say he has some kind of power. Do you think he has her in a hypnotic state? You said she isn't acting like herself."

Hearsay sat up a little straighter. "I don't know. Maybe."

Meddling's back rub became more intense. "Why would Radimar pick Tims of all people?" She looked into the large mirror opposite the couch and appraised her assets. With her full figure and low-cut top, she had so much more to offer him.

Jealousy giggled and turned a brighter shade of green.

"We'll get to the bottom of this," Meddling said with determination. "We just need a plan." She dug her thumbs into Hearsay's shoulders.

"Ow, you're hurting me." Hearsay pulled away and turned around. She gasped when she saw the devious expression on Meddling's face.

"I'm sorry," Meddling said unconvincingly. "Anyway, tomorrow you see if you can get any more information from her. She trusts you. I'll pay a visit to our new neighbor. What are neighbors for?" She snickered.

Hearsay walked down the stairs, pausing at Tims' door. She almost knocked but then decided against it. "Tims will be calling soon to apologize anyways; she always does."

Chapter 17

Timorous slept well again but woke early. She felt regret for how she'd treated Hearsay. She needed to find a way to patch this up. Maybe she'd have time to talk to her before work. Tims had never stood up to Hearsay before, and in the past she'd always made sure to apologize right away. Because she chose not to this time, she worried Hearsay would be even more upset with her. She needed to catch her friend before work started.

Dark clouds gave her walk to work an ominous feeling.

Fright, who hung onto Tims' ankle, worked his way up her leg. Anxiety followed suit on the other side.

Tims noticed how quiet it seemed. "Where is everyone? Are they still in bed?" she whispered to herself, feeling more uneasy with every step.

She looked back and noticed a man about twenty feet behind her. The hairs on the back of her neck stood up. She picked up her pace, and so did he. Tims' heart rate increased. She tried to tell herself not to be afraid, but the feeling grew stronger still. Was he following her? He didn't look menacing, but Tims was alone and vulnerable.

He caught up to her more quickly than she had expected.

"Hey," he called out.

Tims jumped and prepared to bolt when he grabbed her by her forearm, causing her to spin around to face him.

"I'm sorry if I frightened you." Nothing about him looked sorry. In fact, he looked her up and down, making her feel dirty. "Don't I know you from somewhere?"

Tims shrugged off his hand and stared at him. He stood tall and could easily overpower her. *Run. Run!* Her body refused to move.

"Aren't you from Outfit Outlet? One of those girls who met that mystery guy?"

Tims took two steps backward but remained silent.

"What's the matter? Don't you speak?" He frowned at her.

She turned and walked away, searching for support. She quickened her pace.

"Hey, where are you going?" He quickly caught up to Tims again and moved in front of her, walking backward. "Can't a guy ask a pretty girl a question?" Lust radiated from his eyes.

Memories of her stepbrother made Tims feel sick to her stomach. Her heart pounded. She tried to move around him, but he blocked her.

"Please let me pass. I'll be late for work. My boss is waiting for me." Her voice wavered.

"I'm sure he won't mind me walking with you." A grin spread across his face, sending chills down her back. "You know, it's not safe for a pretty girl like you to be out walking alone."

Something about the way he said it sent fear screaming through her body. She pushed hard to get past him and took off running. She heard him several steps behind her. She'd never been a fast runner, but trying seemed her only option. Just as she turned the corner, she tripped, catching her toe on a raised crack in the sidewalk. An old man caught her, saving her from a certain fall.

He steadied her and looked directly into her eyes. "Are you okay, Miss?" His voice was filled with concern.

Shocked she hadn't knocked him down and struggling to catch her breath, she hung onto the old man for dear life. "I'm . . . sorry. That . . . man . . . was . . . chasing me." As she pointed behind her, she turned around, but he had disappeared. Shocked, relieved, and a little embarrassed, she pulled herself away.

"Well, it looks like I showed up just in time," the old man smiled.

Now Tims could see him clearly. When he smiled, all his wrinkles smiled with him. He seemed really old. Strange, because very few old people still lived in Uncertainty. She had never seen him before.

He had a full head of white hair and a whiskered face. His walking stick looked as ancient as he did. A good six inches taller than Tims but hunched over from age, he might have been quite tall in his youth. His rough, callused hands spoke of a hardworking man. No wonder she hadn't knocked him down.

"Thank you." Tims felt heat rise to her face. "I don't know what would have happened to me if you hadn't shown up. I mean, there really was a man chasing me."

"I believe ya. I saw the snake hightail it out of here when he saw me. I guess I'm scarier than I thought." He chuckled, putting Tims at ease.

"Would you mind walking with me to my work? I mean, if it's not out of your way. It's not far." Tims didn't want to tell him she wasn't going to leave his side until she had safely arrived at work.

"Sure. I'm just out walking for exercise. I like to walk early before the hustle and bustle of the town begins. My name is Warder." He pointed behind him. "I live on the very outskirts of the Uncertainty near Obscurity."

Tims' steps faltered. "Isn't that rather dangerous, living so close to Obscurity? I've heard some pretty scary things about it."

"Na, nothing out there ever bothers me. Why would they? I'm just an old man in an old log cabin." He smiled again, his wrinkles smiling with him.

Tims loved the twinkle in his eye, but she was unconvinced about living close to such a scary place. She would never do that. "My name is Timorous, but you can call me Tims." She wondered again at her newfound courage to introduce herself to a complete stranger.

"Well, Tims, which way do we go?"

"That way." Tims pointed in the direction he'd been coming from.

FRIGHT AND ANXIETY began to descend, arguing with one another. Frustrated, her little companions had no choice but to quickly climb back down her legs and then followed from a short distance.

"Who is that guy?" Anxiety asked. "He's definitely been in the presence of our enemy. Look at him glow. I've never seen a human glow that brightly before. What do you think?"

"I don't know, but it can't be good. What should we do?" Fright asked. "Lust had this until this guy showed up."

"We need to find a way to get her away from all these encounters with the enemy."

TIMS ASKED A FEW NONINTRUSIVE questions. Warder didn't seem to mind answering them. Concerned someone his age walked by himself, she became bolder and asked if he had anyone who might walk him home. He told her his family had left him for a better place. She wanted to ask what he meant but decided against it.

"Nope, it's just me and my cat, Cozy. She makes good company, a great listener too. Never complains or asks for anything except to be fed." Warder laughed.

He was the nicest old person she'd ever met. Not that she knew any older people, but some came through her line at work. Tims understood what it felt like to be alone.

"Would you like to come over for dinner sometime?" *My gosh. What has gotten into me*? She'd never invited anyone over except Hearsay. Her cheeks warmed again.

"I don't get out much. My legs give me problems. These morning walks are all I'm able to do. Getting around just isn't practical for me anymore. But thank you for asking." His smile warmed her heart.

"Maybe I could bring you dinner sometime?" she suggested.

"Sure." Warder's face brightened. "I'll give you my number when we get you to your work. You can call when it's a good time for you. Bliss only knows, I'm always available."

Glad she'd made the offer, Tims still found his last statement very strange. Actually, it scared her a little. No one talked about Bliss or even mentioned it. She wanted to ask him about this but just as they reached her store, Officious emerged.

"There you are." His voice boomed across the parking lot. "I've been waiting for you." He quickly ushered her away from Warder, who smiled and waved as she looked back. Officious rattled on about some new TV advertising campaign. Tims felt sad she had missed the opportunity to get Warder's number.

The next thing she knew, Officious sat her down in a chair and a makeup artist began powdering her face.

"Wait. What?"

"Haven't you been listening to a word I've said? We are making a commercial to promote our campaign of 'Important People Shop Here.' You, my girl, are one of the stars of our commercial." Officious grinned from ear to ear.

Tims jumped out of the chair. "No. I can't do this."

Pushing her back down, Officious kept his hands on her shoulders. "Yes, you can. You'll be great. I have it all here in your script. Just say you met Radimar and that Outfit Outlet is his favorite store to shop at. Done, simple and easy."

Tims didn't like how close his face came to hers, but mostly she felt terrified of speaking on camera. "I really can't do this. I won't be able to speak."

Fright smiled at Anxiety.

"Nonsense, my girl, this is easy." He waved his hand in a dismissive gesture. "Hearsay has already done her part. It went wonderfully. I'm sure you will be just as good."

"But he never said this was his favorite store. We hardly spoke." Tims' voice rose in protest, and she feared she might cry.

"Now, that's not true. Radimar did purchase items from this store. Who knows? Outfit Outlet may be the *only* store he shopped at. Wouldn't that make it his favorite store? It's all about business. The point is, he did come here, and we need to take advantage of this while it's still of interest to the public."

Tims didn't have time to respond because they quickly moved her behind one of the checkout counters and held up cue cards for her to read. The makeup artist did one more touch up, and the director yelled, "Action!"

Tims stood there, swallowed hard, and opened her mouth, but nothing came out.

"Let's try this again," the director said. "Just be yourself and share how much Radimar loved the store. Action."

Still, she stood there motionless and mute. She could feel the blood rushing from her head. Officious walked up to her and grabbed her by the shoulders just as she felt faint. He gave her a little shake. Getting right in her face, he whispered through his teeth, "Timorous, you do this now. Your job is on the line. Don't embarrass me like this."

His breath smelled like tobacco, coffee, and donuts. She felt sick.

After several failed attempts and one quick run to the bathroom, she just could not make herself speak.

Both Anxiety and Fright rode high on her shoulders speaking all kinds of horrific ideas into her ears.

What if people came looking for her? What if that man who chased her came looking for her? Everyone will know who she is. Everyone would recognize her. They were all looking at her now.

She noticed everyone's disapproving stares. She felt like such a failure, just like she'd always been. She scanned the crowd. All her fears seemed to come crashing down on her.

Fright and Anxiety gave each other a high-five.

After one last failed attempt to shoot the commercial, Officious screamed, "You're fired! Get your things and leave . . . permanently." Everyone scurried away, leaving her to go to her station, gather the few personal items she had, and placed them in a small box. With her head down, she walked to the exit.

It was almost opening time, and she hadn't even seen Hearsay. Everyone avoided eye contact. Tims handed her keys and name badge to Armor.

Before she turned to leave, Armor handed her a piece of paper. "The old man who came with you wanted me to give you this."

She cautiously opened the paper. It read, "Warder Harmless 777-1212 Give me a call sometime."

Armor pointed at the note. "He seems like a nice guy." With his military training in profiling, he would know how to judge a person. It gave her a little reassurance. She thanked him as she stuffed the note in her purse. With her head down, she began the walk back home feeling defeated.

WARDER LEFT FEELING happy to finally have met the chosen one. Radimar and Essince talked about her nonstop, sharing all the nice things about her. Now he understood why. She was perfect, sweet, and kindhearted. Warder recognized the Messengers sweeping in and out giving her courage. It created an almost halo effect around her pretty little face, even if Timorous didn't recognize the activity all around her. No doubt Peccadillo's crew would continue their pursuit to stop her from finding her way, but he knew King Iam would make a way.

Chapter 18

Meddling decided to visit the new neighbor to check Tims' story. "What would a neighborly visit be without a welcoming gift?"

She rummaged through a box of items she had no use for. Not the type to spend money on anyone but herself, she searched until she found some potpourri her mother had given her. After plopping her secondhand gift into a used flower print gift bag, she marched down the stairs to do some inquiring.

She knocked confidently on the door. Essince opened it quickly. Her radiant smile almost blinded her. Meddling stepped back, unable to speak.

In the presence of King Iam's intense power, Snoop and Duplicity jumped off and ran to the other side of the hall. They now understood why Anxiety and Fear were having such a difficult time.

"May I help you?" Essince asked sweetly.

Meddling quickly recovered and handed her the gift bag. "Oh yes. I'm Meddling, your neighbor from upstairs." She motioned in the direction of her apartment. "I wanted to welcome you to the complex."

"How nice of you. What a friendly place this is."

Still stunned, Meddling worked to begin her investigation. "We do like to think of ourselves as one big happy family. Have you met any of the other tenants? Like, maybe Timorous?"

Essince nodded. "Yes, I have. She seems like a very sweet girl."

Meddling hoped for a bit of gossip, but this gal refused to make it easy. "Well, yes, she is quite sweet." She looked over Essince's shoulder to see into her apartment. "But have you heard? She might be secretly seeing that man everyone's been talking about."

"What man is that?" Essince put one hand on the doorjamb and the other on the door, blocking most of Meddling's view.

Meddling gasped. "Where have you been? It's been all over the news. Radimar, that's who I'm talking about."

"Oh, I think she might have mentioned him." Essince frowned. "I don't remember her saying anything about dating him."

"We aren't exactly sure. Um, could I come in?" Meddling got on the tips of her toes, trying to get a glimpse of the apartment to see if things were unpacked as Tims had said.

"Unfortunately, I'm just heading out. Maybe another time." Essince stepped out of her apartment and locked her door. "Why does it matter?"

Now we're getting somewhere, Meddling thought as she followed Essince down the hall. "Tims has been acting a little strange lately. I'm concerned it's because of her contact with Radimar since some really unusual things seem to happen whenever he's around. You really haven't heard of Radimar?"

Essince stopped and stared at Meddling. "Tims can date and hang out with whoever she wants."

Meddling looked away from the woman's intense gaze. "We are a little concerned for her . . . the other tenants and me. By the way, your place seems so neat and tidy for just having moved in. You must have had some help?"

Essince squinted. "You have a lot of questions. I haven't noticed anything unusual about Tims. Have a great day." She walked away.

Frustrated because she'd failed to get the information, Meddling whispered, "Better to not involve her anyway. She's absolutely gorgeous. I don't want her around when I meet Radimar."

DOWN THE HALL, SNOOP and Jealousy were surprised to see Timorous entering the back of the apartment building with Fright and Anxiety riding on her shoulders and high-fiving one another. They hopped down as Tims entered her apartment and ran to tell their friends of their victory.

"You should have seen it." Fright squealed with delight. "We worked her like a puppet."

"Hold on, you two." Snoop glared at them. "We just met the neighbor."

Fright and Anxiety immediately shut up.

Snoop and his partner shook with fury. "What the Abyss do you think you are doing? That's Essince of Iam." They all spat on the floor. "No wonder the Toadies are here.

This is too big for us. We need their help. If they learned we knew about Essince and didn't tell them, it will for sure be the end of us."

"If you won't go to our superiors, we will." Jealousy spat again. "You dragged us into this mess, and we aren't going down with you."

"COMMANDER DEAMON." Usher bowed respectfully. "I have important information for you."

Deamon left Usher in his bowed position much longer than necessary, still sour over the swap of assistants that had left him to deal with Peccadillo's pitiful Head Attendant. Usher's began body to shake from holding the position. Deamon did whatever he could to make Usher miserable. "What is it? I don't have time for your trivial information."

Usher straightened. "We have a firsthand account that Essince of Iam—" He spat on the ground.

Deamon followed suit.

Clearing his throat, Usher continued. "She's *moved* into the cluster of Nowhere."

Deamon stood, towering over Usher. "Moved in? Why the Abyss would she move into Nowhere?" Deamon cursed.

Usher took a couple of steps away just in case Deamon was in a hair-grabbing mood.

"And who supplied this information? Bring them to me at once."

"As you commanded, I have sent groups of Toadies out to each cluster. The Toadies in the cluster of Nowhere have interrogated some of the underlings."

"Bring in the underlings to me for questioning *immediately*. Get to it, Usher. You're wasting precious time."

Usher called the Obliterists to bring in the informants. Fright and Anxiety looked very small in comparison to the rest of the Guard.

Deamon paced back and forth, glaring at Usher, as if he were annoyed Usher was prepared for the order. A lost opportunity to further punish him. Finally, the Commander sat down on what he liked to call his throne. The other Obliterists and Toadies in the room drew closer to observe.

The underlings were the size of tiny rodents with gnarled hands and beady black eyes that were too close together to be normal. Underlings were not only the smallest but the lowest in the chain of command. Fright and Anxiety both shook so badly they almost looked like a blur.

Before they could even bow to him, Deamon shouted, "Announce yourselves."

They fell, groveling to the ground. Anxiety tried to muster his courage. "I'm Anxiety and this is Fright. Our assignment is Timorous Hominid." He peeked upward and saw Commander Deamon leaning toward him. He rushed on. "She has not given us any problem. Very timid, never venturing out. But there has been a recent change." Anxiety paused, casting a glance at Deamon's angry stare. "It seems Timorous has encountered Essince . . . and Radimar." After Anxiety and Fright spat on the ground, they held their breath.

Everyone stood still, all eyes on Deamon, waiting to see how the Commander would react. His body went rigid with controlled anger. After what seemed like forever, he finally spoke, calmly and almost kindly. "And how long have these encounters been occurring?"

Encouraged by his soft reply, Fright spoke up. "About a week, my Lord." He bowed down again.

Deamon jumped out of his chair and paced the room, screaming obscenities. Everyone scattered. As he raged, he threw whatever he could get his hands on and punched and kicked everything in sight.

Deamon finally stopped and stood still, breathing heavily.

Anxiety took one step closer and weakly offered, "We were unaware of their identity because we were so certain the Obliterists who guard Obscurity had blocked their way."

Usher hid his grin behind his hand.

Deamon stepped dangerously close to the two underlings. "Are you saying I am not doing my job?" With every word he got louder and louder.

Rushing on, "N-No Sir. We are just underlings and know nothing of how the Great Commander Deamon and his Guard works."

Deamon would have squashed them right then but knew the Prince would not approve. These two miserable fools were their only lead, so they needed to use this information to their advantage.

Fright and Anxiety fearfully clung to each other.

"Usher!" Deamon shouted, pretending he had left the room, to further humiliate him.

"Yes, my Lord." Usher immediately stepped forward.

"Prepare to leave for Netherworld and provide transportation for our small friends here. Call the Leaders of the

Guard. Now that we know our enemy's main target, we must move to apprehend and interrogate her to find a way to weaken our enemy's influence and stop these breaches of security in all the clusters.

Elated, Usher did little jig, obviously happy to be heading back to the Netherworld.

Deamon scowled. "Make sure some of our best Toadies cover for these underlings while they are gone."

"Yes, my Lord. I have already assigned them." Usher bowed, proving once again how accomplished he was at his job.

As usual, Commander Deamon ignored him.

Chapter 19

Stunned from being fired, Tims unlocked her apartment door. After setting the box of personal items on the table, she slumped down on her couch. Wrapping her arms around herself, she began to rock back and forth. "How did all this happen?"

Not only had she lost her job, she had probably lost her only friend. Hearsay didn't even make an effort to see her during the disastrous filming for the TV commercial.

Brokenhearted, Tims began to cry.

FOUR TOADIES WATCHED Timorous.

"I don't see what the big deal is. She doesn't seem to be a threat. Why were we called to do the work of some nobody underlings?" complained a Toady.

"Our orders came directly from Commander Deamon. It's not ours to question, but we can definitely make life more difficult for her. We will show all the underlings in this cluster how it's done."

The Toadies increased her emotion, but Timorous had made their job easy. She had stated her fears out loud and her body language spoke volumes concerning her anxiety.

Each Toady had an Amplifier and carried communication devices that only worked within the clusters. The Amplifiers were long with a point at the bottom end and widened to a ball near the top to fit the Toadies large greenish-brown leathery hands. By command of the Prince, only the Toadies were allowed to use these devices.

The rod was placed near their victim's head while the Toadies continued to feed the negative emotions. Humans were unaware they were being victimized by the enemy. Most gravitated toward the rod, like a small bug to a bright light at night.

Foolishly humans often joked about their fears or misgivings. The moment Toadies caught even the slightest hint of negativity, they spoke thoughts into their minds to confirm these fears in order to increase the emotions.

They all stood around Tims with evil grins as they watched her rock herself on the couch. She held her hands to her face, saying over and over, "Why, why did this happen to me? I always mess up. Something must be terribly wrong with me."

The Toadies relished watching her suffer. Often, they could back off and on their own, the humans continued feeding their own negative emotions. At this point they were not a threat to Peccadillo's kingdom and were left to their own personal Abyss. But at this point they were having too much fun.

Leaning in, the Toadies held their Amplifiers closer to Tims. The rods crackled and hissed like live electricity. The lead Toady held his rod even closer to Tims' shoulder to amplify her sense of defeat.

Using their Amplifiers, they created an emotional heaviness around Timorous. She curled up into a tight ball on the couch. "I wish I could die."

The Toadies laughed. They pushed thoughts of stupidity and worthlessness into her mind.

Timorous moaned. "What has gone wrong these last few days? What has changed?" After a moment she whispered, "Radimar. Everything had been fine until I met him."

The Toadies spat and pressed harder to convince her their sworn enemy was the cause of all her problems. Prince Peccadillo's takeover had been achieved using the same tactic. They laughed at the ease of this assignment.

"Maybe he did wonderful things for some but did awful things for others, like, um . . . like . . . sneaking up on me at the park and making me drop my wallet. Wasn't he the reason I lost my job? If I'd never met him, none of this would have ever happened."

The phone rang. The Toadies held her in deep negative thought. Timorous stumbled to find the phone, disoriented as the phone continued to ring. She tentatively picked it up, "Hello?"

"Tims, this is Hearsay. What happened? I heard they fired you. Why would they do that?"

Tims paused to blow her nose. "They released me for not properly performing my duties at work."

"What? You're always on time. Your money till always balances. This doesn't make sense." Hearsay gasped. "No. You didn't refuse to be in the commercial, did you?"

"No, I didn't refuse. I just couldn't do it. My anxiety was so high that I struggled to get any words to come out."

This meant Hearsay was the lone star of the commercial. Half-heartedly she said, "If you come back right now and do it, they would probably give you your job back."

"Hearsay, I can't do that. I'm going to go now. I'm not up to talking about this right now."

"Well!" Hearsay sounded offended. "It seems to me you aren't up to talking about anything these days. Call me when you are." She paused. "How could you do this to me? We've been friends forever." She hung up, leaving Tims holding a silent phone.

Grinning, the Toadies watched Tims' face fill with shock and confusion. She stared at the phone in her hand. Hearsay turned this whole thing around. "Maybe Hearsay is right; maybe I am the one at fault." She started crying again.

The Toadies giggled as they watched her torment herself.

The moment she hung up, the phone rang again. She quickly picked it up. "Hearsay, I'm sorry. I'll tell you everything if you come over tonight."

Nothing but silence on the other end of the phone.

"Hearsay?"

"Hi, Timorous. This is Essince. Are you okay?"

Thankfully Essince couldn't see the red that crept into her face.

"Tims, are you okay?"

"Uh . . . yes, I-I'm fine. What can I do for you?" Tims sniffed.

The Toadies loved how easy she was to read and continued to poke and prod her with their rods.

"I didn't know if you were at work or not."

Tims said nothing.

"Are you sure you're okay? I could come back home if you need me." Essince offered so kindly, Tims' tears ran down her face silently.

"No, that's okay, I'm fine," she managed to say.

"Your neighbor, Meddling, came to welcome me to the apartment complex this morning."

"What? Welcome you? Meddling?"

"Yes. She said the complex likes to think of itself as one big happy family."

Tims laughed once. "What a strange thing for Meddling to say."

Essince sighed. "Yeah, I thought it kind of strange too. But even more strange were the things she said about you."

"About me?"

"That's Essince!" a Toady shouted and extended his rod to the back of Timorous' ear, intensifying her anxiety. "Get her off the phone," one of the Toadies yelled. "This is why we are here—to stop these interactions."

All their rods crackled loudly, as if a lightning storm swirled about in Tims' apartment.

She started scratching her body as if she were itchy all over. "I've got to go. I'll talk to you later." She abruptly hung up the phone. The itchy sensation seemed to create great agitation. She grabbed her purse and ran out the door. She didn't even remember to lock her door.

The Toadies weren't far behind. "Now you've done it. You've got her so worked up she didn't stay put where we were commanded to keep her."

"We needed to get her off the phone with our enemy." Now they were all screaming, yelling, and accusing each other while they ran after their charge.

NOT FAR FROM WARDER'S place, Radimar met with Captain Valiant. He held the highest rank of all the Legionnaires and was considered the most powerful and bravest of all. He was more than twenty feet tall, but at the moment he knelt down on one knee conferring with his Prince.

"Time is growing short, Val. The enemy is aware of our presence." Radimar spoke with confident urgency. "We must work quickly. Timorous needs more guards. You are to be very discreet as you increase your presence."

"Yes, my Lord. I was informed to bring in no more than two Legionnaires at a time. Although even at that, it may create more risk for her."

"She has already been exposed. Make sure your troops stay in the background but nearby if needed. We must make sure she finds her way to the *Book of Actualities* and ultimately to the quest. Assign her your top warriors and try not to draw any unnecessary attention. Peccadillo looks for any reason to make war."

Captain Valiant bowed as Prince Radimar dismissed him. Standing again, Valiant became almost invisible, the outline of his frame visible only when the light hit it just so. He moved like a light breeze on a summer day, unnoticed; yet at a moment's notice hecould become a mighty hurricane force on the command of King Iam.

WHAT SHOULD SHE DO now? Hearsay had been Tims' only trusted ally. Now she couldn't even call her. She walked for a few hours, not even caring which direction she headed. Her stomach growled, reminding her of how hungry and thirsty she was. It had to be well past lunchtime.

Seeing a grocery store ahead, she decided to buy a bottle of water. At the counter, she rummaged around in her purse for her wallet. The clerk cleared her throat impatiently. Tims struggled to keep her panic at bay. "Sorry."

When she finally pulled out her wallet, a piece of paper fell to the ground.

The Toadies tried to hide the note, but just as they were about to kick it under some shelving, a flash of light stopped them. All the Toadies fell back, blinded, and rendered temporarily powerless. "Essince," they groaned.

"Miss, I think you dropped something," said a sweet voice.

Tims turned to say thanks but did a double take. "Have I met you before?"

A cute, strawberry blond girl about ten years old handed Tims the note, then stood with her hands behind her back, twisting side to side as she smiled up at her. Something about her eyes, or maybe it was her smile that stirred a memory, but Tims couldn't quite place her.

"No, I don't think so. Bye." She waved and ran off.

Essince could easily change her form as needed. The Toadies were so focused on Timorous not finding the note they were blindsided and now lay paralyzed on the floor. They had never experienced being so close to Essince. Not only were they unable to move and grab their Amplifiers, but it seemed the rods had stopped working altogether. Confusion, fear, and anger filled their black hearts.

Tims left the grocery store and sat on a nearby bench to drink her water and study the piece of paper. "Call me sometime" stood out to her. Somehow, she felt more at peace. Maybe she just needed a short rest. Should she call Warder? But calling someone she'd just met and inviting herself over created a challenge for her.

Without Fright and Anxiety at her side and the Toadies temporarily stunned, Timorous decided to do something she never done before—be courageous.

The Messengers could fly quite fast, but today they had extra speed as they flew through the air with an extra push from the strong Legionnaires. This made their job faster and much more fun. At this speed, most of the enemy troops were unable to see them coming or going.

Timorous found a pay phone. She carefully dialed Warder's phone number. It rang for what felt like forever. She almost hung up when a gruff voice answered. "Hello, who's calling during my afternoon nap?"

Tims felt her courage waver. "Hi, Warder. It's me, Timorous. You met me earlier this morning." She clutched the phone nervously with both hands. "I'm sorry to have woken you. I can call back later."

"Timorous, I'm so glad you got my note." His tone grew cheerful. "Don't worry about a grumpy old man. The only ones who ever call me are usually trying to sell me some kind of nonsense. Are you coming over for dinner?"

"I . . . um, I guess if you want me to. What would you like me to make?"

"Make? Oh, yes, you offered to make dinner for me. How about you be my guest tonight. I already have a good turkey roasting. I'm not a half-bad cook, ya know." Warder chuckled.

Tims imagined him smiling, wrinkles and all. She found herself smiling too. "Okay, that sounds great. What time do you want me to come?"

"What time are you off work?"

After a short pause, "I'm not working for the rest of the day." At least she didn't lie.

"Great. Why not come over now and keep me company while dinner is cooking." He paused for an answer, then added, "I don't get much company, you know."

Tims couldn't turn him down. She knew what it felt like to be alone. "Okay. Can you tell me how to get to your place? And can I bring anything?"

"Just yourself." He chuckled. "Just yourself."

Chapter 20

Warder rattled off the address and directions to his place. Tims hoped she had jotted it all down correctly on the back of the note. Once she hung up the phone, she remembered Warder said he lived right on the edge of Obscurity. A cold shiver ran down her back. Could she really go so near that scary boundary? But she'd just promised Warder she'd come. Looking down at her notes, she took her first steps into the unknown. Even though she felt a little nervous, she just couldn't disappoint him.

Around her, the unseen group of Messengers arrived quickly and pushed as much encouragement and hope from King Iam into her before she began her trek toward the enemy lines.

WHEN THE TOADIES WERE finally able to move again, they limped along, dragging their rods behind them. Arguments broke out about whose fault it was for missing Essince's arrival. They had no desire to report this humiliating attack. They still searched for Timorous and knew they were getting closer. With their keen sense of smell, they detected their target's scent.

Then their communication device started beeping. "Uh-oh. Usher ordered a status update," the lead Toady announced. It was the only technology the Prince allowed because it only worked in the clusters. It also made for faster communication in emergency situations like this.

"We can quickly move into Obscurity and pretend we didn't receive it," one of the other Toadies suggested.

"Someone would surely tell and that would be then end of us."

The six-inch pentagon-shaped communication device made out of black stone, held six inset buttons that controlled different types of communication. The lead Toady held it to his ear. "Yes, Royal Assistant Usher, what can we do for you?"

"You are late on your report," Usher snapped. "You know the protocol. Do you have your assignment under control?"

"Please accept my sincerest apologies. Yes, we have thoroughly discouraged our assignment and she presents no problems."

"No encounters with the enemy?" Usher asked suspiciously.

"None whatsoever." The Toady forced confidence into his voice.

"I find that odd since, for some reason, the enemy seemed determined to interfere with her. Are you sure you haven't missed something?"

The veins in the lead Toady's neck bulged and pulsed with fear at being caught in his lie. "Absolutely. We will contact you the moment we suspect something, Sir."

"Tell me then, you slimy ball of mush, why some underlings in her apartment reported Timorous left running while all of you fell all over yourselves to catch up with her? How could she be in her apartment if she is out running around town? Hmm?"

Silence reigned for a few short moments.

"Oh. Yes. Allow me to clarify. I never said she didn't leave, just that she presented no problem. Her friend called and discouraged her further—with our help, of course. In her disheartened state, she left for a walk." He cringed, awaiting Usher's response.

"*Do not* let her out of your sight!" Usher screamed. "We have eyes everywhere. If you can't handle this, call immediately." He paused for effect. "Your reward will be waiting for you." The call ended abruptly.

The Toadies shifted their eyes here and there, wondering who watched them and had reported back to Usher.

"He didn't mention the store incident," one Toady reasoned. "Maybe he doesn't have eyes everywhere."

"This must be extremely important." The lead Toady marched away cursing, the other Toadies ran to catch up with him.

TIMS WONDERED IF SHE should go home to get her car. An uneasy sense about going back home kept her moving forward.

Essince sat in a nearby tree in the form of a blue jay and sprinkled some wisdom on Timorous. Tims saw nothing but felt a slight change in her reasoning. From the unseen world, this looked very much like gold dust.

She knew the Toadies were several blocks back, lying on their slimy bellies to move more quickly in their frantic search for Timorous.

Working to make it more difficult for them, Essince called for some Messengers to slow them down by tripping them, knocking their Power Rods from their hands, and throwing out different scents to confuse their path. Any delay gave Tims more time to reach Warder's house.

Timorous made her way closer to Obscurity, noticing most of the buildings appeared abandoned. Panic seeped into her mind. This wasn't a good idea. *What was I thinking?* I hardly *know this man.* She studied the directions Warder had given her.

In the distance, she saw Obscurity's thick, dark green, fifty-foot high foliage. She'd never been this close to it before. The more she second-guessed her decision, the slower her pace became. Eerie noises sounded from the edges of Obscurity.

How did the old man make it all the way into my neighborhood? Didn't he say he had bad knees? The sound of chains falling to the ground reached her ears and caused the ground to shake. Simultaneously, a flock of blackbirds flew out of Obscurity. Tims ducked, barely avoiding them.

Before she turned to run, she heard a faint, faraway, "Hello." She glanced over her shoulder. The gruff voice repeated, "Hello."

The person was waving something in the air. She squinted, trying to see if it was a weapon or a guard telling her to stop,

"Hello." The sound drew closer, so did the person. He continued to wave whatever he held like a crazy person.

The weapon no longer waved and the greetings were fewer as well. He seemed to be struggling. "Timorous." He bent over, leaning on the object he'd been waving.

Warder!

Sighing with relief, she hurried toward him. When she reached him, he was wheezing from the exertion.

"Here." She pointed to a bench on the side of the street. "Let's sit down and rest a bit."

Warder struggled to catch his breath but finally spoke with joy in his voice. "Thank . . . you . . . I . . . was . . . afraid . . . you . . . wouldn't . . . come."

"Of course, I would come. I told you I would." Timorous didn't want to admit how close she'd come to turning back. "Warder, I was wondering. Your home is a long way from where we met this morning. How do you do it? How do you walk that far each morning?"

"Well." He laughed gruffly, finally breathing normally. "I don't usually go running." He winked at her. "I decided to come see if you got lost. Earlier today, someone dropped me off in town to walk. It served as a nice change of scenery, and I got to meet you." He gave her a kindly smile.

Tims was felt thankful that she hadn't turned back. "It took longer than I anticipated because I didn't expect it to be out this far, but I'm here now. That's what matters."

Chapter 21

All the Lead Guards of the clusters gathered in Prince Peccadillo's meeting hall again. Tensions were high among them as they anxiously awaited their prince.

Deamon noticed the table had been replaced, this time with a thicker slab of dark gray granite. Black snake-like designs and diamonds, embedded for eyes, covered its surface. Jagged, uneven edges bordered its oval shape.

When Prince Peccadillo entered, everyone rose and bowed. "All power and authority to our Prince Peccadillo." He waved a careless hand, and they took their seats.

"I assume I've been called to this meeting because something has been mishandled. Or are we here to celebrate?" Prince Peccadillo scanned the room, his lips twisted in a sadistic grin.

Miss Enchantress glided her way into the room. All the Guards rose and looked lustfully at her beauty. She chose to wear a charcoal black dress to match the Prince's black suit.

Deamon frowned jealously. She belonged with him.

Her gown ran to the floor, elegant and sensual, with lace see-through material in all but the most purposely placed opaque material. The snake with diamond eyes pattern of her dress mirrored that of the table, giving everyone an uneasy feeling of being watched.

"Hello, my dear." The Prince kissed her passionately, then took the kiss deeper with controlled violence. As he moved his lips down her neck and to the base of her neckline, she leaned her head back and moaned.

The Guard growled and shoved each other as they watched with pleasure.

When he finished, Miss Enchantress could barely stand. The Prince smiled as lust and jealousy rose in the room.

Deamon moved quickly to begin his report. Miss Enchantress stood behind the Prince, draping herself over him as he sat at the head of the table. From where Deamon stood, he had a perfect view of the exposed curves of her velvety skin. She smiled at him knowingly.

Pulling himself to his full height, Deamon began. "While there are still some reports coming from other clusters, only the cluster of Nowhere has confirmed sightings and seems to be the most active. They report multiple sightings of Radimar and that Essince has moved into town."

After they all spat, Deamon turned his head toward the Lead Guard of Nowhere. "I think it only fitting to have the Vacuity continue this report." Taking one last look down Miss Enchantress' dress, Deamon took his seat next to the Prince.

Usher flushed with visible admiration in respect for Deamon's scheming.

"Why in the Abyss would our enemy move into a cluster?" roared the Prince. "Speak up, Sergeant Vacuity."

Sergeant Vacuity sat near the end of the oval, directly across the table from the Prince. He stood slowly. "Prince Peccadillo, our underlings only recently came forward with information concerning their assignment. They reported the one of interest had a few personal encounters with Essince. Radimar seems to be staying in the background. There are no recent sightings of him—only rumors as of late." He paused as if gauging the Prince's response.

"And?" Prince Peccadillo's face looked guarded, as he continued to seductively pet Miss Enchantress' arm.

Vacuity's hands shook. "The underlings felt they had things under control—at least until Essince moved into an apartment across the hall from their charge."

The Prince stood clinching his fists.

"What the Abyss?" the Prince roared. Everyone leaned away from Vacuity. Prince's breath blasted Vacuity's hair back, leaving it singed on the ends. "Why did you allow Essince," he spat, "to move into your cluster? Were your lines not secure?" He glanced at Deamon.

"It appears she did not travel through Obscurity but found some other route." When the Prince's eyebrows raised, he hurried on. "Our borders were well protected—I guarantee that."

"What other route is there?" The Prince breathed heavily as he waited for an answer.

Vacuity remained silent.

"Tell me, you must have apprehended the one of interest since our enemy seems so set on being near her." He squinted and spoke through gritted teeth.

"We sent our best Toadies to discourage further activity with the enemy, but it seems they became overzealous. She ran from her dwelling. Some underlings happened to witness an unusual occurrence that may or may not have involved Essince." They all spat on the table. "The underling said the Toadies were incapacitated for a time."

"What? Sergeant Vacuity, you idiot. You're telling me you put your expert Toadies in place, causing a fearful human to run, and then they were taken off-guard by our enemy? Your lack of leadership and incompetence is a disgrace to my kingdom." With his hands behind his back and a scowl on his face, Prince Peccadillo paced.

"My Prince—" Deamon spoke cautiously. "Because of their idiocy, the one of interest is now in one of the last safe houses in your kingdom."

Without so much as a glance, Prince Peccadillo snapped his fingers and sent Vacuity to the Abyss. Nothing but a small whiff of black smoke remained and quickly dissipated. The Guard drew in a collective breath but remained still.

"Deamon, I want you to personally oversee the cluster of Nowhere and apprehend the one the enemy is hiding at first opportunity." The Prince's eyes turned blood-red. The intensity in the room was palpable.

"Prepare the Obliterists to advance on Essince as well. We must find out why the enemy is so interested in this mere human who lacks courage.

HEARSAY VISITED TIMS, hoping Radimar would be there. She knocked on the door. "Tims, I know you're in there. I know it must feel like the end of the world, but I'll help you find a new job." She put her ear to the door but could hear nothing. "I promise."

When no answer came, she dug through her purse. "I can't believe I'm doing this again." Just as she found the spare key, Meddling bounded down the stairs.

"She's not home. I don't think she's been home all day. What's going on?" Meddling stood against the post of the staircase, her arms crossed over her chest.

Hearsay gave her the short rundown of the day. After the story, Meddling had a smug look.

"What are you not telling me, Meddling?"

"Not much, but I did have a chat with our new neighbor, the one Tims alleged she helped yesterday."

"What do you mean 'alleged'? What did you find out?"

"Well, for starters, she refused to let me into her apartment. In fact, she didn't seem to want me to even see in. Don't you think that's strange? I even took her a welcome gift." She huffed out an angry breath. "She said she met Tims but didn't say anything about getting any help from her."

Hearsay moved closer with anticipation.

"She also said Tims mentioned meeting Radimar but didn't know anything else. In fact, she acted as if she hadn't even heard of him."

Hearsay's face fell. "That's it?"

"Well, I think my new neighbor is lying. Who hasn't heard of Radimar?" Meddling continued, "Tims is keeping secrets. She needs to tell someone, because you just have to tell someone, so you tell someone you don't even know."

"I don't know." Hearsay's brows came toward each other and she tightened her lips. "That's not like her. Maybe something bad happened and she's afraid to tell. You think she shared a secret with her neighbor rather than, me, her closest friend?" Hearsay rubbed her worried brow.

"Of course, it's not like her. She's hiding something. And yes, I think that's exactly what she did. It makes perfect sense. No one acts normal when they're keeping a big secret. You know how elusive Radimar has been. Now she is exclusively interacting with him."

The maintenance man came around the corner. "Hi ladies," he tipped his head when he passed them.

"Wait," Meddling almost shouted. "Mr. Ons, right?"

"You can call me Hands," he replied.

Meddling smiled, trying to be as cute as possible. "I just met our new tenant this morning. She seems really nice."

"New tenant?" Hands scratched his head. "I haven't heard anything about a new tenant."

"Sure. She's in 1C, and her name is Essince." Meddling spoke a little too dramatically.

Hands moved down the hall to 1C and rifled through his keys. "I heard the new tenant wasn't moving in until next month." He opened the door and swung it wide. "See." He waved a hand toward the empty apartment.

Hearsay and Meddling stared inside the empty apartment.

Meddling pushed her way in. "I swear she stood right here this morning and the place was filled with all her things." She blinked in confusion. "She even took my welcome gift."

"I don't know what you're talking about, but I've got work to do. Apartment 3F has a clogged sink." Hands Ons left the two women and went about his work.

The corner of Hearsay's mouth went up. "But I met her. Maybe Essince is someone bad and lied to her. What if Tims is in trouble?" She inserted her key in the lock of Tims' apartment but found it was already unlocked. "That can't be good," she said to herself.

Meddling followed her into Tims' apartment. "Really, Hearsay, you've got to believe me. Her neighbor was there and quite beautiful. She wouldn't let me in, but the place was full of her stuff. Maybe she's helping to hide Radimar too?"

"I don't know what to think."

Meddling's face turned red and she put her hands on her hips. "Look, I don't know what kind of trick this Essince gal is trying to play, but she and Tims are somehow in this together."

Hearsay scanned the room. "Tims, are you here?"

There was no answer.

Meddling sat on the chair and put her feet up on the ottoman. "Okay, let's say I didn't meet this mystery neighbor. Why would Tims lie about that?"

Hearsay frowned and sat on the couch. "I'm really concerned. This isn't like Tims. Maybe Radimar isn't a good guy. Maybe he's a bad guy. Maybe he swept her off her feet and . . . . and—" She trailed off, as if not wanting to think the worst. "Tims is such a simple girl. It wouldn't take much." Tears welled up in her eyes.

"Maybe she has to keep his whereabouts a secret." Meddling held her hand to her chin as she worked to solve the mystery. "He just shows up here and there. They've got to be connected somehow."

Hearsay gasped. "Tims refused to talk about him on the commercial at work today. I thought it was just nerves, but maybe you're right."

"We'll get to the bottom of all this and make Tims come clean."

Hearsay nodded halfheartedly. "I think I will wait in her apartment. She'll have to come home sometime. Right?"

"Good idea," Meddling agreed. "Call me the moment she gets here. I'm going to see what I can hear on the streets. I'll check back in about an hour."

Meddling headed out, while Hearsay set up camp in Tims' apartment. "Please come home, Tims," Hearsay pleaded out loud.

Chapter 22

Tims put her arm around Warder's waist and his arm over her shoulder, helping him stand and walk slowly back to his home. Tims tried not to look up as they came closer and closer to the edge of Obscurity but found it hard to keep her eyes on the path before her.

"Child, you're trembling."

She looked at him wide-eyed.

"I promise you, we're safe, even though the overgrowth hanging above us makes it feel like we're actually in Obscurity."

Tims looked down. Warder's arm over her shoulder gave her some sense of safety.

Warder's cabin sat near the five-foot-wide white line that separated human life from the dense forest of Obscurity. The line perfectly sculpted the edges of a portion of his yard. Nothing grew on the white powdered boundary line, not even a weed.

Rosebushes lined the last ten feet of the path leading to his front door. "These are beautiful. Did you grow them?" Tims worked to keep herself from thinking about the eerie sounds coming from just past the boundary.

"Why, yes. I grow them in memory of my sweet Serenity. She loved them and was so good at making them grow. After she passed, I had to work hard to figure out how she did it. They almost died that first year." He chuckled, a warm sound Tims had grown fond of. "I guess that's what life was like for me at first too. I didn't think I'd survive, but I did. I would have never made it without King Iam's comfort."

"I'm sorry for your loss." Tims stiffened at his mention of King Iam.

"No worries. I'm at peace with my life and the coming Gathering." He smiled.

She smiled back, still confused. Something rubbed against her leg. She jumped and let out a small shriek.

Warder almost lost his balance, but he held onto her and laughed. "Sorry about that, Missy. This here is Cozy, my cat I told you about."

Cozy rubbed her furry body along Warder's pant leg, then went to back to Tims'. She reached down to pet Cozy, enjoying the feel of her soft fur.

Warder opened the door and the wonderful aroma of a turkey roasting came rushing out. Once they walked inside and shut the door, Timorous felt at ease, no longer hearing the eerie sounds.

Warder sat down in a worn chair. "I'm bushed. Have a seat, my dear. It will be a little while before dinner is done."

Tims stood awkwardly for a moment before sitting on an overstuffed love seat. How odd to feel so at peace with a stranger. His home felt homey. Two walls were lined with floor-to-ceiling bookshelves. A small desk rested against another wall, and the two doors on either side of the desk probably led to bedrooms.

There was a small kitchen just to the left of the entrance. A large fireplace in the kitchen was formed by a tall arch, so high Tims could almost stand in it.

In the flaming fireplace, a large turkey rotated on a rotisserie powered by a small motor. Pots hung from the ceiling. One small cabinet with a countertop for preparing food and one porcelain sink with a shelf above it for storing plates and glasses completed the area.

"How long have you lived here?"

Warder gazed at her from under his bushy eyebrows. "Well, that depends. Do you want to know how long I've owned this place or how long I've been living here as a permanent resident?"

"Why not tell me both stories?"

"I don't suppose you remember what life was like before the time of Prince Peccadillo."

She tensed. What had she gotten herself into?

"Don't worry, Missy. This here is a safe house, off-limits to Mr. Peccadillo. It will stay that way till I die, which I don't plan on doing, by the way." He chuckled to himself.

Timorous didn't feel comforted by this strange talk.

"Where do I start? Before I can even remember, my great-grandfather owned this place. He passed it on to my grandpappy, who passed it on to my father, who passed it on to me. Now there is no one left to pass it on to. I think King Iam is keeping it standing for my sake.

"We used to come here each summer and play in the lake that sat just beyond the border of Obscurity. A happy time in history. Mr. Peccadillo began making appearances, traveled around the world having long conversations with leaders in the communities, focusing especially on the young people, going from one college campus to another encouraging students to question why things were the way they were and working his way up the political ladder back then. Yep, it wasn't long before he became a top official. At that time most people still looked to King Iam for direction." Warder looked out the window and sighed.

"King Iam is still looking out for the best interests of us, his people. People loved him for it, back in the day. But I'm getting ahead of myself. Before Peccadillo moved in with us people and created the clusters, he resided in Bliss. He became jealous of King Iam and started spreading lies about how King Iam held out on folks, how'd they'd be better off with him instead. About a third of his fellow workers believed him and they plotted to take over Bliss. But Peccadillo and his lot were caught and banished from Bliss by King Iam himself."

Timorous had never heard this story before. "Bliss is real?"

"Bet your bottom dollar on it. Yes, sirree, Bliss is as real as the couch you're sittin' on."

Timorous wanted to believe it but felt Bliss had always been more like a fantasy. Maybe he was just a nice old man telling stories.

"As you can imagine, Mr. Peccadillo grew angrier and angrier at King Iam. He decided to try and take from him what mattered most, King Iam's people. With his forces, he began to convince the people there must be a better way. They stopped listening to King Iam and followed Peccadillo.

Eventually they named him their new prince. Not everyone agreed but enough did. Some were promised high positions. Others who opposed him, mysteriously disappeared. Rumors spread about their deaths. Those who still disagreed became afraid. They forgot King Iam held all power but chose not to force us or manipulate us as Peccadillo did.

"Then, as you probably know, strange vegetation grew into Obscurity. It grew at an unnatural pace and divided the clusters, airwaves and air travel were cut off. There were those from my time who tried to rebel. They ventured into Obscurity, never to be heard from again.

"Peccadillo and his forces would lead us to believe everyone who tried to travel through Obscurity died, but I know it's not true." Warder stopped and shook his head. "It only took a few people running back out of Obscurity and telling of the horrors that lay beyond the boundary for people to stop trying.

"Peccadillo and his forces went on a mission to remove all *truth* from the people. They burned all copies of the *Book of Actualities*. At least Peccadillo thinks so." Warder winked at Tims mischievously. "People were imprisoned and executed if they were found with it."

"What's this book you are talking about?" Tims wrung her hands. "I don't remember hearing about any of this in school."

"I'm sure you didn't hear about it in school. They removed all that history long ago. The *Book of Actualities* holds the absolute truth of our history and more. That's why Peccadillo set out to destroy it."

As he related the story, Warder had gotten a little worked up and stood. Tims' eyes grew large with apprehension. He calmed himself and after sitting back down, he took a deep breath and continued.

"Yep. Every cluster holds at least one copy in a safe house like this. Every copy is guarded by an old-timer like myself who has remained faithful to King Iam." Warder punctuated this with pride.

"I have vague memories of my mother talking about a king." She glanced around, wondering who might hear her and what might happen if they heard her say his name. "So, *you* own a copy?" A feeling of nervous excitement filled her, and she sat on the edge of her seat. She read often. Reading helped Tims escape from her fears. This book sounded so intriguing she'd probably stay up all night reading it.

Warder looked toward the kitchen. "Looks like the turkey is ready to come off the spit. Would you mind giving me a hand?"

Disappointed he hadn't answered her question, Tims planned to ask again later—maybe after dinner. She really wanted to know more about this book.

As they sat down to eat, Warder closed his eyes and bowed his head. Tims just stared at him not knowing what this meant. She saw his lips moving but heard nothing. When he looked up again, she asked, "Are you all right?"

"Sure. I was just thanking King Iam for the food we are about to partake of and for you being with us."

Tims glanced around nervously. "Is King Iam here?"

"King Iam is everywhere all at once, like air. He sees all and knows all." Warder took a bite of his turkey. "Mmm, cooked to perfection."

Tims began to eat but the thought of someone being able to see and hear everything made her uneasy.

Warder reached out and patted her hand. "King Iam loves us so much. Every detail of our lives is important to him. I'll explain more to you later."

After dinner, feeling full and satisfied, Tims said, "I don't think I have ever had such a wonderful meal. Thank you, Warder."

He grinned. "Don't forget, next time it's your turn."

Tims looked at the clock and gasped. "I'd better get going. It's getting late, and I don't want to walk home in the dark."

"What kind of a host would I be if I sent a pretty young woman like yourself home without an escort? Remember I told you I got a ride into town from a friend? It's a long way. This friend of mine will be here in about an hour. Wait till then and he'll take you home."

"He? No, I don't want to impose." Tims stood up and backed toward the door.

Warder waddled her direction and looked her in the eyes. "Tims, do you think I would ever put you in harm's way? You can trust me. This is one of my dearest friends. He's completely honorable."

She never felt safer than she did right then. After a moment of indecision, she agreed, "All right. I'll wait. Thank you."

As they settled into their seats, both felt a little sleepy from the meal. Tims still wanted to know more about the *Book of Actualities.* Maybe she'd ask after a short nap.

Warder had already slouched down and was quietly snoring. She curled up on the love seat and laid her head down on one of the overstuffed armrests.

HEARSAY SAT ANXIOUSLY in Tims' apartment, waiting for her friend to return. It wasn't like Tims to be out of her apartment, let alone out so late. Something bad must have happened. Hearsay had called the police, but they refused to take any action until it been at least twenty-four hours. Tims was an adult, they said.

As she sat in the living room, Hearsay picked at the little fuzz balls on an old blanket. She decide to call Meddling. She had failed to contact Hearsay in an hour as she had promised.

Meddling picked up right away. "Is she there?"

Before Hearsay responded, the phone clicked and within a couple seconds, Meddling burst in. After a quick visual sweep of the room, her expression fell. "I thought she was here. I told you to call me when she got here."

"Don't be mad at me. You said you'd check in, and it's been hours," Hearsay huffed. "I wondered if you'd found out anything."

"I've been out investigating, and you've been just sitting here. Call me when you hear from her." She stormed out, slamming the door behind her.

Chapter 23

Warder laid sleeping in his chair and Timorous slept peacefully on the love seat. He heard a light knock on the door before Radimar quietly walked in. Warder's eyes popped open. Radimar quickly put a finger to his lips, motioning to Warder to stay quiet. Warder quietly pulled himself out of the chair and joined Radimar by the table. "Have you prepared her?" Radimar whispered.

"I've begun the process, my Prince, but she knows nothing. This may take longer than I expected." Warder glanced Tims' way. "She seems open and hungry for the truth. She's been able to receive the information without the evil underlings hanging on her, yet she is still questioning."

Radimar nodded. "You're a great teacher."

Warder's chest swelled with pride.

"You are the right person to help her. The underlings were replaced with more powerful reinforcements. But don't worry—we will not be defeated."

Warder's brows furrowed, and he pulled his lips in causing his whiskers to stick straight out. "Do we have to send her back? You know they will be all over her." He eyed her with concern. "Why not let her stay here with me, allowing for more time to train her."

"It is all part of her preparation. 'Easy' is not what will help her overcome the enemy. She needs to face the enemy with the power of King Iam. It's the only way she can be strengthened to withstand the journey ahead of her. Remember your own journey?"

Warder snorted as he thought of his past.

"You would not be in the place you are now had you not been trained to believe in the power King Iam gives you."

Warder sighed at the memory. "True. I just dislike that the path is so difficult. 'King Iam, protect this dear girl. The enemy isn't going to be easy on her.'"

A VERY GROGGY TIMOROUS began to stir. She sat up, a little disoriented at first, trying to remember where she was. Then she saw the clock and her eyes widened. She rose from the couch in a panic, "I need to go. It's so late."

"Now, don't you worry Tims," Warder said. "I promised you an escort home, and he's here now."

Radimar stood right there in front of her.

Did he glow, or was it just the fire behind him? Overwhelmed to see Radimar, she took a step back, almost falling back onto the love seat.

"Hello Tims." Radimar held out his hand to shake hers. "I'm so glad to see you again."

Tims didn't remember taking his hand, but she definitely remembered the surge of power that coursed through her at his touch. She stared, mesmerized by his eyes and his radiant smile.

Warder cleared his throat.

"Um, hello," Tims finally said. "You two know each other?"

Radimar slapped a hand on Warder's shoulder. "Yes, we're longtime friends. I stay with Warder whenever I'm in town."

"Friends? It's true that you travel between the clusters?" Wide-eyed, Timorous glanced back and forth between the two of them.

"On a regular basis," Radimar shared.

"But how? It's not allowed." The words came tumbling out. "It's not possible. Warder said so himself."

Radimar chuckled. "One of these days I will show you how. For now, just trust me. Nothing is impossible when it comes to King Iam."

Tims' mind raced. Her whole sense of reality tilted on its head. "I don't really know much about that, but do you know this king Warder's been telling me about too?"

Warder and Radimar exchanged knowing glances. Warder stepped forward, looking Timorous in the eyes. "Timorous Hominid, allow me to properly introduce you to Prince Radimar, son of King Iam." He bowed slightly as he swept his hand toward Radimar.

Tims tried to curtsey, quite awkwardly but stopped, worried they'd laugh at her.

Radimar gave her a reassuring hug. "That is not required, but thank you for honoring me." He took her by the hand and urged her to sit on the love seat beside him.

Warder returned to his usual chair.

Tims leaned away from Radimar, but he still held her hand. A prince held her hand. The sensation of the power felt amazing. *I must be dreaming. This can't be real.*

Radimar leaned toward her. "So, now that we've been properly introduced, I need to give you a little instruction." He studied her for a moment. Even though Tims stared at him, she wasn't sure she could really focus on what he was saying as wave after wave of power swept through her.

"Timorous, do you remember when I told you I had chosen you?"

Here she sat, next to Prince Radimar. This had to be a dream she'd wake up from at any moment. Unable to speak, she just nodded her head in bewilderment.

"It is true." He gazed at her intently. "You are very special, and I have chosen you for a specific purpose. I know this might be hard to grasp since we've had so little time together, but you are deeply loved by my father, King Iam, and me."

Had she heard him correctly? Could she really be loved by someone so amazing? Her mind spun trying to take it all in—the power, the craziness of it all. Why didn't she feel like running? It finally dawned on her. She felt pure love, something she'd never truly experienced before. Something deep in her broken heart began to bubble up, something she couldn't contain. Was this . . . joy? Staring at Radimar in awe, she gave a short nervous laugh. She'd never felt so *loved.*

She looked at Warder and he laughed, too. "Ya better believe it, Missy. He's totally in love with you."

Timorous started laughing again, in short little spurts then in a true full-on belly laugh. A laughter full of unmeasurable joy. At one point, she even snorted, putting her hand over her mouth in embarrassment. That only lasted a second before she started laughing again. Then they all started laughing. In that moment, it didn't matter if she understood everything. She was safe; she was loved. She had found someone she could truly trust.

They laughed until tears rolled down Timorous' cheeks. She settled down and wondered what it meant to be chosen? What would be required of her?

Radimar leaned in. "The question is will you *choose* to trust me?"

With a little hesitation, Timorous swallowed. "I think I can, but I'm not sure how." She pulled away. "I believe you are trustworthy, but I'm not sure I am." What if she made a wrong choice? She had truthfully answered his question. She had never fully trusted anyone before. She looked down at her hands, embarrassed by her confusion. "I'm sorry. I know this shouldn't be so hard."

"I like your honesty," Radimar reassured her. "Timorous, here's the thing. I trust you. Your trust in me will grow, and we will grow closer."

Timorous quickly glanced at him and blushed. What did that mean, this growing closer thing? She knew she wanted it but feared the unknown territory.

"For now, let me take you home." Radimar stood and reached out to her.

Timorous placed her hand in his, enjoying once again the warmth of their contact.

TIMS WALKED WITH RADIMAR down Warder's path feeling no sense of fear, only an acute awareness of Radimar's nearness and the peace she felt next to him. She glanced sideways at him a few times and looked away quickly each time. She wondered why a prince might have any interest in her, an ordinary girl. The thought thrilled and confused her.

"Do you come here much?" she finally asked.

"Only when I have important people, like you, to see." He leaned down and gently tucked a loose strand of hair behind her ear. She felt goosebumps rise at the power of his touch.

They reached his car, and he opened the door for her. She slid into the beautiful leather seats. He continued to hold her hand as they drove. The power of love radiated from him. Radimar spoke, but Tims struggled to focus. He said something about needing to be careful.

"There is an unseen world. Prince Peccadillo's abilities to create trouble in the clusters, using his unseen forces, will be looking for ways to stop you. But don't fear, you will not be alone. I and those who serve King Iam will be near. It won't always feel like this because we are also a part of the unseen world, fighting against Peccadillo's realm. When you feel alone, trust we are near. Warder will explain more to you tomorrow."

"What do you mean by the unseen world? This is all so confusing. I've seen Prince Peccadillo on TV, and I've seen you. So, who are the ones who aren't seen?"

Radimar golden eyes seemed to pierce her. "I promise you it will be explained soon. For now, just believe there are forces who are working against you—forces you can't see.

Often the things you do see and experience are influenced by the unseen. Trust me."

She wanted to trust him. "Okay." She'd wait for Warder to explain later. Today had already been filled with more information than she knew how to handle. About a block from her apartment, Radimar pulled over. He explained that their being seen together created more risk for her.

"Warder is preparing to instruct you in the *Book of Actualities* tomorrow." Tims was surprised to step out of the car and find herself stepping right into Radimar's embrace. She melted into the safety of his arms. He made her feel so secure. He held her for a long moment. She didn't want it to end. He kissed her on the cheek. "Go in the power of King Iam. I'll be in touch." He left quickly.

She watched longingly as he drove away.

Was this what it felt like to be loved? The power of Radimar's love made it hard to keep her balance as she walked toward her apartment complex. Thinking about his embrace and kiss on the cheek caused goosebumps to reappear and a warm blush to rush to her face. Everything about him seemed perfect. The smile on her face refused to disappear.

"WHERE DID SHE JUST come from? She wasn't here and then she was?" a Toady snorted. How were they supposed to explain her disappearance and reappearance to Deamon?

"Can't you see, you moron? She's glowing with the presence of Iam."

They all spat.

"They've kept her under their cover. We will need to keep our distance until the power subsides. We must find a way to dim this light quickly and move her into Obscurity for the Obliterists to apprehend her."

WHEN SHE ENTERED HER apartment, Timorous found Hearsay sitting on the couch, wringing her hands, her eyes red from crying.

"Tims." Hearsay ran to hug her. "Where have you been? I have been so worried I even called the police."

Tims returned the hug as she looked to see if Meddling was around. "I'm sorry, Hearsay. I felt so upset about everything that happened last night and this morning. I just had to get out." Even though she usually told Hearsay everything, she felt a strange new caution about sharing too much.

Hearsay wiped a few tears away and studied Tims. "Where were you all this time? It's 1 a.m. I felt sure something bad happened to you."

"I'm sorry." Tims hugged her again. "I know this is going to sound strange, but I met a new friend. He's an older man and really swee—"

"A new friend?" Hearsay gasped. "And a man. Tims, you've got to be kidding. Don't forget I've been with you since you were small. I know your past. I know you never make friends with men. You never even made friends with men you knew at work." She crossed her arms and narrowed her eyes suspiciously.

"Like I said, Hearsay, I know it sounds strange, but it's true." She led Hearsay back to the couch. "Something is changing inside me. I can't explain it. Maybe losing my job is the beginning of something new for me—something good."

"I don't know about that but you do seem especially happy."

Tims felt warmth color her cheeks.

"Meddling made some interesting observations today that seemed more plausible than I'd originally thought." Hearsay crossed her arms.

Tims' brow furrowed at the thought of Meddling filling Hearsay's thoughts with lies. "Remember when I worked at The Burger Joint? I was happy to stay there, but you wouldn't let me settle. You helped me to find the strength, even when I didn't want to, to improve my situation."

Nodding, Hearsay uncrossed her arms.

"Maybe you were right about me coming out of my cocoon . . . a little. The last couple of days I feel like I've taken another step forward. Is this making any sense?"

"Well . . ."

"Like going for a walk in the park by myself, or when I dropped my wallet, going to get it from Radimar." Her face warmed again at his name.

Hearsay stared at her with squinted eyes. "Does this have anything to do with meeting Radimar? Is this the new friend you're talking about?"

"No and yes. A little, I think."

Hearsay's lips tightened.

"No, he's not the new friend I'm talking about, and yes, I think meeting Radimar has caused a change in my life. Look, I lost my job today because I met him and wasn't able to talk about him in front of a camera. Hearsay, a freaking camera. When would that ever work for me?"

Hearsay nodded knowingly. "Okay, so you haven't been spending all day with Radimar? I'm just checking because Meddling made some pretty convincing arguments."

"No, I'm not. And you believe Meddling over me?" Tims didn't try to keep the hurt from her voice. "You hardly know her, but you've known me forever."

"Okay, I believe you. You do seem different. I want to hear about everything that's happened over the last few days. I don't care if it takes all night. I'll call in sick later this morning."

A sudden banging on the door made both girls jump. Hearsay hurried over and looked out the peephole. "It's Meddling," she whispered. "She's been trying to help me find you."

Tims shook her head. "No. I just can't deal with her right now."

Chapter 24

Meddling continued banging on the door. "I know you're in there. I saw Tims coming home."

"She's going to wake the neighbors, Tims," Hearsay whined. "I've got to let her at least see you. She tried to help me all day." Not waiting for permission, she unlocked the door.

Meddling pushed past her and stood in front of Tims, hands on her hips. "So, did you have a nice day, Timorous?" Sarcasm dripped from her lips.

Hearsay put a protective arm around Tims. "Meddling, it's been a rough day for Tims. She doesn't feel up to talking right now, but I'll fill you in tomorrow,"

"Oh, really? A hard day?" She huffed. Her face grew red. "It's been a hard day for us too, Tims. I've been all over town looking for you. What have you been doing all day? Or should I say, who have you been with all day and maybe yesterday as well?"

Tims blinked in confusion and looked at Hearsay.

"Really, Meddling," Hearsay explained, "this isn't the time. She's tired. We can talk about this later." She pulled Meddling by the arm toward the open door.

Meddling resisted, yanking her arm out of Hearsay's grip, only to have Hearsay grab it again and continue to pull her toward the door. This time she allowed herself to be moved but grabbed the door and held on, even when Hearsay tried to push her out.

"How did you get home tonight, Tims, hmm? Have you told Hearsay how you got home?" Meddling shouted over Hearsay's shoulder.

Hearsay turned and squinted at her. "How did you get home tonight, Tims? You didn't walk, did you?"

"Um, a friend drove me home."

"A friend? Really? Is that what you call *him*?" Meddling's words felt like maliciousness daggers thrown at her.

While Toadies were unable to prod Timorous at this time, they worked overtime on Meddling.

"Meddling," Hearsay said angrily. "Tims already told me about her new friend, so just drop it. We can talk about this tomorrow." Hearsay pushed Meddling out. She shut the door, locked it, and then leaned her head against it, a little out of breath.

Muffled through the door Meddling continued, "Did she tell you about the embrace and the kiss?" Hearsay's head snapped up and she stared at Tims in disbelief.

"It's not what you think. It was just a good-bye hug and a kiss on the cheek." She left out the part that it came from Radimar.

"This new friend drove you home?" Hearsay's tone was guarded.

"He wanted to make sure I got home safely." She didn't lie.

"You let him hug and kiss you? How old did you say this friend of yours is?" Hearsay spied her suspiciously. "I don't ever remember you hugging anyone but me. Not to mention, I don't think you've been kissed since someone cornered you in ninth grade."

Tims gulped. "Geek Weed? Don't remind me. It was awful."

"Really, Tims. How old is this guy, and how do you know he's not just trying to use you? You're pretty naive."

A Toady stood by prodding Hearsay.

Tims sighed, "He's really old, and he's been kind and appropriate with me. He even saved me from some guy who started following me to work yesterday. I ran and he chased me, but just before—"

"What? I can't believe someone tried to attack you and I'm just now hearing about it. How could someone so old save you?" Hearsay rushed toward Tims.

Tims took a deep breath, tired of Hearsay's relentless inquisition. "He just happened to be in the right place at the right time. As soon as I turned the corner, I almost knocked him over. Once the guy chasing me saw I wasn't alone, he took off in another direction."

"Well, I'm glad someone rescued you, but you let him hug and kiss you? That's just weird, Tims. Are you all right?" Hearsay put her hand to Tims' forehead as if checking to see if she had a fever.

Tims told her about leaving early for work and how her attacker had approached her. Hearsay loved a good story, but the exhaustion from the day finally overtook her. Barely able to keep her eyes open, Hearsay yawned and curled up on the couch with the blanket. "We'll talk more in the morning."

Tims climbed into bed and lay there thinking of Radimar. "I hope that protection for me is near. I don't even understand what exactly I'm being protected from." Still sensing his presence, she fell asleep, remembering the love she felt and wondered what it meant to be chosen.

STILL IN THE NETHERWORLD, Commander Deamon and the Lead Guards of the clusters leaned over the table piecing together information to confirm sightings to look for any patterns.

"Excuse me, Commander Deamon," Usher bowed.

"What is it, Usher? Why not just come out and speak what you have to say? No wonder the Prince would rather work with Miss Enchantress." The rest of the Guard laughed.

Usher remained calm—one of his strengths and how he'd made it to this high position. "Do you prefer I enter without giving appropriate respect?"

Deamon jumped at him. "What did you just say?"

Usher bowed lower. "I just asked for clarification on how you would like me to enter when I report important information to you." He spoke as submissively as possible.

"How to enter? I wish you to enter dead. You will treat me with the utmost respect, you little peon. Give me the information and be gone before I kill you myself."

The Lead Guards snickered.

Usher ignored the threat. "We have word on the one of interest, Timorous. She is back on the grid and at her apartment. The Toadies are standing back as you requested, but they also have no choice at the moment."

"And why is that?" Deamon sighed impatiently.

"Because she glows with the presence of Iam—quite brightly they say."

Everyone spat.

"Hmm, not surprising, since she's been in the safe house. Summon the Guard of Obscurity nearest the safe house." Deamon barked. "I want reinforced guards on all sides at all hours. And send in Deceit. He will be helping me with a few key Toadies in Nowhere."

"As you request." Usher bowed again.

Deceit must have expected the call. Usher rounded the corner and there he stood, grinning smugly.

He's spying on me. Usher would put an end to that. "There you are Deceit. I've been looking everywhere for you. Commander Deamon called for you. He's not be happy with the delay. You really need to be in your office ready to receive important calls like this."

Deceit's smugness quickly disappeared. "I was just on my way." Trying to pretend he already knew, Deceit ran into the meeting room, sure he was late.

Usher stayed to hear Deceit grovel.

"Commander Deamon, I'm sorry for the delay. I came as quickly as possible."

Usher laughed at his joke, knowing Deamon would take advantage of any exposed weakness. He didn't wait to hear more. He wickedly grinned knowing his little trick had worked.

Unfortunately, he had the unpleasant task of heading back out to Obscurity. Once there, Usher scurried to his desk in Deamon's lair and called for Sergeant Terror. While the Obliterist despised Usher, he did outrank most of them and could demand their respect.

Terror behaved himself, since he'd been selected next in line for Sergeant Vacuity's position over the cluster of Nowhere.

"Usher." Sergeant Terror bowed slightly.

"Sergeant Terror, Commander Deamon requests you place a heavy guard at the safe house in Uncertainty at all times. Make sure you are ready if anyone so much as steps a foot over the line." He didn't bother looking up from his desk.

Usher heard a low growl and glanced up in time to see the hatred in Terror's eyes before he took his leave.

WITH THE HELP OF THE Legionnaires, Messengers were in and out of Tims' apartment all night long.

"It looks like a freaking fireworks display," one Toady complained. Their attempts at swatting down the Messengers never quite hit their mark.

Chapter 25

Tims left the next morning before Hearsay woke up, leaving a note to let her know she'd be home after dinner and promised to call her. She grabbed her things and a couple of bags of food from her kitchen and stepped out, quietly locking the door behind her.

Meddling leaned against the hallway wall waiting for her. "So, what are you up to today?" As usual, her comment dripped with sarcastic accusation.

Tims didn't answer and tried to leave.

Meddling blocked her path. "I saw you embracing and kissing Radimar last night."

Timorous abruptly stopped and her heart raced wildly.

"I wouldn't say you're a cute couple. You'd have to be cute for that. You're as plain as cold toast. What does he see in you?" Meddling scowled and ran her hands down her curvaceous sides. "I have so much more to offer him. Anyway, I don't know how you'll explain your way out of this with Hearsay."

"She's right," a Toady whispered in Timorous' mind. "Who are you to think you could be special? How could anyone so amazing choose you? You are less than ordinary. You are nothing."

"Oh, and I know Hearsay thinks you're a great friend, but she knows you lied to her about spending the day with the new neighbor."

Tims' brow creased. "What do you mean?"

"Yah, that's right. Hands Ons told us the new tenant isn't moving in until next month. He even showed us the empty apartment." Meddling snickered at Tims' bewildered expression.

Just then, the door to Apartment 1C opened wide to reveal a beautifully deCorrated room. Essince stepped out, closing the door behind her. "Hi, Tims. Hi, Meddling. Have a great day." Off she went, leaving Meddling with her mouth hanging open.

TIMS SMILED. "I'VE heard that's a great way to catch flies." She swiftly turned and walked past Meddling. She'd figure things out with Hearsay later.

She hadn't driven her car lately, but it always worked perfectly. *The Toadies stood by waiting to cause trouble. Tims' glow had dimmed a little, but they needed to stay discreet. Messing with her car seemed easiest.*

She turned the key, but it barely turned over. She tried two more times. By the third try, it only clicked.

The Toadies snickered.

Her hands tightened around the steering wheel. She knew Warder was expecting her. She couldn't carry the groceries that far. As she got out of the car to head back into her apartment, a car pulled up behind hers.

The window rolled down. "Need a lift?"

Tims saw Essince smiling.

The Toadies backed away and screamed their disapproval. "No fair, no fair."

Essince beckoned with a wave of her hand. "Come on Tims. I don't mind."

Tims hesitated but then grabbed her bags and hopped in. The moment the door shut, she felt the same peace she'd felt sitting next to Radimar and sighed with relief.

"Where to?" Essince put her car in gear and pulled ahead.

Tims considered her options. Go to Warder's? Get her car fixed? Go home? "I don't know. I probably need to get my car fixed. I'm going to be needing it more than usual."

"Really, why is that?"

Tims didn't really hear Essince's question. "Why what?" Her face warmed with embarrassment. "Sorry, I was lost in my thoughts."

"Why will you be using your car more? Did you get a new job or something?" Essince peeked her way.

"Something like that. It's kind of a new career path. You might say I'm in training." Tims thought it best to stop there. Radimar told her to be careful, but what did that mean? This unseen world thing seemed strange and maybe a little made-up to her.

"I know," said Essince. "I'll call my dad. He's really handy with these things. I know he'd love to help."

"No, I can't impose like that." Timorous never asked for favors. That would be risky. They might expect a favor from her in return, and what if it she felt uncomfortable with obliging? She preferred not to put herself in a situation like that.

"Do you have your own mechanic?" Essince seemed eager to help. *Working with the realm of the unseen, she was making sure Tims didn't miss her appointment with Warder.*

"No, but this isn't your responsibility or your father's." Tims hoped Essince understood. "But thank you for offering."

"My dad will be happy I asked. You just leave your keys with me, and I'll have him look at it this afternoon. Okay?"

Tims reluctantly handed her the keys. *Maybe just this one time*, she reasoned. "I guess. If you don't think he will mind. I can't pay a lot."

"No worries, he really likes helping people out. Now where am I taking you?" Essince' asked enthusiastically.

Tims exhaled, relieved to have her help. But as far as sharing where she needed to go, she refused to tell her the exact location. "Just drop me off near that abandoned school." It was not far from Warder's cabin. She could walk the rest of the way.

"Sure."

To Tims' relief, the trip only took fifteen minutes. Essince stopped by the two-story building and didn't ask why she'd chosen a spot that looked like a ghost town.

"Thanks for the ride." Tims grabbed her grocery bags and started to climb out of the car.

"Listen, Tims." Essince held out a business card. "If you need a ride home, just give me a call."

Tims took the card and waved good-bye. She read: *Essince, The Freeing Spirit, Here to help you! 777-8888.*

"Strange. I wonder what kind of work she does," Tims mused.

She walked the distance to Warder's cabin, but the closer she got, fear crept up her spine, as it had yesterday. The same eerie sounds she'd heard seemed much louder today. She looked up at the great dark canopy of vegetation. Her legs shook. Something appeared to move through the trees, or was it just her imagination?

For some reason, her feet refused to move. She just stood there, as if cemented to the ground, her arms full of grocery bags. The more she looked at the vegetation of Obscurity, the more it took on shapes, like clouds when you stared at them long enough. But these weren't puppies and bunnies. Something with broad, gigantic shoulders appeared. She thought she saw eyes. A cold swift breeze blew past her, sending shivers through her body. When she dared another peek at the vegetation, she dropped her bags. Were those teeth? No, her mind must be playing tricks on her.

She needed to go home where it felt safe. She turned to leave when she heard someone whistling a happy tune. It sounded familiar. Yes, her mom used to sing that song when Tims was small. What were the words? She worked hard to remember. Hum hum hum . . . something about the whole world in his hands. She couldn't remember the rest, but she knew it had to be Warder. She grabbed her bags and ran the rest of the way, trying to hum along with his whistling, never once looking at the overgrowth.

THE TOADIES THOUGHT they had a firm grip on Tims. Then something struck them. Stunned, their power weakened.

"Ow. What was that?" One of the Toadies yelped.

Another asked, "What the Abyss just happened? That had to be the work of our enemy." The group stood silently for a moment, looking around. Not wanting to admit the truth that they once again missed their opportunity.

The lead Toady grunted. "Couldn't you have done more than blow some wind at her?"

"Well, maybe if you started singing one of our songs, it might have stopped the old man from reeling her in with a song of our enemy."

"Why didn't you trip her or something?" the smallest of the group complained.

"Commander Deamon isn't going to be happy," the lead Toady whispered.

Several of the Toadies shuddered at the thought.

"Who says we have to tell him? We still have time to put an end to this. We're staying right here and plan our attack."

The Obliterists in Obscurity probably witnessed the whole scene, but none of the Toadies mentioned it. They moved off the main road to a more secluded location, but not before one unfortunate Toady took one last look toward Warder's cabin. Seeing the Guard of Obscurity looking angrily in their direction, his skin turned to a cold pale green and he hurried to catch up with the rest.

"GLAD YOU COULD MAKE it." Warder welcomed Timorous with a smile and a hug, pleased the enemy had failed to keep her from coming. "How did things go last night?"

"Fine, I guess." Tims relaxed right away in peace of his home. "My friend waited in my apartment for me and asked a lot of questions." Now, why had she said that? Her trust in this kind old man seemed to grow stronger the more time she spent with him. It felt good to know she had another friend.

"Did you keep to the basics?" His expression was serious.

"Yes, but my neighbor, Meddling, saw Radimar drop me off last night, and I don't think she's going to let it go." Timorous blushed, remembering Radimar's hug and kiss. Warder didn't say anything.

"Hmm, we'll have to think of how this can best be handled. I'm sure the enemy is planning on using this Meddling or anyone he can to get to you."

Tims stiffened. "What does it mean, the enemy is planning to use her? Will Hearsay be safe?"

Warder patted her arm. "Don't you worry. She'll be fine. You're the one the enemy is interested in." He paused, glanced down, his brows pulled together. "We'd better get to work. You have a lot to learn."

Tims gave him a wry look. What an understatement. She had *everything* to learn.

MEDDLING COMPOSED HERSELF quickly. She had no intention of letting some plain, simple girl like Tims get the best of her. She caught up with Hearsay on her way out. "Hi, Hearsay. You going to work?"

"No, I overslept and called in sick."

"Look, I'm sorry about last night. Why don't you come to my place for breakfast?" Hearsay's eyes had dark circles under them from the lack of sleep. Meddling put an arm around her and comfortingly guided her upstairs.

Soon they were seated at Meddling's kitchen table. She poured Hearsay a second cup of coffee. "Why did Tims leave you out of all of this? You're her best friend. I don't think it's wise to trust someone who isn't willing to tell the truth." Meddling pretended to be concerned.

"Tims explained all that to me last night."

"Really? So, she told you Radimar dropped her off last night?" Meddling blinked innocently.

"Radimar? No, she said an older man who befriended her yesterday did. She even told me he hugged her and kissed her on the cheek." With a look of confusion, Hearsay sipped her coffee to avoid saying more.

"Did she give you the name of her new friend?"

"No, but I believe her. She has no reason to lie to me. Can we just drop it now?" Hearsay half frowned at Meddling's meddling.

"Hearsay, you can believe what you want." She stared down at her cup. "I'm just telling you I actually saw who dropped her off, and he wasn't old. The hug and the kiss were a whole lot more than she is leading you to believe." Meddling shook her head before taking another sip.

"Are you sure you saw her with Radimar?" Hearsay shot Meddling a suspicious look.

"Yes, it was him all right. At one o'clock in the morning, hugging and kissing outside of his car. They stood not far from a street lamp, parked down about a block from my window. I saw it all. For sure it was Radimar." Meddling paused and watched Hearsay process this new information. "Think about it. Tims said she spent the day before with the new tenant, but Hans proved no one lives there. Who do you think she's been spending all her time with?"

"Didn't you say you talked with the new neighbor?" Hearsay asked.

"That's beside the point. We both saw the empty apartment. I think the 'new' neighbor is in on this." Meddling stood and paced. "There really must be something big to hide." Meddling thought the neighbor might be with Radimar in this intrigue. But if she wasn't the focus, then why not turn it into a mess for Tims. "She should have told you. Why do you think she didn't?" Meddling looked sideways at Hearsay. When Hearsay hesitated, she added, "Maybe it's like I said. She needed someone she didn't know to share the secret with."

Hearsay stood and angrily stomped toward the door. "Tims said she met this old man yesterday while being chased by some dangerous guy. Do you really think she made that all up too? She tells me everything." Hearsay waved her arms around as she ranted.

"I hate to break it to you, but Tims is up to something. Maybe she knows she wouldn't stand a chance with a guy like that with you around." The very idea that Radimar would even give Tims a second thought irritated Meddling.

A very ugly jealousy Toady stood next to her, its rod crackling near the base of her neck.

"She chose to lose her job over it. And where is she today? Did she tell you?" As her anger rose, Meddling crossed her arms and tapped her foot.

"She left me a note but never shared her destination . . ." Hearsay trailed off.

Chapter 26

When Warder noticed Tims trembling, he knew the enemy was up to his no-good tricks. He closed and locked the door behind them.

"Warder, do you ever hear sounds coming from Obscurity?" Tims grimaced. "Or maybe it's just my imagination playing tricks on me. I heard sounds and thought I saw something out there."

"I used to hear them a lot too but not much these days. They leave me alone most of the time. They figure I'm so old I can't do much damage and will die off pretty soon." Warder laughed.

Tims didn't think it was funny. "It's not my imagination? Things live in Obscurity?"

"They're a part of the unseen world that answers to Mr. Peccadillo. I wouldn't worry your pretty little head over it. They can be mighty scary, but they can't get to you here, like dogs barking on the other side of the fence. Peccadillo has a whole guard of Obliterists watching over Obscurity, but remember, this here is a safe house protected by King Iam."

"What is an Obliterist?" Tims wrapped her arms around herself.

Warder rubbed his whiskered chin, trying to decide how to answer her question honestly without frightening her. "I've only seen one or two in my life. Most people never see any creatures from the unseen world. Peccadillo doesn't want people to know about these horrible beings or what they're up to. Obliterists are very big and ugly. They hold some of the highest ranks in Peccadillo's kingdom and are very dangerous if you don't grasp the power you possess in King Iam."

Tims turned a little pale. "I thought Obscurity created safety for the clusters. It's in all my history books. This land all belongs to Prince Peccadillo, including this cabin, right? How is it a safe house *from* him?"

"Aren't we full of questions today," Warder chuckled. "But it's to be expected. I'm sure you're going to ask a lot more as we work today. You were taught in school what Peccadillo wants you to believe. But trust me, all the land, including Obscurity, belongs to King Iam. For now, Peccadillo rules over it.

"On the day the world declared Peccadillo their new prince, those who clung to the truth lost their voices and their knowledge of the power to make change. A great celebration took place by the multitudes who openly accepted and almost worshipped Prince Peccadillo. That will change when the time is right. You don't need to fear Peccadillo's forces if you believe in King Iam and the *Book of Actualities*."

"But who's the enemy Prince Peccadillo speaks of?"

Warder's brows shot up. "You still don't know? Peccadillo views King Iam as the enemy." He gestured with his thumb to his chest. "But we're the good guys, Tims. He's the enemy."

"What? Wait. You're telling me that Prince Peccadillo is bad, even though he reigns over all the clusters and brought peace to us?" Her voice rose in disbelief.

"It's okay, Tims. I'll explain everything. I know I'm throwing a lot of new information your way." He patted her arm, then he slowly moved to the fireplace. Getting down on one knee, he struggled to pull the heavy stone out from under the hearth. Behind it laid a very large package wrapped in velvet and tied with silver string. After pulling it out, he pushed the stone back in its place with a grunt. Dust covered the package, as if it hadn't been taken out in a long time.

Warder struggled to stand. Tims hurried over to help him.

"Thank you, my dear. These old bones don't work as well as they use to. Would you mind picking that up?" He pointed to the package still sitting on the floor. "Put it on my desk." He wiped his forehead and worked to catch his breath.

Expecting the package to be heavy, Timorous almost threw it across the room. It felt featherlike. "How could something so big be so light?"

"Careful," Warder chuckled. "Actualities may not always be easy, but they are light in comparison to the burden of lies."

She laid the package on the desk, which seemed far too small to hold such a large item.

Warder waddled his way over to it. Slowly and almost reverently, he untied the silver string and began to unfold the velvet cover, revealing a mysterious-looking book. "I haven't pulled this out in some time." He gently brushed a hand over the old, leather-bound cover, which read *Book of Actualities* in bold, gold lettering that almost glowed.

"It's so old," Tims noted.

"Indeed, it is. It's been passed down through many generations. This here book tells the whole of the truth, the history, the victories, the falling away, and the future to come." Warder gazed into her eyes. "Tims, you've been chosen. Do you know what that means?"

"I . . . um . . . I really don't have any idea. I'm sorry." A slight blush colored her cheeks.

Warder patted her shoulder. "No worries, Missy. That's what I'm here for, to help you learn. It's a high honor to be chosen. Many are called but few truly follow. Radimar believes in you. We are so proud of you."

She stared down and scuffed her shoes on the floor. "But, why? I haven't done anything."

"Sure, you've done something. You're here, ain't ya?"

She shrugged.

"Tims, it took courage to come to me today. That's a strong first step. Be proud of yourself." Warder pulled up a chair. "Now, sit down, and we'll get started."

TIMS NEVER THOUGHT of herself as courageous. Was she . . . today? Had it been courageous to stand up to Meddling? Had it been courageous to accept a ride from Essince and help from her father? Maybe she could be considered brave for coming to Warder's home, especially because of its closeness to Obscurity. A warm feeling passed through her and healing ebbed into her heart.

"It's time you learn what's been kept hidden from you. Let's start at the beginning." Warder reverently opened the large book and read: "King Iam created the heavens and stretched them out. He created the world and everything in it. He gives breath to everyone, life to everyone who walks on the land." Warder explained that King Iam had created all things, including Prince Peccadillo. "See Peccadillo doesn't want us to know the truth about his being thrown out of Bliss."

"Why would Peccadillo—or anyone for that matter—ever want to leave there?"

"Missy, he didn't want to leave. He wanted to take it over, to overthrow King Iam. He convinced himself and others he was better than King Iam." Warder shook his head at the foolishness of such an idea. "See, Peccadillo was one of King Iam's most beautiful creations and held a very high position. He convinced many under him to follow and bow to him. King Iam gives us the choice to follow him or not—even Peccadillo. Peccadillo chose his own fate.

"King Iam banished him from Bliss and sent him here to our world. All his beauty melted into the ugly truth of his hatred and jealousy. The same fate happened to all who chose to side with him."

Warder went on to explain how Peccadillo's hatred for King Iam drove his desire to destroy the humans, taking vengeance on King Iam. He deceived the humans, much like he had his followers. His deception finally paid off, growing so strong, most people no longer believed in King Iam. He finally took over and separated the clusters. "So, you see, Peccadillo wants us to believe he succeeded."

"Well, didn't he? I never hear anyone talk about King Iam. I've only heard a few people even risk whispering the word Bliss." Tims felt nervous just mentioning the forbidden word. "I've never heard of anyone successfully making their way through Obscurity."

"Peccadillo is really good at deceiving us. See, King Iam gave us the power to overcome him." Warder held up his gnarled index finger to make his point. "People have forgotten the Truth."

Tims' mind flashed back to her last customer of the day at Outfit Outlet. The man in the black suit and sunglasses. She remembered his warning and the evil radiating off him. A shiver went down her spine. "Warder, do you think the Prince, I mean, Peccadillo ever shows himself in public?"

"I'm sure he is able if he wanted to, but mostly he sends his army to take care of the feet-on-the-ground kind of work, if you know what I mean." Warder chuckled. "Why do you ask?"

Tims looked down and fiddled with her hands. "Well, the first day after I met Radimar, customers came and asked me all kinds of weird questions—even silly ones. I felt relieved when the day finally came to an end. Then my last customer showed up at my register. He looked a lot like Peccadillo in his perfect black suit. I didn't get a good look at his face though. His behavior intimidated me. He warned me not to have contact with Radimar."

Warder brushed a hand over the white stubble on his chin. "Could have been someone who is a Peccadilloist, a human worshiper of Peccadillo. They act and dress like him. Peccadillo personally assigns beings to them to make them appear to have special powers. Their hearts are as black as his." He paused. "Hmm . . . Peccadillo has known of you since fairly early on."

The comment increased Tims' concern.

Warder took her hand and looked into her frightened eyes. "Timorous, you need not fear. All those who choose King Iam, as you did, have been given power to overcome Peccadillo and his forces."

"But how?" she questioned. "If we have the power to overcome him, why don't we?"

Warder studied her for a moment. "Because Missy, Peccadillo convinced almost all humans there is no need to overcome him—that he is on our side. Never forget, Peccadillo is our enemy, no matter what you hear." Despite his age, Warder stood tall like a warrior ready for war. "Shall I continue?"

Tims' mind raced. "Peccadillo, the enemy? Is there anything safe in this world?"

"After Peccadillo's banishment from Bliss, King Iam offered him a wager. Peccadillo gladly took it, thinking he had the upper hand. Of course, King Iam won. Peccadillo lost what little power he did have. All he has left is deception—and he's quite good at it."

"What wager?"

"King Iam bet Peccadillo the life of his son for all the humans and all they had lost because of Peccadillo. But there was a catch."

Timorous waited on the edge of her seat.

"His son had to come to our world to live as a human, paying for our mistakes in full."

"You mean Radimar?" Tims ask hopefully. "Can he help fix this mess we're in?"

"He has, but we have a responsibility in making things right too. It's all a part of the bigger plan that King Iam has in mind."

Tims squinted as one corner of her mouth rose.

Warder continued. "Many years ago, Radimar came, but people didn't recognize him. Those who'd been waiting expected some kind of a royal grand entrance. Only those he'd chosen saw him for the prince he is. He allowed those who did not believe to sentence him to death."

Tims gasped. "When was this? How did he get away? Are they still trying to kill him?"

"Radimar came a long time ago but didn't get away." Warder spoke matter-of-factly. "He came to win the wager. That meant he had to die."

Timorous frowned and tilted her head in confusion.

Warder scooted forward, sitting knee to knee with her. He stared into her eyes intently. "He *allowed* them to take his life."

Timorous stood abruptly. "How could can that be? I just saw him last night." Tears filled her eyes. "How is dying, winning? You're telling me there's no hope. He lost."

Warder took her hand and encouraged her to sit again. "Not so fast. I haven't told you the twist in the story. Let me finish." He patted her arm reassuringly. "See, what Peccadillo didn't realize is the power of King Iam lives in his son, Radimar. Nothing is greater than that."

"Peccadillo's kingdom celebrated the death of King Iam's son, but very quickly it became clear something had gone terribly wrong. Peccadillo personally threw Radimar into the Abyss. No one ever escapes from there. But a ruckus began, and they heard shouts of joy. Peccadillo's kingdom shook with fear. Radimar not only came out of the Abyss but brought back many humans who were held captive there. They walked right out victoriously, leaving Peccadillo in a tizzy."

Tims furrowed her brow. This all sounded like a fairy tale. She understood that Peccadillo and his forces lived in the Netherworld, and the Abyss represented the place people went when they died. It sounded horrible to her. "You're telling me people came back from the dead."

"Yes, some did. And what's more, he took the last of Peccadillo's power, leaving him only with the ability to deceive. Never forget that, because he's very good at it."

Warder leaned back. "So here we are today, living our lives thinking truth is what we see around us. People nowadays don't even realize there is a whole world of unseen things going on around them. And in this unseen world, the enemy is looking to destroy us while King Iam and his kingdom are looking to help us overcome. We have eyes, but we don't see."

This all sounded quite strange and unbelievable to Timorous. She didn't think she could ever believe this crazy story as much as Warder did.

Chapter 27

Hidden away in an abandoned building not far from Warder's cabin, the Toadies plotted to increase Tims' fears and cause her to run from their enemy. The slimy fiends stood shoulder to shoulder in deep discussion.

One Toady shouted above the rest. "We'd better come up with a plan fast. We're running out of time."

Each shared their evil schemes. When they disagreed, they fought and bit one another. One reminded them all how the stench of their open wounds would bring the attention of the Obliterist. They quickly focused and formulated a plan.

"I SHOULD GO." FEELING rather overwhelmed by the story, Tims stood and stepped toward the door. "I need some time to think about this."

"It's a lot to grasp." Warder's forehead creased with concern. "You're not going to walk home, are you?"

"I have a friend who's going to pick me up."

"A friend?" He seemed a bit alarmed.

"Her name is Essince." She chose not to tell him she'd have to walk a bit and maybe even wait awhile for her.

"Ah, very good." He visibly relaxed. "Now remember, Tims, Prince Peccadillo and his forces know you're in contact with Radimar. That makes you their enemy. You *need* to remember they really can't hurt you unless you give them that power. You have the power of King Iam in you. All you have to do when you find yourself in a pinch is call out King Iam's name. Do you hear me?"

Still confused, Tims nodded absently.

"AND THERE SHE IS," the Toady on guard yelped. He ran to the other Toadies. "We've got work to do."

In a rush, they all moved, pushing and shoving their way out of the hiding place and into their positions. "She's alone. Now is the perfect opportunity to move," they sneered.

TIMS FELT A CHANGE the moment she stepped outside. Her sense of peace was instantly replaced with foreboding. Even the air felt different. *Had the temperature dropped that much since this morning?* She hugged herself tightly and walked at a quick pace, not looking back at the Obscurity. The noises she'd heard earlier seemed louder and closer now. Her heart rate increased, and she moved even faster. "Keep your head down and move quickly," she repeated over and over.

A light fog moved across the ground, coming straight toward her from the direction of Obscurity.

The hairs on the back of her neck rose up. Petrified and unable to think straight, she wanted to run, but fear caused her to stop abruptly. The fog slowly moved closer and closer. It smelled odd. *Maybe this is what death smells like?* Her throat felt like it was closing up. She couldn't yell for Warder even if she wanted to. She trembled violently.

Run. Run!

Why wouldn't her feet cooperate? The fog was now only two feet away.

From above came a loud screech that shook her from her stupor. She took off running toward the abandoned school.

THE TOADIES LAUGHED at their games. They'd been carefully watching her body language, how she looked toward Warder's cabin, then back to the fog, then out to the school, and back to the fog. To discourage her, they whispered doubts about each escape route. The fear on her face was so easy to read, her rigid body an even easier read. Everything worked as planned. They watched her race toward the abandoned school and swarmed around her, blocking every exit except for the one path they wanted her to take.

BREATHING HEAVILY, Timorous made it to the abandoned school. She planned to call Essince from here, having noticed a pay phone the day before. She hoped it still worked, since cellphones were a thing of the past. She dialed several times but in her frantic state, kept dialing wrong numbers. She tried over and over, keeping a watchful eye on the fog still coming toward her. When she finally dialed correctly, it rang and rang. Essince's phone answered, "This is

Essince. Leave a message and I'll be in touch soon." Tims left her a message.

Where is she? How soon will she get here? Just when she had lost hope, she saw a car coming her way. Relief washed over her. "Wow; that was fast."

As the car neared her, she realized it wasn't Essince. Apprehension seized her. The passenger door swung open and out came the young man who had chased her the other day.

"Hey, there. Nice to see you again. Would you like a ride?" He looked her up and down.

She felt dirty just being near him. She wanted to run, but again she remained motionless.

He took a step closer and reached out for her. "Come on, I wouldn't hurt you."

Tims stepped back.

The Toadies all snickered. Lust worked the young man over, doing his job well.

He took another step toward her as the driver started to get out of the car.

Two men. A new wave of terror passed through her. She had to get away. Tims ran, not knowing or caring where she headed.

The first man chased her on foot while the other hopped back into the car. She ran until her lungs were on fire. She turned several corners and found a large group of bushes to hide behind. She knelt down and tried to slow her breathing and stayed quiet as the car slowly passed by.

What to do, what to do? What did Warder tell me?

She heard footsteps approaching. Their pace slowed and then seemed to change directions as if the person was unsure of where she had gone. He began to move in her direction, getting closer and closer.

Then she remembered what Warder had told her. Feeling a bit silly, she whispered as quietly as possible, "King Iam."

The man stopped. Had he heard her? He now stood only ten feet away.

She whispered again, "King Iam."

The man stepped toward her.

"King Iam." Still afraid, she raised her voice a little.

He parted the bushes and gave her an evil grin. "There you are, pretty lady."

She jumped up and ran down the road faster than she thought possible, now screaming, "King Iam, King Iam." Warder's suggestion failed. Not that she really thought it would work.

When she reached an intersection, the man in the car pulled up and cut her off. She turned to run the other direction, but the other man came up behind her. She was trapped. The men grabbed her arms and pulled her toward the car, laughing. She fought with all her might.

"Get her in here before someone sees us." The man, who had been chasing her on foot, wrestled her into the car.

Heart racing and sweat running down her back, Timorous felt completely helpless. They had succeeded. She was in the car. When the man held a knife to her neck, her fighting stopped.

"That's right, pretty lady. It will be much better if you just stay still."

Her mind surrendered and slipped into an overwhelming blackness.

She dreamed of screaming, "King Iam. King Iam." In desperation, she whispered one last time. "King Iam, where are you?"

A quiet whisper reached her heart. "I'm here. Fear not."

TIMS FELT DISORIENTED when she awoke. She slowly became aware of lying face down and her hands taped behind her back. The tape wrapped around her lower arms until her elbows were inches apart. She was still in the car. She could hear fast traffic passing, but the men were arguing outside the car.

"You idiot, why didn't you make sure we had enough gas?"

"Hey, buddy, this wasn't planned. Remember? The opportunity presented itself, and we went with it."

"We can't do anything with her right here. Too much traffic." The men seemed to be waving a few people off when they slowed to offer help. "Let's just ditch her and the car here. It's stolen anyway."

"But she's seen us. Maybe we need to get rid of the evidence, if you know what I mean."

"She's not going to tell." The speaker sounded exasperated. "You saw how terrified she was. She fainted like a pathetic wimp. That should be enough to keep her silent."

They looked back at her. She pretended to still be unconscious. One of the men shook her hard and demanded she wake up. She trembled but kept her eyes shut.

"I know you can hear me, you faker. If you breathe a word of this to anyone, well, let's just say, we know where you live."

"It's a shame," The other man laughed. "We could have had such fun. Maybe next time, pretty lady." With that, they left.

Tims lay there a long while, afraid to move. When she finally rolled to her side, she realized it was night. How long had she been out, and how far had they taken her? More importantly, how to get her hands untied? Luckily, they hadn't tied her legs.

With some effort, she kicked off her shoes and used her feet to unlock the door. She pushed it open and slid off the seat. She stumbled to the ground and slid into the ditch separating the two sides of the highway. Gravel and dirt ripped her jeans and left a large scrape on her thigh. In pain, she sat up and positioned her legs under her, feeling the wet marsh under her feet. She got herself into a standing position.

The ditch was filled with tall grass, rocks, and prickly weeds. It must have rained recently because it also held an inch or so of standing water. She followed the ditch along the highway, falling multiple times as she tried to walk on the uneven slippery ground. The dark of night made it difficult to see what was in front of her, nor could she catch her falls. A good thirty minutes passed. She shivered in the cold. Hopelessness overshadowed the pain she felt. Cars sped by. Each time, she'd duck down, worried the men might be looking for her.

She had no sense of time or where she headed. It felt like hours since she had started walking. She began thinking about Warder and the power he said she would have if she called on King Iam. Hot tears began streaming down her face.

Is it all a lie? Warder is just a nice old man with silly stories. And what about Radimar? He seemed amazing, but her life had been turned upside down ever since her first encounter with him. Maybe he was the cause of all her problems. How stupid of her to trust someone. She should trust only herself. After all the promises Warder told her about King Iam, how he'd be there for her, was this what she got?

A sense of betrayal and abandonment overwhelmed her. She chastised herself for being so gullible, each negative thought leading her deeper into depression. She wondered if anyone really cared about her. Maybe she would die out here of exposure. Maybe it would be easier than living in this ugly world.

A TEAM OF TOADIES FOLLOWED behind her, speaking lies into her head. Their rods crackling, they told her she had no value, that no one cared, and that she was alone. With each fall, she lost a little more motivation. As tears ran down her face and her shoulders slumped more and more, they congratulated themselves on their success. She had listened and, better yet, had accepted their evil lies as truth.

SHE FELL YET AGAIN, getting a mouth full of some kind of muddy algae mess. She couldn't go any farther.

Looking up, she saw the glow of an advertising banner and recognized the 9-Eleven store across the highway. Could she make it across the highway? She had to try.

She struggled up the embankment, half on her belly and half on her feet. Muddy and exhausted, she slipped and smacked her cheek hard on the gravel as she neared the top. Groaning, she lay there for a moment, blood and dirt mixing together.

A car slid to a stop near her.

"Oh no. They found me." She planned to plunge back into the ditch when a blond young woman came running out of the car.

Essince ran and reached down to help Tims up the rest of the embankment.

"Tims, Tims. Are you okay?" she cried. "I'm so sorry I was late. I've been looking for you everywhere."

Tims began sobbing.

Essince sat down and pulled her into her arms while Tims' sobs grew deeper. She felt comfort in Essince's arms, but in her state of trauma, she still couldn't make sense of what had happened.

Essince used a small utility knife to cut the tape off her arms and wrists. She helped Tims into the car, turned up the heat, and covered Tims with her coat.

Still crying, Tims gradually calmed down. Essince gave her a tissue to wipe her nose.

As they drove off, Essince took her hand. "What happened? Are you okay?"

Tims refused to even look at Essince. She felt relieved to be rescued, but she wasn't okay. She had cried out for King Iam, and he hadn't come. Why did she even try?

Chapter 28

"What happened?" Essince asked again.

Tims stared out the window, silent tears running down her face.

"Tims, it's obvious you were kidnapped. Do you want to go to the police and report it?"

She shook her head "no" and cried harder.

Essince's eyes filled with tears, heartbroken for her. Tims had scrapes on her arms, feet, and face. Patches of red covered her skin where the scrapes had dug deep enough to draw blood. "Can I at least take you to the hospital to be treated for your wounds?"

"No!" Tims scared herself with her explosive response. "No," she said more quietly. "I just want to go home. Please just take me home."

"Okay." Essince kept her eyes on the road. "Do you want to talk about it?"

Tims remained silent.

They drove quietly back to her apartment and Essince walked Tims to her door. "I hate to leave you when you are in shock but I'll only be gone a few minutes. I need to get some medical supplies to clean and bandage your wounds. Will you be okay while I do that?"

Tims nodded and walked emotionlessly through her door.

Essince ached for Tims but knew that only through struggle could her new trust in King Iam grow, much like exercising a muscle made it stronger. King Iam would use this to help her in future battles. The enemy attacks were to be expected. Yet King Iam always found a way to use Peccadillo's assaults to strengthen his followers.

AS SOON AS ESSINCE left, Tims felt guilty. She'd forgotten to even thank her for rescuing her and bringing her safely home. She let the guilt go for now and decided to thank her later. As she stood in her living room, her thoughts felt fuzzy, making everything feel off. She just wanted to shower and go to bed.

Just then, Hearsay, key in hand, and Meddling following, pushed their way through the door, not even bothering to knock. Tims chastised herself for not locking all her locks. The two almost fell over each other as they entered. They both spoke at once, neither really looking at Timorous.

As they talked over each other, Tims understood nothing of what they said. The energy in the room increased in intensity.

A whole new group of Toadies entered with the young women, happy to be creating chaos.

Finally, one voice rang out more loudly than the other. "So, our lover girl finally comes home," Meddling snarled.

Hearsay joined in. "You lied to me. Radimar brought you home last night and he hugged and kissed you." She stopped abruptly, seeing Timorous for the first time. Her eyes took in her bare, muddy feet and the bleeding scrapes on her face and arms. "What happened to you?"

Tims' eyes once again filled with tears.

Hearsay hurried to her and pulled her into a gentle embrace. "Tell me what happened to you." She stepped back quickly and crinkled her nose. "Seriously, what happened? You smell awful." When Tims still did not answer, Hearsay frowned, "You have to tell me. Something is going on, Tims."

Tims opened her mouth but nothing came out. She looked over at Meddling's accusing eyes, then back to Hearsay. Hearsay's posture shifted and her look of concern melted away to a look of suspicion and anger. Feeling more flustered than ever, she twisted her fingers together nervously.

"What are you keeping from us? Why won't you talk to me?" Hearsay crossed her arms. "I've always been there for you? Did Radimar do this to you?"

But Tims, still in shock, said nothing.

"I thought we were best friends. Now you hide things from me. All these years I've been there for you, and this is the thanks I get?" Hearsay spat out her words. "You've never appreciated me."

Feeling like a pathetic mess, Tims crumpled to her knees, while Meddling gloated.

In an almost whisper and without looking at either of them, Tims quietly asked, "Hearsay, could we speak in private?" She glanced up at Hearsay as a tear ran down her face.

Hearsay hesitated.

"No way," Meddling said. "I've supported Hearsay for the last couple days. We were worried. Looking at you now, we had good reason to worry. I deserve to hear the truth, too—if you can handle that." Meddling walked over to Hearsay's side. "Maybe you should just tell Hearsay the truth for once, Tims. Wouldn't that make it so much easier?"

Hearsay looked at her with a mix of concern and distrust but sided with Meddling. "There's a lot of things you've shared with Hearsay that aren't adding up. We know you've been spending the last few days with Radimar. Just admit it."

"No," Tims shot back angrily, unable to take any more. Her body ached, and her head pounded. "I didn't spend today with Radimar or yesterday either."

"Then what did happen?" Both Hearsay and Meddling leaned forward.

A few Messengers made their way through the enemy lines, while several Legionnaires worked in the background to help them meet their mark. Each time the Toadies swung, but their accuracy was lacking.

Courage and indignation rose in Tims' heart. Confidently she stood and raised her chin, "You need to leave . . . now. I'm exhausted and unable to share anything with you in this state."

Hearsay's eyebrows shot up, "Well, I never! Tims, I've never seen you like this. What's gotten into you? I'm beginning to believe Meddling. Maybe you and I are no longer friends." With that, Hearsay whipped her shoulder-length ponytail around and headed out the door.

Meddling gave Tims one last condescending glare, making it clear she would return to retrieve the information she sought.

Timorous locked the multiple locks on her door and slowly trudged to her bedroom. Throwing herself on her bed, she sobbed uncontrollably. Her mind filled with every lie the enemy could throw at her. Nothing good had come out of meeting Radimar. In fact, everything was falling apart around her. In utter despair, she ignored Essince's knocking at her door.

"Tims, I'm here for you. Just call if you need anything."

She heard Essince's muffled offer of help through the door but didn't have the energy or desire to respond.

Stripping off her filthy clothes, she stepped into the shower. Her wounds stung as the water ran over her scrapes. Blood and dirt made little rivers down to her toes and into the drain. She didn't do any scrubbing but just stood numbly under the hot water until it ran cold.

"Why did I lay on my bed before showering?" she moaned. She pulled off the dirty covers and threw them in the corner. Grabbing her favorite blanket, she wrapped it around herself before she fell into a fitful sleep.

HAVING RECEIVED MULTIPLE reports of enemy interference, Deamon returned to Obscurity. He grew more livid with each report. Usher hoped his news would cheer him a bit. It was bad enough working with him when normal activity was taking place. More recently, it had become unbearable.

Usher found the Commander in the meeting room and pacing back and forth. "Commander Deamon, the Toadies have regained control of the one of interest." He smiled, waiting for some sort of praise.

"Is that so?" Deamon continued pacing.

Usher's smile faltered. "Yes, my Lord." He rechecked his notepad. "She is at her apartment completely defeated."

Deamon snorted, making light of it.

Usher frowned. "I would think you'd be pleased with this progress."

"So, you have figured out what the enemy plans?" Deamon toyed with Usher. "Seems to me that Prince Peccadillo cares little about someone so insignificant and more about what our enemy is planning."

Usher responded with controlled irritation. "Yes, my Lord. Yet my first responsibility under your command was to stop the influence of the enemy on the one they seem most interested in. I have done my job. As you are my Lord and wise leader, I thought the responsibility of grasping the enemy's plans was yours."

Faster than Usher could blink an eye, Deamon, in all his fury, jumped on top of him. "How dare you scrutinize my leadership, you imp." He spat into Usher's face.

Usher struggled to breathe beneath Deamon's crushing weight.

"My dear Deamon, is that how you treat Prince Peccadillo's top assistant?" Miss Enchantress leaned against the doorframe in all her glory, taunting him with his former words to her.

Deamon heaved heavy, raging breaths over Usher as Miss Enchantress sauntered over and looked down. She leaned over Deamon's shoulder. "Look Deamon, Usher is turning blue." She put on a pout of fake pity.

He didn't budge. Usher laid nearly at the point of fainting.

She took Deamon's beast-clawed hands and drew him a few steps away.

Usher glanced in her direction to gaze at her beauty briefly as he drew in his first shallow breath. He stayed on his hands and knees for some time, head down and gasping while trying to regain his strength.

"What brings you here, my dear?" Deamon said as he shot a glare at Usher's pitiful crumpled form on the ground.

Miss Enchantress drew him close to her and pushed out her lower lip. "Don't be mad at me, my sweet. You know I am as bound to follow Prince Peccadillo's orders as you are. I would much rather be here with you." She wrapped her leg around Deamon's.

Usher watched Deamon take his first real look at Miss Enchantress. Thankfully, his interests were swayed. He wrapped his arms around her and pulled her in tight. "Remember who you really belong to." He kissed her neck. "You still haven't told me why you're here."

She laughed as she leaned her head back. "The Prince requests Usher's presence, and I offered to assist you while he's away."

Without bothering to look at Usher, Deamon shooed him away with his hand.

More than happy to leave, Usher slowly and painfully crawled out of the meeting room. Once he made it to his own room, he finally stood to his feet. With no desire to stay and let Deamon finish him off, he packed as quickly as his injured body would allow.

Would Deamon put out an order to get rid of him as he went? It wouldn't be the first time something like that happened. As stealthily as possible, Usher left the lair and headed to the Netherworld.

Chapter 29

Timorous tossed and turned the whole night. She finally decided it was useless to continue trying to sleep and got out of bed just before dawn. As she sat drinking her tea, she resolved to end all communications and interactions with Radimar. She never understood the plans he had for her anyway. It didn't matter that he chose her. Things were just getting worse.

The phone rang. She jumped and stood by it, trying to decide whether or not to just let it ring. Her answering machine picked up and gruff voice spoke. "Hi, Tims. This is Warder. I'm worried about ya. Are ya still coming today? I've got a great stew a-brewin'." He laughed a little but then spoke seriously. "Really, Tims. I know the unseen enemy is probably working overtime."

At that point, Tims snatched up the phone. "Hi, Warder. I don't think I'll be coming anymore."

"What's going on, Tims? Talk to me." His tone was filled with concern and she felt her resolve waver.

"I don't feel like talking right now. I'm sorry, I have to go." With that, she hung up.

She stared at the phone. If she distanced herself from this whole Radimar thing, maybe life would get back to normal. But she couldn't quite remember what normal was—or if she had actually ever been happy. Since meeting Radimar, life had changed. Maybe it wasn't all bad.

The Toadies worked hard to push negative feelings and thoughts about Radimar and Essince into her mind, wanting it to be difficult for Tims to remember any good moments with the enemy. The Toadies kept screaming, "Liars. Betrayers. This is what life will be like if you continue with them."

WARDER STARED AT HIS phone, surprised she'd hung up on him. He sat down by the desk. "King Iam, I know you know what you're doin', but please help Timorous through her first steps of trusting in you."

A SHORT WHILE LATER, someone knocked quietly on Tims' door.

"Why won't people just leave me alone?" Timorous moaned.

She tried to just ignore it, but whoever knocked, quietly persisted. She looked through the peephole. Essince smiled her "the sun is rising" smile, as if she knew Tims had seen her.

Timorous turned around and leaned on the door, wondering what to do.

Being overly confident, many of the Toadies had been dismissed, thinking things were under control. Now only four were left to guard her. The Toadies saw Essince at the door and screamed obscenities. "No. She is ours. She has given us room." They put their Amplifiers near her neck.

"Quick, call the others back," one yelled in a panic.

They worked to create a cloud her mind with anxiety and confusion.

CAPTAIN VALIANT SENT three of his top Legionnaires to clear out the enemy and watch the perimeter. The order had come the instant Warder's request reached King Iam.

The Toadies rods crackled like electricity, increasing confusion and chaos in Timorous until a flash of brilliant white light surrounded them. The Toadies temporarily lost their sight and crawled around reaching for their rods.

When they were able to see again, all three Legionnaires stood with drawn swords of light, ready for battle.

The Toadies, faking confidence, taunted them. "You're not welcome here. This one belongs to us. She gave us room last night."

"You are mistaken. She's been chosen, and you have only confused her. You may not return to this place," one Legionnaire ordered. The guards grew brighter and brighter until the Toadies could no longer endure it. They fled. Their exit was almost comical as they tripped over one another, pushing each other out of the way.

ALMOST WITHOUT THINKING, Timorous opened the door and invited Essince in.

Essince pulled Tims into a protective embrace. "Timorous, I've been so concerned for you."

Immediately peace filled Timorous. She began to relax. For the first time, she wondered if this peace actually came from Essince.

"Are you better this morning?"

Tims turned and walked away. Essince followed her and waited patiently.

When Tims turned to face her, tears welled up in her eyes. "I guess not," she barely whispered.

Essince, her face filled with compassion, gently took her hand.

A new rush of comfort filled her.

"How about I make us some more tea and you share whatever you feel comfortable with?" Essince moved to the kitchen and went to work.

Tims sat down. "I tried calling you from the abandoned school where you dropped me off yesterday, but you weren't home. Not that you were supposed to be available for me. But I got so scared." It seemed easier to talk when Essince was busy doing something else.

Essince brought two cups of tea to the table. "I'm so sorry, Tims." Her piercing gaze seemed to comprehend Tims' pain. Tims sensed loving concern wash over her.

Essince's gentleness soothed her, and Tims found the words tumbling out. "A car pulled up and at first, I thought you came but it wasn't you. Two men chased me." Tims clutched her teacup, her fingers turned white.

"It's okay, Tims. You don't have to share anything you don't want to. You must have been so scared."

"I was." A tear dropped to the table. "I don't remember much after they got me in the car. I guess I fainted."

Essince came around the table and gently hugged Tims. Again, peace and comfort flooded her body.

The red scrapes on her cheek, arms, and leg were still oozing. Essince grabbed the first aid kit she'd brought and began to apply ointment and bandages while Tims continued her story.

Tims told her how she had gotten out of the car and struggled to walk through the ditch. "Then you showed up." She sighed, relieved to finish her story. She'd purposely left out a few details from before the kidnapping, including the strange noises and unusual fog that seemed to chase her.

Essince handed her a tissue. "Do you think you should call the police?" she asked.

The question caused Tims to tremble, and her tears returned.

"Tims, what are you afraid of?"

"Um . . . they made some threats and . . . and I really don't want to talk about it."

"Okay, we don't have to talk about it anymore, and I won't tell anyone." Essince gave her a reassuring smile.

"I'm sorry, Essince. I don't know what to think these days. I feel so confused." Tims slumped in the chair.

Essince calmly took a sip of her tea. "What are you confused about? Maybe I can help."

Tims looked into her eyes and then back down at her own teacup. "Have you ever been told something wonderful—something unbelievable—and then found out it might all just be made up?" She felt silly even mentioning it.

"What wonderful things have you been told?"

"I'm not sure I should say." Tims paused. "If it's all lies, why not tell. But if it puts me—or you—in danger, then I shouldn't." she reasoned out loud.

"Why don't you share, and we'll work it out together."

"Maybe you're right. I need to talk to someone. I don't have many options right now." She laughed weakly. "Someone told me to do something if I found myself in a . . . ah . . . difficult situation like last night. I tried it, but it didn't work. So now I just don't know." Her cheeks warmed with embarrassment.

"So, it's kind of like believing in something you can't see?"

Tims thought for a moment, then nodded.

"How are you so sure it didn't work? What I know of the unseen is that it's very different from trying to live the way we do every day here. Maybe the answer looked different from what you expected. I mean, if you were in a difficult situation and the answer came in a different way than what you expected, but an answer was still provided, doesn't that mean it did work?"

Timorous thought about last night. She cried out to King Iam, but the bad men found her and dragged her to the car.

Essince continued. "So last night you were captured . . . abducted . . . but then later were let go. If this thing you were told to do in a difficult situation was meant to get you out of that situation, then didn't you get the answer?"

Tims gasped. "Then you showed up. Maybe part of the answer was you, Essince. Maybe it did work." Hope bubbled up inside her.

"I think you may be right. I don't know how I would have found you without King Iam's help." Essince said innocently as she took another sip of tea.

"Shhh." Tims never once had spoken to Essince about King Iam or the unseen world. "You shouldn't say that out loud." She looked around nervously and whispered, "You know of King Iam?"

"Oh, he's been a part of my life, like forever." Essince beamed, almost literally.

Awestruck, Tims took a few moments to collect herself. "What do you know of things . . . uh . . . unseen?"

"I know quite a bit." Essince spoke as if it were everyday knowledge. "My father taught me. I know it's easy and hard, simple and complicated. But the most important part about the unseen is to trust in the truth, especially when it doesn't make sense in the seen world."

This whole seen and unseen thing confused Tims.

Essince glance at the clock on the wall. "I need to head out. Before I go, is there anything you need from me?"

"No." Tims shook her head. "But thanks."

"Okay, I'll be back later and help you change your bandages.

"Thank you, Essince, you really helped me—again." Tims smiled shyly. It felt strange to have someone supporting her.

Chapter 30

Thirty minutes later, Tims dressed and headed out. She found her car in perfect running condition.

She needed to thank Essince and her father for fixing this. She had been such a comfort and had helped her think more clearly.

She headed off to Warder's house. When she arrived, she forced herself to stay focused on Warder's cabin rather than on Obscurity looming ahead. She pulled slowly onto the gravel driveway and parked. The area still creeped her out with the overgrowth from Obscurity hanging over Warder's property.

The sounds were even louder today—and angrier. Feeling the hairs on her neck rise and her heart rate increase, she didn't waste any time running up the path to the door. She hesitated with her sore knuckles inches from the door. She stopped, wiped her sweaty palms on her pants and prepared to knock again just as Warder came around the corner of the house.

His white bushy eyebrows shot up. "You came."

Tims jumped a little. She hadn't expected him to appear outside the house. "I'm sorry. I should have called first. I'm sorry I hung up on you. I guess I got confused and had some doubts." She smiled apologetically at him. "My friend, Essince, helped me to . . . um . . . understand a little better."

Warder's eyebrows shot up again. "So, you're spending regular time with Essince?"

"No, not really. She's my new neighbor. But don't worry. I haven't told her anything. I didn't want to cause problems for her too."

Warder laughed heartily. Tims' brow creased.

He gave her a fatherly hug. "All is well, Tims. I'm just happy you came back. Now, let's go inside for another lesson."

CLEARLY PERTURBED, Prince Peccadillo sat slumped on his throne with one leg over the armrest. He didn't often sit there except for making video appearances to his officials of the differing clusters, especially his human officials.

When Usher entered the throne room and saw Peccadillo in a funk, he thought to cheer him. "Have you heard? Our enemy's target is back under our control?" He stood straight and proud, waiting for some praise.

"What makes you so sure, Usher?" The Prince didn't look at Usher but continued swinging his leg and biting his sharp claw-like nails at the end of his perfect fingers.

"H-has there been a change? My last report states—" Usher feverishly checked through his tablet for the details. "I mean, they reported to me that the one of interest was confined—"

At that moment, a large group of Toadies, the very ones who reported to Usher, came rushing in unannounced. They groveled at Prince Peccadillo's feet, all talking at once.

"Silence!" The Prince stood in all his dark glory.

They obeyed immediately.

Hands behind his back, Peccadillo walked slowly around the group. With penetrating gray eyes rimmed in blood-red, he had the ability to burn them to the ground for their lack of respect. "To what do I owe this disrespectful disturbance?"

A Toady scurried forward. "We are sorry for our rash entry, but this is an emergency, and we could not wait." He bowed low. "We came directly to you, our Prince, who should know first. We held the one of interest under full control. Unwilling to even open her door to the enemy."

Usher stood off to the side, desperately looking through his tablet for any error these bumbling buffoons had caused.

"But?" The Prince's tone dripped with venomous evil.

The Toadies' trembling increased.

"Speak up or I will send you all to the Abyss."

"Essince stood at her door," a Toady bellowed in a panic. They all spat on the floor. "We worked our charge hard, and she refused to open her door."

Another continued. "We were so focused on her, we did not see the Legionnaires enter from behind us."

The Toadies stared in disbelief at the one who spoke. They'd planned a much more elaborate story to cover their failure.

After a long pause, Peccadillo roared, "You idiots. Why did you not have your own rearguard?" His eyes turned blood red, as they often did when he became especially infuriated.

They all answered in a rush. "These Legionnaires are not the kind we underlings usually encounter." They looked at one another in fear.

One Toady continued. "They were the High Legionnaires of Bliss, their power too great for us. That is why we swiftly made our way to tell you in person." He ended his statement sounding more like a question, hoping they'd made the right move.

And they all ducked, looking like a mass of trembling green mush.

One more comment came from the back of the group. "They told us she was chosen."

The Prince stood still for a long moment, then began to pace, tapping his chin. "Interesting." He paused again. "You are dismissed. But give a full report to Usher."

They left hurriedly.

After watching them scurry out, Usher was aghast and asked, "Will you not punish them?" He'd suffered at the Prince's hand for far less an infraction.

"Usher, if we destroy all our underlings, we will have no army. Be gone. You are as simpleminded as they." Peccadillo turned his back and made his way back to his throne.

Usher left just as swiftly in his own foul mood. "Simpleminded? Humph."

WARDER WASTED NO TIME walking over to the *Book of Actualities.* "Let's continue our lesson."

The day before, they'd gone over the beginning of all creation, the rebellion of Peccadillo, and the wager King Iam had won. Today Warder wanted to take her through the trials and victories of those who chose King Iam.

She hesitated at the door, a little out of sorts.

"So, what happened after you left yesterday, if you don't mind me asking?" Despite his concern, he kept his tone light.

Tims had removed the bandages Essince had put on her face, hoping it would be less obvious, but she couldn't hide the all bruises and scrapes. She avoided his assessing gaze. "I'd rather not talk about it."

An awkward silence filled the room. She marched over to the little desk and sat down, pretending to study the cover of the *Book of Actualities*.

Warder considered her for a moment, then sighed. "Okay then. Let's begin."

They read about the former battles that occurred and victories won. Tims saw a theme arising. It seemed all the people in this book experienced problems of different kinds. Depending on their choices and their reliance on King Iam, the outcome would be good or bad. She asked a few questions, but it all still felt very much like a tall tale to her.

By the time they broke for lunch, Tims had relaxed.

As he sipped from his bowl of stew, Warder asked, "So tell me about Essince."

Tims looked up. "Why do you want to know? Do you know her?"

Warder patted her arm as he often did when he wanted to reassure her. "I'm not trying to pry, Missy. It was just something you said that sparked my interest—something about how you didn't want to cause problems for Essince too. What kind of problems are you talking about?"

Tims stared at her bowl of stew, deciding if she wanted to share. Since Warder spent all this time trying to teach her things he really believed, maybe it would be okay to share.

"Ever since I met Radimar, I've had nothing but problems." She looked up, but Warder sat expressionless. "I don't want others to have those problems too." Her shoulders slumped. "I question whether or not I should continue with this." Without meeting Warder's gaze, she waved in the direction of the *Book of Actualities*. "If this—this way of living—is so difficult, I wouldn't wish it on others." She hoped he wasn't disappointed in her. "So, I shouldn't tell anyone about Radimar or Bliss or the *Book of Actualities*, right? Isn't that why you and Radimar told me to be careful?"

Warder took in a deep breath. "Not exactly, Tims. You don't need to be careful for others, but for your own sake." Warder leaned forward.

"What kind of problems are you having?" His look of concern spoke volumes of his desire to protect her.

"Well—" She paused, building the courage to continue. "My name got spread all over the news. That's not good. I lost my job and my best friend, who thinks I'm a liar. My car broke down. I've been attacked by the man you saw chasing me the other day. I've been abducted and barely got away. Look at me. I have scrapes and bruises covering most of my body." She clutched the edge of the table, not wanting to go into more detail.

Warder reached over and took her hands. Tims winced. He turned her hands this way and that, noticing her wounds. His expression changed to anger.

"Dag-nabbit, that enemy of ours didn't go easy on you." He spoke more to himself than her.

"You know those men?"

"No, no. Those men who abducted you aren't the enemy, although the enemy did use them. I'm talking about the unseen enemy, Peccadillo and his cohorts." He shook his head slowly. "I'm sorry all this has been so difficult for you. Whenever anyone begins to take steps toward King Iam, the enemy is going to try to stop them. This is why we told you to be careful. This is what we were trying to prepare you for. Peccadillo uses circumstances or people to make us feel confused and discouraged. Am I correct in assuming you are feeling that way now?"

Tims nodded numbly.

"These problems you mentioned prove you are on the right track. The question is what do you do about it now?"

"But why? Why follow Radimar and King Iam?" She slouched in her chair, feeling frustrated.

"Ah, that's the right question." Warder smiled at her.

Tims remembered Radimar also saying "why?" was the right question.

"Maybe I've been pushing a bit too hard. For me, the real test of trusting King Iam came as Peccadillo gained power. The intensity of the attacks back then had me questioning whether I should continue on this path." Warder looked into the distance as he remembered. "Especially after my parents passed."

Tims sat up. "Well, what did you do? How did you make the . . . um, *attacks* stop?"

"Stop the attacks? The enemy hasn't ever stopped. But King Iam is always with me, giving me the strength to overcome. I learned to fight the unseen enemy, which is what I want to teach you."

The idea that the attacks would never end frightened Timorous. "I think I'd like to leave now." She gave him an apologetic shrug. "I can't live like this."

Warder smiled sadly. "I know how you feel. Really, I do. Let me tell you one more thing. It's all been worth it. See, in the end, Radimar helped me grasp the *why* behind following him. I'm sure he'll do the same for you." He patted her hand. "You've already begun reading about how King Iam's people overcame attacks in the past."

A quiet knock came at Warder's door.

Warder chuckled. "Come on in, Radimar."

"Radimar." Tims sat up. "It's Radimar?"

When the door opened, Tims abruptly stood. Radimar moved to her side and wrapped one arm around her waist.

A rush of power coursed through her. Embarrassed, she looked down. "I'm sorry."

An awkward silence hung in the air until she looked up. Once she looked into his eyes she never wanted to look away. Pure love, pure security, rested in him. She never wanted to be away from that.

Radimar smiled at Warder. "Looks like I got here just in time."

"Looks like it to me too." Warder returned the smile. "I think I'll go take a short nap while the two of you have a visit."

Before Tims could protest, Warder went to his bedroom and shut the door behind him.

Chapter 31

Meddling was waiting outside of Outfit Outlet when Hearsay got off work.

"What are you doing here?" Hearsay's sighed with annoyance.

"I wanted to make sure you're okay. I thought you'd appreciate my concern." Meddling crossed her arms and frowned.

Hearsay had learned that Meddling always had an agenda. But worn out from the day at work, she went along with it. "Okay, I'm sorry. I'm fine. Thanks for checking on me."

At this less than convincing apology, Meddling gave Hearsay a condescending look. Hearsay spun around and walked briskly toward her car.

Meddling stomped after her. "So, I've been doing some digging about Radimar."

Hearsay shrugged her shoulders and kept walking.

"Don't you want to know what I found out?" Meddling moved in front of her, hands on her hips.

Hearsay glared at Meddling. "I don't know, Meddling. No one has seen him lately, and besides, I feel bad about how I've treated Tims. She looked like someone beat her up, and . . . I . . . I'm a horrible friend."

"Most people haven't seen Tims lately either," Meddling pointed out. "Anyway, I've heard rumors Radimar is an enemy of our government. It's kind of exciting, if you ask me. But Tims might be in a lot of trouble. Maybe we need to find her and convince her Radimar isn't the guy for her."

Hearsay stopped in her tracks and stared at her.

"Why don't you come to my place?" Meddling offered. "If Tims isn't there, we'll wait for her."

"How about I go home, and you call me if she's there or when she arrives?" She needed to do something for Tims, but she didn't want Meddling's help.

Meddling's face grew bright red. "I guess you really are a horrible friend. I'd do whatever it takes to help, but you apparently won't."

Hearsay ignored the insult and walked away without looking back.

RADIMAR ESCORTED TIMOROUS to the small couch and sat with her. "How are you feeling about these new changes in life, Timorous?"

"I . . . um, don't quite know how to answer that." She had just confessed her doubts to Warder. Now, being so near to Radimar, she doubted her doubts.

"Why is that? Have things been difficult for you since we last spoke?"

How did he know? Tims forced herself to look away. "Things have been difficult since I first met you." She stared down at her hands. "It's strange. When I'm with you, I feel safe and loved." She blushed at this admission. When she glanced up, he smiled. "But as soon as you're gone it's like . . . like—"

"Like everything that could go wrong, does?"

"Exactly. I can't explain it, but things seem to be getting worse since I met you. There must be something wrong with me. What am I doing wrong?"

"Timorous, look at me."

She didn't want to look at him. Or maybe she didn't want him looking at her. Radimar was like no one else. He was perfect. The word "pure" came to her mind. She immediately felt shame for her past. If he could really see her, he would see how imperfect, used, and dirty she was?

"Timorous, look at me."

When she still didn't look up, he took her hands. She felt warmth building in them. With her own eyes, she watched as the scrapes and bruises disappeared. Her eyes widened. "How . . . how did you do that?"

He released her hands. She finally looked up; he standing in front of her. Light radiated out of every part of his body. This was no illusion. He stood smiling, smiling at *her.* "There is nothing wrong with you. Peccadillo is working to defeat me, even though I have already won. Remember I told you I'm a part of the unseen world. Anyone who chooses to follow me is also Peccadillo's enemy because he is also a part of the unseen world. Timorous, you have to choose whom

you will believe and whom you will follow."

She gazed at her hands in amazement. "I didn't think I believed in anything. I've never trusted anyone."

"Everyone believes and follows something. For some, it may be their own intellect. For others, it may be what they can get or own. For you, Timorous, fear rules your life. Every decision you've made has been based on fear."

She struggled to take it all in. His radiance, his perfection, the words he spoke about the fear that dominated her life. Could he be right? Had fear ruled over her?

"Remember how Warder told you King Iam made a wager with Peccadillo and lost?"

"Yes. King Iam told Peccadillo he'd send you, and if he could destroy you, he and those with him would have total control over the clusters and destroy all the humans forever. But after they killed you." She crinkled her nose at the crazy story, but since he was standing right in front of her she continued, "They were unable to contain you. You came back from the Abyss, freeing many who been trapped there and won the wager."

"That is correct."

"And you did all this to set people free."

"That is also correct."

"But why?"

Radimar smiled, "Isn't it clear? Because we love you."

He held out his hand to show the scars she'd seen the first day she'd met him. "Timorous, what do you choose? A life of fear or a life of truth? Both are difficult, but one way comes with many rewards."

"I choose you." In that moment, the world shifted, and something inside her changed forever. She didn't want this to ever end. "Can't I stay with you all the time?"

Radimar laughed and took her in his arms. It felt wonderful to be held. "There will be a day, Timorous, when you will be with me forever. But for now, we have work to do.

There will be challenges, but you have the power of King Iam in you to overcome whatever you face." He kissed the top of her head. In that moment, any pain or injuries from her abduction disappeared.

"Timorous, as you carry out King Iam's plans, the unseen enemy will try to stop you. Don't be afraid. Now that you work for King Iam, you have greater power in you than the power of this world."

Chapter 32

"Turn on your TV," Meddling shouted over the phone to Hearsay. "Prince Peccadillo is about to make an important announcement."

Hearsay hurried to turn on her TV. Meddling was right; something was happening.

KILZ Nightly News had just delivered an emergency broadcast signal. Corra Spondance stood nervously with her hand to her earpiece, waiting to be cued. Finally, she got the signal. "We interrupt your regular programming for breaking news from our worldwide capital, Netherworld. As you know, ladies and gentlemen, it is rare for us to receive messages directly from Prince Peccadillo himself." Excitement shown in her flushed face. "I don't have to tell you all that we need to take the following information very seriously."

She paused, appearing to listen to instructions through her earpiece. Then she nodded. "Now ladies and gentlemen, I give you Prince Peccadillo."

The screen opened to Prince Peccadillo surrounded by tens of thousands of people all applauding and cheering. He lifted his hands to calm the crowd and a hush rippled through as the Prince stood.

Hearsay thought he looked extremely handsome. His jet-black hair, cut in the latest fashion, highlighted the angular cut of his cheekbones and square chin. His intense gray eyes, set under perfectly shaped eyebrows, stared piercingly into the camera. His dark gray suit coat was hand-tailored to fit his muscular torso; slacks outlined the well-sculpted muscles in his long legs. His elegant appearance concluded with his high-fashion shoes.

As the crowd pressed in, two women standing near the front of the stage fainted at the sight of him. Others reached out, begging him to take their hand.

He spoke in a clear, smoothing tone. "Ladies and gentlemen, many years ago we defeated our enemy who dominated and controlled our people." He paused as the crowd cheered. "We brought order after the destruction our enemy brought to our world. We created laws to protect us from anyone and anything that resembled this former, devastating way of governing."

Some in the crowd booed the past he referred to.

Again, Prince Peccadillo paused for effect. "As you know, we conquered the enemy. Yet, they have not given up and we have evidence of the enemy working to infiltrate our glorious clusters."

Gasps of shock and concern rose from the audience. People mumbled amongst themselves.

Hearsay slid down to her knees to be closer to the TV.

"We have decided to take action by informing you good people of each cluster to keep a careful eye out and to report to your authorities if you see or hear anything suspicious."

Prince Peccadillo's piercing gaze seemed to come right through the screen.

Hearsay felt as if he was talking directly to her. She quickly sat back on the couch.

"If you hear someone speaking of a fanciful place or any other king, you know you are speaking to the enemy. If you have encounters with people who seem to be acting strangely as if they have spent time with the enemy, you shouldn't hesitate to call the authorities. If you know someone who spoke about being healed or other such nonsense, they need to be reported to the authorities immediately. They have been infected by the enemy. The enemy bites not with teeth but with what appears to be deceit. But it will only bring you death."

Fear ripped through the clusters.

"They speak lies to trick you into believing your government and my protective reign over you is something very bad. Could anything be more absurd?"

The crowd responded with laughter.

"If the good people of the clusters were to believe their lies, it would mean an end to life as we know it. The safety of clusters are at stake. We need each good citizen to be alert and contact the authorities about anything out of the ordinary, no matter how small it may be. I trust the best defense is for us to work together. I bid you good day."

As if on cue, the people chanted, "Live forever, our Prince."

The cameras faded out just as a flash of red flared in Peccadillo's pupils.

Meddling muffled a scream. "Hearsay, they're talking about Radimar and the things he's done. It's so clear, don't you see?"

"I'm not completely sure. They didn't say his name. Wouldn't they have said his name?" She thought for a moment. "Radimar seems like a great guy. Surely, he isn't the enemy."

"They didn't have to say his name, silly," Meddling continued. "It's everything we've been hearing these last few weeks. Weird stuff happens when he's near people." She paused. "Didn't you say Radimar held your hand and kissed it? Maybe we should take you in to get checked out? Maybe you've been infected?"

"With what?" Hearsay snapped back. "The measles?"

"I don't think others will see it that way."

"Do you see me acting abnormal?" Hearsay felt a little queasy. No one, especially not Meddling, knew she'd lied about Radimar kissing her hand.

"Well, you touched him," Meddling scoffed reproachfully.

"Actually, I never touched him. I mean, he never touched me. I've never even spoken to him. I made it all up to get attention." Hearsay bit her lower lip. Better to feel embarrassed for lying than for Meddling to turn her in to the authorities.

"I didn't want Timorous to get all the attention. I took the chance and became a celebrity—if only for a short time. I did see him . . . but not close up. You aren't going to report me, are you?"

Still on the phone, Meddling smiled wickedly, along with her evil companions.

After waiting for a moment, long enough to make Hearsay sweat, Meddling finally said, "No, I'm not going to report you . . . yet. I think you've been acting fairly normal."

Hearsay wanted to ask what that meant but kept silent.

"I'm more concerned about Timorous."

Hearsay sat up straight, "You're right, Meddling. She's acted strangely, and she spent time with him. What should we do?"

"I'm not sure, but you've spent quite a bit of time with her." Meddling made another dig. "If she's infected and you are her closest friend, well—"

Hearsay's evil Toady gave her a poke. "Oh my gosh, Meddling, you've been spending time with Timorous too." Hearsay injected fake surprise into her tone.

"Don't start throwing lies around. What I meant to say was, not that I think you are a threat, but you've told everyone that you've been with Radimar and they saw you on television. A lot of people know about this, whether it's true or not." She calmly closed her case.

The wheels in Hearsay's head began to spin. People would recognize her. The store promoted the new TV commercial multiple times a day. People had already been stopping her on the street for autographs.

"Oh no, you're right." Hearsay's eyes brimmed with tears. "What should I do? You have to help me Meddling. You're the only one who's been with me from the beginning of all this mess." Reminding Meddling again of their close involvement might keep Meddling from reporting her.

"Calm down. Why don't you come to my place and we can figure it out?"

"Okay, I'll be right over."

Hearsay took extra care in how she dressed. She put on a shawl she never wore, a large straw hat, and big dark sunglasses.

IN THE NETHERWORLD, the cameras went black.

Prince Peccadillo stepped down from the podium that stood in front of a large green screen. "Usher."

Usher came quickly and bowed. "My Lord?"

"I want to see this message broadcasted multiple times today."

"Yes, my Lord. Might I add, your speech and the background crowd were quite impressive. The clusters will eat this up. I'm already hearing panic and calls have already been coming into the cluster authorities." He smiled devilishly. Usher caught a slight smirk on the prince's face as he unnecessarily straightened his perfectly pressed suit coat.

"I want hourly reports from each cluster. Let's see how many weak-minded humans our enemy plans to use."

Heading to his office, Usher rounded the corner and ran into Deceit once again. "What the Abyss, Deceit. Are you spying on me?"

"Why no. But if you would like me to, I would be happy to oblige."

Hands behind his back, Usher prowled around Deceit. "The Prince sent me to find you."

"Do tell." Deceit's excitement nauseated Usher. "I am happy to be in the service of our great prince."

Usher crossed his arms. "The Prince is very displeased with your work."

Deceit's smile wavered.

Usher found it funny how easily he took the bait. "You must be more vigilant in getting your reports to me from Uncertainty. The Prince expected you to have subdued the one of interest by now."

The color drained from Deceit's face. Sweat beads formed on his brow, and he kept wiping his hands on the sides of his long coat. "I-I'll get right on it. Please tell the Prince he can count on me." Abruptly, Deceit turned and walked briskly down the dark hall.

Laughing, Usher made his way to his office. Unfortunately, he still had to report to Commander Deamon.

Chapter 33

After Radimar left, Tims spent the rest of the day with Warder, learning from the *Book of Actualities*.

"The land is still under Peccadillo's power for now, but everything belongs to King Iam. Each person still must choose King Iam and acknowledge Radimar as the true prince. But Peccadillo's deception is still widely accepted. It's been this way for a long time. People just assume this is the way life is supposed to be. There is almost no memory of what life was like with King Iam." Warder sighed as he looked down at his mug and shook his head. "It's hard to understand at times. That's why you must trust King Iam in what you can't see."

He shuffled back to his chair. "Let's sit over here for a spell."

Tims obediently rested herself on the sofa.

"Now, where were we?" Warder wrinkled his brow in concentration. "Ah, yes. People have no memory life with King Iam. This is where you come in."

"Me? How? What am I supposed to do? I'm just beginning to learn." Tims thought it made a lot more sense for Warder to be the chosen one, since he was more knowledgeable.

Warder chuckled. "You're probably wondering why I am not the one he's chosen? Am I right?" His wrinkles and whiskers smiled with him. Timorous lowered her eyes. "Here's the thing, Tims." He scooted to the edge of his chair and leaned close. "I'm chosen too." He proudly pointed his aged index finger at himself.

Tims felt confused until she remembered how Warder said many were chosen but few followed. "Are you going to lead the way for me and others?"

"Blessed Bliss, no." Warder's laughter erupted. "Radimar is leading the way. But we each have been given a specific job. Mine is to teach and prepare you for your journey. Radimar chose you to be a Gatherer. It's a high calling indeed."

"What's a Gatherer?"

"We'll get to that. But let's say for now that you'll be helping others find the same peace and love you've found with Radimar."

A warm breeze came rushing through his home. When it stopped, Essince stood in the center of the living room. Beaming with light and floating in midair, she appeared almost translucent.

Timorous jumped and stumbled over the sofa to hide behind it.

"Holy Bliss, Essince, you about scared our insides out." Warder awkwardly rose to his feet and peered over the sofa at Tims.

Rushing to her in a blur, Essince stood Tims up and stared into her eyes with intensity. "Are you okay, Tims?"

Warder chuckled. "Tims, I believe you've met Essince."

Tims leaned away and took a second look at Essince. She seemed her normal self now, smiling as usual. Essince gave her a hug. "Relax, Tims; it's me."

"How . . . Where . . . How did you get here?" Then as if speaking to herself, she said, "I guess I shouldn't be surprised. You all have the same, the same—" She struggled for the word. "The same something," she finished weakly.

Essince laughed. It filled the whole room with joy. Soon they were all laughing. Tims didn't even know why, but it felt good and eased her awkwardness.

"I thought I'd stop by and see how you're doing on your new career path." Essince winked at her.

"You knew about all this?" Tims waved her arms, gesturing at Warder, the ancient book, and the cabin.

"Yes. And I came to see if I could help. You are so very good at sensing things unseen. Now you need to learn to use that sense for King Iam to help others."

Perplexed, Tims looked from Essince to Warder and back again.

"Tims," Warder said, "let me properly introduce you to Princess Essince. She's like a sister to Prince Radimar."

It finally dawned on Tims. No wonder they seemed so similar. No wonder she felt the same sensations when she was in their presence.

"Nice to meet you, neighbor." Essince plopped down on the sofa and gestured for Tims to sit next to her. Essince turned to Warder. "We need to move our plans up. Peccadillo decided to go public and sent a broadcast to all the clusters to turn in anyone who had contact with us. I'm sure Timorous is their main target. But others are sure to suffer because of his antics."

Warder breathed in sharply, clearly shaken. He smoothed his whiskers with his hand. "He actually said your names?"

"No. You know the enemy refuses to speak of the one who defeated him. But he gave enough information to put many, including Tims, in danger." Essince squeezed Tims' hand. "Don't you worry. We've got this. Peccadillo always thinks he's trapped us, but we know all his tricks."

Her confidence gave Tims a little bit of encouragement.

"Warder, give her the crash course version. She's starting her journey a little sooner than we had anticipated."

Warder shook his head. "I don't like this, not one little bit. It's too soon. She needs more time."

"Warder," Essince scolded him lightly.

They stared at each other. Finally, Warder conceded. "You're right. The power of King Iam is strong enough to help anyone overcome Peccadillo and his minions."

Tims' head spun with a new set of questions. "Journey? I don't think that's a good idea. I really don't like traveling." Her voice faded as she saw Warder and Essince's expressions.

She had made her choice to believe them. Now she needed to trust them.

HEARSAY ARRIVED AT Meddling's as quickly as possible. Even with her disguise, Hearsay felt exposed.

A large Toady, especially gifted at paranoia, followed her very closely. He kept his rod crackling near the base of her neck. Hearsay kept looking from side to side.

When she finally made it to the apartment foyer, she flung herself inside and leaned on the wall. Sweat ran down her back. She waited a moment to catch her breath before she sprang up the stairs, taking two at a time to Meddling's place.

She knocked quietly but incessantly, not wanting to draw attention to herself, but wanting to get inside immediately. "Meddling, are you there? This is Hearsay."

As soon as Meddling opened the door, Hearsay rushed in and quickly slammed it shut, making sure all the locks were secured. With a sigh, she leaned on the door and closed her eyes.

"What the Abyss has gotten into you?" Meddling took a step away. She scrutinized Hearsay as if she were an alien.

This only made Hearsay more uncomfortable. "Please, Meddling. Nothing is wrong with me. I'm just nervous. I feel like everyone is watching me and trying to decide if they should call the authorities." She ran to the window and peeked around the curtain. She held out a hand. "See? I can't stop shaking."

Meddling carefully kept a healthy distance from Hearsay, as if she thought Hearsay might be infected. "Calm down. Why don't you sit down over—" She paused, looking around the room. "Over there." She pointed toward a chair in the far corner by the door.

Hearsay frowned and narrowed her eyes at Meddling.

"What? We want to keep you out of sight," Meddling said. "You know, to keep you safe. I'll make you some tea."

Hearsay awkwardly took her spot in the corner. The chair wasn't very big, more of an accessory, but she didn't question it. The spot kept her away from the window and behind the door in case anyone came to see Meddling.

"By the way," Meddling asked, "did you happen to mention me to anyone? Your coworkers?"

"What? No. Why would I do that?"

"I'm only thinking of your safety. If you haven't told anyone you know me, no one will come looking for you here."

Hearsay gave her a skeptical frown.

Meddling set a cup of tea on the table for Hearsay to retrieve. "Here's your tea."

Hurt, Hearsay stared at the cup. Why hadn't Meddling handed it to her?

Meddling stared at her, "Well, I need to make my cup. Is it too much to ask for you to come get yours?"

The Toadies in the room were having fun.

Meddling's dismissive response left Hearsay feeling very small. She stooped down and almost crawled to her cup of tea and then back to her chair.

Chapter 34

Meddling settled onto her couch on the opposite side of the room from Hearsay. "I think what we need to do is get the focus off of you. Don't you agree?"

"But how?" Hearsay sighed. "Even you don't want to be near me." She pulled her knees up to her chest and mumbled tearfully into her arms. "Maybe I should just go home."

"That's the first place they'll look for you."

Hearsay sniffed back her tears. "Okay, so how do you propose we shift the focus off me? I am, after all, a local celebrity."

"Maybe, but you aren't the only target." She stood and tapped her chin, pretending to contemplate. "Let me think. Who else had contact with Radimar? Outside of you, of course." She gave Hearsay a sideways glance.

"But I told you, I didn't have contact with Radimar. Only Tims did." Tears rimmed Hearsay's eyes as she realized what Meddling was driving at. "I can't do that. I can't hurt Tims."

Meddling blinked innocently. "I would hate to have all this fall on your shoulders alone."

Hearsay covered her face and began to cry again.

Several Toadies surrounded her, unseen but very present. They used their rods to place all sorts of lies, half-truths, and justifications into her head. Each thought rippled through her brain like a pebble in a puddle.

A firm knock on the door startled Hearsay. Calmly, Meddling walked to the door and opened it. Sergeant Lawman and two other police officers filled the doorway. The sergeant was a big man with thick black hair and a full mustache, clearly a take-charge man.

"Hello, Miss." He tilted his hat to her, then hooked his thumbs onto the edge of his utility belt.

"Hello, Officer. I mean, Sergeant Lawman. What can I do for you?" Meddling said, taking care to stand with her shoulders back, showing off her full-busted figure. She flashed him a shy seductive smile. Hearsay watched as the other officers rewarded her with a quick glance at her ample cleavage.

Sergeant Lawman cleared his throat and glared crossly at the other officers. "We're here to investigate. We received an anonymous report that someone in this complex has been acting rather strangely. This is serious business, as I am sure you've heard Prince Peccadillo's report recently."

She pushed her dark curls back from her face. "That does sound serious. How can I help you? Would you care to come in?" She opened the door and waved them in.

Hearsay sat stunned on her little chair in the corner. Did the anonymous report come from Meddling? She seemed so at ease, while Hearsay felt completely out of sorts.

The men didn't hesitate, but entered and walked around slowly, trying to act as if this were normal behavior, but they looked more like they were investigating.

"Can I get you men some coffee?" Meddling swayed her wide hips on the way to the kitchen.

"No, Miss. We won't take much of your time. We have a lot of people to speak to today."

The other officers seemed more interested in watching Meddling, but the sergeant focused on his mission. He scanned the room, his gaze landing on Hearsay. Her knees were pulled up to her chest, and she sat rooted in her position. His intense assessment made her quiver. He approached her slowly as one would approach a wounded animal.

Opening his notepad and clicking his pen, he said. "Miss, do you mind if I ask you a few questions?"

Sitting as she was and her hair a mess, Hearsay felt sure they'd consider her infected. She looked to Meddling, then back to the officer.

Fear spread through her body, literally, as a Toady's rod crackled up against her back. She knew she needed to relax but swallowed hard as the officer watched her suspiciously.

THE TOADIES FILLED the room, but they all made way when an Obliterist entered. Bowing slightly, the lead Toady asked, "Were we not doing our job to your liking?"

The Obliterist sniffed hard and grimaced. "As much as it displeases me to be among those so inferior to myself," not referring to the humans, "Commander Deamon sent me to make sure the job got done properly this time. We can't afford any more mishaps." He spat with disdain. "Continue. I am only here to observe, unless you are unable to complete your mission."

The Toadies mumbled insults under their breath. They didn't like being babysat.

The Obliterist's presence made it harder to concentrate their efforts, but before long the energy in the room rose to a palpable level. At one point the electricity in their rods caused a flicker in the human's lights. The Toadies quickly glanced toward the Obliterist, who seemed rather bored. Luckily, it only caused more suspicion from the sergeant and his men. The interrogation was going better than planned.

Chapter 35

Sergeant Lawman stood patiently waiting for Hearsay to reply.

Meddling came and stood next to him. "This is Hearsay Blather. She's an acquaintance of mine but doesn't live here."

The sergeant studied Hearsay. "Miss Blather, you look familiar. I never forget a face. Aren't you the one I saw on KILZ News and, more recently, in Outfit Outlet's commercials?"

Hearsay uncurled herself, quickly stood, and tried to smooth her hair. "Yes sir, Sergeant Lawman; that is correct. Nice to meet you." She put out her hand, but he just looked at it. She dropped it and smiled weakly.

Sergeant Lawman eyed her up and down then wrote something on his notepad. Hearsay tried to lean over to look but he pulled it away.

"Miss Blather, there's been a lot of interest around this fellow named Radimar, who you have spent some time with." He stopped for a moment and watched her reaction. When she just stood there blank-faced, he continued. "You do know who I'm talking about?"

Hearsay shook inwardly but tried to appear confident. "Yes, sergeant, but I haven't spent any time with him."

His intense blue eyes held hers. "Your news spot and commercial would say otherwise." He stared her down like she were prey.

Looking away, she again tried to straighten her unruly hair. "Well, yes, I know what it must look like to you. But it was really a cover-up for my friend Timorous." She watched as he wrote this down.

"Please explain yourself." His harsh tone made her jump.

"You see, Timorous works with me and is quite shy." She didn't want to admit how close they were. "Radimar came to her counter at our store and had a brief conversation with her. I really wasn't close enough to hear. When he left, I wanted to find out what they spoke about. Timorous barely talks to anyone, especially not men, so this seemed very unusual for her."

"Hmmm." The sergeant's face gave no sign of whether or not he believed her. After a few uncomfortable moments, he asked, "How do you spell her name?"

Happy to comply, Hearsay spelled it out for him.

"So, what did Miss Hominid tell you?" He tapped his notepad with his pen.

"She refused to tell me anything. At the time, she feared having to talk to the media with all the hype, so she asked me to. What was I supposed to do? She's been my friend for such a long time."

Her admission to being close to Miss Hominid didn't go unnoticed by the sergeant.

"I thought there would be no harm in talking for her. I just made something up. You'll notice I did mention her in the news spot." Hearsay tried to act as innocent as possible.

"You can even ask Meddling here. She's her neighbor and sat with us when it first aired."

Meddling glared at Hearsay.

The sergeant looked to her for a statement.

"Timorous is just my neighbor downstairs in apartment 1B." She waited as he wrote. "But I don't spend any time with her. Hearsay is her friend, and I just happened by the door they left open after seeing Hearsay on the news. Then she was right here, in my own apartment complex. I just couldn't resist seeing a local celebrity." She smiled, giving Hearsay a knowing look.

Sergeant Lawman and his officers watched this interaction closely. "So how do you explain the commercial?" He directed his questions to Hearsay.

"Well, you see, our manager of Outfit Outlet wanted to make the most of the situation. It's not every day a famous person walks into our store. This, of course, happened before we knew this Radimar guy might be a part of the enemy forces."

The sergeant interrupted. "We never said Radimar was a part of the enemy forces."

"Well, I-I thought that . . . I mean, I assumed from the description of strange happenings that Prince Peccadillo referred to that Radimar was a part of it all. There's been so much on the news lately about him." She finished in a rush.

He continued to eye her skeptically. "Hmm, I can see you are very perceptive."

Hearsay's heart pounded.

"That still doesn't explain why you were on the commercial and not Timorous."

"Oh, our boss wanted her too, even demanded it. But Tims refused to say anything. Don't you think that is kind of strange? You can even check with my boss, Officious. They fired Timorous. She's not been herself lately. When Tims refused to share anything or even talk about him on camera, I had to. After my boss fired her . . . well, I need my job. At the time, I didn't see any harm in it." She blinked innocently at Sergeant Lawman.

Lawman looked unconvinced as he wrote in his notepad. "I'll be checking into this information, Miss Blather." He spoke as if he'd already decided her guilt.

Hearsay rushed on. "In fact, Timorous told me directly she's spent time with Radimar on several occasions. She might even be with him now. But I've only seen her with him at the store. Meddling saw them together one other time." When the sergeant said nothing, Hearsay continued frantically. "I got caught in this mess accidentally. You've got to believe me."

Sergeant Lawman continued to stare suspiciously at Hearsay.

A large Toady stood next to Lawman. Suspicion filled his mind as the Toadies worked on him.

"Miss, I think I'm going to need to take you down to the city station for more questioning."

"But I'm innocent." Hearsay sat down before she fainted and looked even crazier.

"I didn't say you weren't. But it sounds like you have a lot of information that might lead us to locating the enemy. Are you willing to cooperate?" His commanding pose spoke volumes.

"Sir, you might want to make sure Hearsay is back here before tonight." Meddling sauntered up to him, putting her hand on his forearm. "Timorous left Hearsay a note saying she would be back after dinner. Since Timorous is so shy, Hearsay might have a better chance at getting information from her than you and your team. No offense, but you are rather strong and intimidating." She looked up at him with a flirtatious smile.

"Hmm, you might have a point. What did you say your name is?"

Meddling not only gave her name but also her phone number. When he resumed his questioning, she stepped back.

"You also saw Radimar?"

"Yes," she admitted reluctantly.

"Would you be willing to come to the office to make a statement as well and, if need be, work as an informant?"

Meddling stood tall, pulled her shoulders back as if she were a soldier on duty and purred, "It would be an honor. Especially an honor working with you, Sergeant Lawman."

Seeing a chance to turn this a little more in her favor, Hearsay moved quickly to Meddling's side. "Sergeant Lawman, I'd be happy to cooperate as well. It's so important we work together like the Prince said. It will be good to have Meddling make a statement, too." She grabbed Meddling's arm like they were best friends.

Looking at Hearsay in horror, Meddling jerked her arm back, wiping her arm with her hand as she stepped away.

Two officers walked Hearsay out to the vehicle.

MEDDLING FELT A TAP on her shoulder just before she walked through the door. She looked back up at Sergeant Lawman with anticipation.

"I have a few questions before we head back to the station."

Meddling turned around and smiled seductively at him.

He took in a deep breath but kept his demeanor professional and serious.

Meddling immediately adjusted her expression to match his. "Miss Blather's behavior seemed rather strange when we arrived. Have you noticed a change in her behavior since you first began interacting with her?"

An ominous smile rose on the face of the Toady who stood next to Meddling. Her face mirrored that of her unseen partner.

"I'd be happy to share about Hearsay's strange behavior of late."

Chapter 36

Usher took a deep breath before entering the conference room.

Prince Peccadillo and Commander Deamon, now back in Netherworld, bent over maps spread over a large table.

"I believe the enemy's adherents hide in all these clusters." Deamon pointed to several different clusters with his claw-like finger. "Our plan to flush them out is working well."

Standing on opposite sides of the table, neither the Prince nor the Commander acknowledged Usher's presence. He knew they were ignoring him. After bowing for several moments, he cleared his throat. "Prince Peccadillo and Commander Deamon, I bring you an update. The cluster of Nowhere seems to be making some headway. A group of Toadies has intercepted the one of interest. Should I prepare the questioning chamber?"

"Finally." Prince Peccadillo scowled. "It's time we gain knowledge of our enemy's plans."

Usher added, "I thought it especially brilliant of Commander Deamon to send in an Obliterist to help."

Prince Peccadillo's fisted his hands. "What the Abyss, Deamon!"

Deamon stepped back several feet but stood confidently at his full height. "My Lord—"

"I did not give you clearance for this act of war. This will most certainly compromise our mission, you moron." The Prince grabbed the nearest underling by the throat and threw him across the room.

Commander Deamon bowed slightly and took a sideways swing at Usher, who quickly avoided his reach and ran to the opposite side of the table.

"My Prince," said Deamon. "I meant no disrespect. The Obliterist attended only to give the Toadies motivation to complete their task properly. I assure you, he stayed in the background, uninvolved."

"They needed extra motivation? Is my command not motivation enough?" The Prince took on a menacing glow and his voice became louder.

Usher ducked under the table, gripping the edge with his scrawny fingers and keeping a watchful gaze on the other two. The Prince paced around the room. Everyone shifted their positions as he stomped one way, then the other. Even Usher moved around under the table like a scared animal, working to escape the wrath to come. Commander Deamon stood his ground, seemingly unmoved by the Prince's rant.

Deamon stepped closer to the table, taking another side swing at Usher. Usher dodged again but he saw the look of hatred in Deamon's eyes.

"My Prince," said Deamon, "it was merely a precaution. Would you have me take a chance?"

The Prince breathed heavily, and his eyes smoldered with fury. He slammed his fist on the table. "He stayed only in the background?" the Prince shouted accusingly.

Deamon took a step closer. "Yes, my Prince. He stayed out of sight and made no moves to bring attention to his presence. It's only fair as the Legionnaires are near." Deamon spat. Others followed suit. "We felt a show of strength on our part was important."

Peccadillo leaned over the table on his fists and his head down. Everyone went silent. Finally, he spoke with a growl. "You have taken an unnecessary risk."

"A tactical move, my Prince, I assure you." Commander Deamon said matter-of-factly. "You can trust me. We pursue the same goal."

Peccadillo's nostrils flared. "Deamon, future decisions *must* first be brought to me. Do you understand?"

"Understood." Deamon bowed but sent Usher a look of promised retaliation, causing him to shudder.

They took a short break. Usher made a quick exit to his personal lair to grab his dagger.

At his hasty entrance, the door hit Aide, toppling him over.

"Where is my dagger? Where is my dagger?" Usher shouted in a high-pitched tone.

Aide still worked to get to his feet when Usher kicked him. "Where is it, you idiot?" He pointed to his now-empty wall where he kept his knives.

"I-I, uh, I thought to polish your knives, your greatness." Aide cowered in the corner with his hands over his head.

"The knives are on the table." He pointed in the direction with a trembling hand.

"You're cleaning my knives of the blood of my enemies?" Usher's scream reverberated throughout the room.

Aide ducked but said nothing.

"You know that is my favorite thing about them!" Usher ran to the table, relieved to see Aide had not yet begun. He quickly found his dagger and tucked it in his belt. "Aide, you put these back on the wall as they were, immediately. Do you hear me?"

"Yes, your greatness. Right away, as you command."

Usher grabbed his knife, his tablet, and cloak before heading to the door.

"Is there anything else I can do for you?" Aide called after him.

"Yes, lock the door, and don't let anyone in."

COMMANDER DEAMON ARRIVED right after Usher's rushed exit. He began kicking the small door. "Usher," he bellowed. "I will have a word with you. Open this door immediately."

Deamon persisted until the door splintered, finally flying off its hinges and across the room. Seething, he crawled through the short doorway but stopped halfway, unable to fit through.

From his hiding place in the utility closet across the hall, Usher watched. Deamon scanned the room until he saw a shivering green blob with bulging, frightened eyes holding a small knife, hiding under the table.

"Where is he?"

The little knife fell from his hand with a clang.

"Answer me, you twit, or it will be your life I take."

"H-he . . . he's n-not here." Aide's lower lip quivered.

Deamon eyed him suspiciously. Growling through his teeth, "You tell your asinine master he is to report to me immediately." His voice rose to a scream. "Understood?"

Aide jumped and hit his head on the underside of the table. "Y-yes, my Lord," Aide groveled.

Deamon swept one long arm through the room, destroying anything within reach. Many of the swords were broken or bent. He almost crushed Aide by the impact. Deamon retreated without a word.

Usher knew he had barely dodged Deamon's wrath this time, but he couldn't forever. He was, after all, Prince Peccadillo's top assistant.

Chapter 37

Warder shuffled over to the *Book of Actualities*. "I don't like the idea of giving you a crash course with you having so little knowledge of the unseen world. But we'll just put our trust in Essince and Radimar. They've never been wrong before. Let's get to it."

Essince's brief appearance helped encourage Timorous. Several times, Essince had assured her that for whatever she lacked, the power of King Iam would provide at the right time.

Tims expressed her confusion over the seen and unseen worlds with Warder. "I've *seen* Radimar and Essince, but you say they are a part of the unseen world as well. It's still so confusing."

"I know it's confusing at times. Sometimes they allow us to see them in the world we know and see." Warder creased his eyebrows together. "Now, I know you think you've seen Prince Peccadillo too, but you've only seen his façade. The unseen world has two sides, good and evil. Peccadillo and his forces are the evil side and constantly battling King Iam and his army. Both sides are intertwined with our seen world. Peccadillo and all those exiled just won't quit. While you can't see them, Peccadillo's minions have specific jobs to do and are assigned to specific humans to prey on their weaknesses."

Tims raised her eyebrows.

Warder patted her hand, "Don't worry, Tims. King Iam is also at work with his unseen army to fight for us. King Iam is more powerful than the enemy."

"But what are they fighting over?"

"They are fighting over what King Iam treasures most—us humans."

Tims sat back in shock. "Us? Why us?"

"Because, little Missy, King Iam created us, and he loves us deeply."

"If he loves us, then why doesn't he just stop all of this?" She waved her arms around. "All this mess and suffering?"

"King Iam will never force you or trick you into believing him, as Peccadillo does. King Iam gave you the power of choice, to choose to follow him or not. It's a beautiful gift he's given us." He let out a tired laugh and rubbed the back of his neck. "I don't always understand King Iam's timing. Sometimes it frustrates me, like rushing you through your training, but I still choose to trust his plan. See, we don't need to know all the answers to follow King Iam. We just need to believe his plans are good."

"When bad things happen, is that part of his plan?"

"No but it doesn't catch him by surprise either; and he is always working to provide a solution. Just because it ain't easy, doesn't mean he ain't in control. This is very important to know for your journey. Remember, what you see doesn't always represent the truth."

"Now Peccadillo is a different story. His ultimate goal is to destroy us all, slowly and painfully. Even hoping we'll take others down with us. You can be guaranteed he's been a big part of any suffering you've experienced."

She looked at him, wide-eyed. "Peccadillo and his unseen forces are the cause of the bad things I've gone through?"

"You got it." Warder smiled proudly.

Tims shyly smiled but it dropped quickly as she wondered about what was ahead for her. Could she take this journey? Maybe it wouldn't be so bad. Maybe it would be like winning a prize. "Am I traveling to Bliss?" she asked hopefully.

"At some point, yes, but not this time. I'd be lying to you, Tims, if I told you this journey will be easy, but you're going to do great. Radimar and Essince both believe in you."

She slumped in her chair. "I don't really know what Radimar wants me to do."

"You don't have to understand it all; you just have to trust in the power of King Iam. He'll reveal the plan as you go. Rarely does he tell us everything when we're just beginning." He struggled to stand up. "Now, we need to get dinner made. We have important guests joining us." He moved slowly to the kitchen as if he were tired, but his eyes danced with excitement.

Tims' barely heard his comment about dinner. "Don't you see? I don't take risks." Her voice cracked. "I'm really afraid I will disappoint you all."

He circled around the table and gave her a reassuring hug as a kind grandfatherly gesture. Tims began to cry.

"You are not alone in this. Do you remember what Essince said?" He handed her a tissue.

Tim nodded, wiping her nose.

"It's going to be a great adventure, and the reward will be worth all the hard work that lies before you. If King Iam himself didn't know you're able to do this, he wouldn't have sent Radimar and Essince to speak to you directly."

"I guess you're right. They did seem to seek me out."

"They sure did and over all others here in Uncertainty." Warder laughed. "Now I'm going to get started on our dinner while you keep studying."

As she studied the *Book of Actualities*, Tims' eyes grew heavy. Her head rested on the book, and she fell asleep.

In her dream, Timorous was in a fragrant garden full of flowers of every color. She felt herself float. Feeling the kiss of dawn on her cheek, she slowly began to remember where she really was.

She awoke abruptly to find Radimar's face inches from hers. Startled, she lurched upright in her chair.

Radimar's gentle laugh brought her back to her senses.

"What just happened? I feel like I've been sleeping for days."

Warder set the main course on the table. "What a wonderful gift Radimar just gave you. One of many more to come, I'm sure."

"Hi, Tims." Essince stood on the other side of the table. "Let's eat our last dinner together."

"This is our last dinner together?" Timorous panicked.

"Not forever," Essince drew out. "But the last for some time."

She gave Tims' hand a squeeze. Peace immediately wrapped around her.

Warder served a wonderful meal. Tims watched the three of them talk about past times, laughing throughout the evening. It was like the family she always wished she'd had but even better than she had ever imagined. These were important people, Prince Radimar, Princess Essince, and their trusted friend, Warder. She spoke only when they asked her a direct question to draw her into the conversation. That night would always hold a special place in her heart. She didn't want the evening to end and wished they all could just stay there forever.

Warder's cabin was filled with the presence of King Iam. Not aware to Tims, many of King Iam's servants crammed into this small space.

With dinner finished, they moved to sit in Warder's cozy living room. Radimar sat next to Tims on the small couch, with Warder in his usual chair because Essince refused to take it. Essince sat on the floor crossed legged, right next to Timorous.

"How are you feeling about your training?" Radimar asked.

She recapped all the stories. Her report lacked some details, but she summarized the history of King Iam and Peccadillo. All three listened intently. When she finished, Tims felt a little embarrassed to be the center of attention. "Did I get it wrong?"

"You did great." Radimar flashed her a smile that melted her heart. Warder gave her an I'm-so-proud-of-you look, and Essince clapped her hands in joy. Timorous smiled shyly at the praise. "I'm just beginning to learn about the unseen world. I just don't understand it very well."

Radimar took her hand in his. "Do you believe I am King Iam's son and have overcome Peccadillo and his forces?"

"Yes, I'm clear who you are and what you have done." She gulped, hoping her next comment wouldn't ruin everything. "But I still struggle with some doubts. Is that a problem?"

Radimar smiled, and it felt like the sun was shining inside the little cabin. "No, Tims. The important thing about this journey isn't knowing all the answers but knowing the one with the answers."

Chapter 38

"It's time to go," Essince called to Timorous from the cabin door.

Now several hours past dinner, Tims wondered how upset Hearsay might be when she finally got home.

Warder gave Tims a long hug. She felt like he was saying good-bye forever. Tears welled up in her eyes, and in Warder's.

Hands on her shoulders, he stared into her eyes. "Now you don't worry, little Missy. You're gonna do great."

A moment of awkwardness hung between them.

Then Warder's face lit up. "I just remembered. Before you leave, I need to give you something."

He shuffled over to the table, carefully wrapped the *Book of Actualities,* and reverently handed it to Tims. "You need to take this with you. You're gonna need it."

Tims' brows shot up. "Oh, no. I can't. It belongs to you and to this safe house. It's been in your family for years. What if I'm found with it? It will be lost forever." She held her hands up and backed away.

"You're my family, Tims. I can't think of anyone else I'd want to give it to. I'm sure Radimar and Essince agree."

Tims looked to Essince for support. She nodded her head and grinned.

"Thank you." She reluctantly allowed him to put the book in her arms. "I feel honored to be entrusted with something so valuable."

"It's all part of the plan, Tims. Trust me and our King." He smiled with all his whiskers and wrinkles joining in.

Essince drove Timorous home in an expensive-looking car with dark tinted windows. Neither one of them spoke. Tims focused on the quest before her. Could she actually have the courage to venture out beyond Uncertainty? What if she failed?

As if sensing her thoughts, Essince put a hand on her knee. Tims felt what she now recognized as King Iam's power giving her strength through Essince's touch.

"You can do this, Tims." Essince assured her. "We chose you. We believe in you. You don't have to see the plan to run after it. Trust us. Things are happening all around you, even though you can't see them. We will fight on your behalf, but don't confuse not seeing us with thinking you're alone." She glanced her way. "You can't always trust your feelings, but you *can* trust us."

Essince's soothing voice helped Tims calm down. "But why can't I see the unseen world? I mean, I see you."

"We allow you to see us. We have no doubt the unseen evil ones will also show themselves when the time is right. They'll do it to deceive and frighten you. Those are their only tools. They hold no real power over you, only what you give them. Normally, even they would not show themselves. But because of the journey you are about to take, you should be prepared to see things you've never seen before."

Tims normally would have been a wreck at this point, yet somehow Essince made it sound so doable. Tims had taken more risks in the last few days than in her entire life. *I can do this,* she thought—and for the first time, she believed it.

Essince explained the first step of the plan and reminded her she'd always be near. "You will enter Obscurity."

"Obscurity?" Tims gasped. "No, that can't be right."

"Obscurity is the only way to get to where you are going. You hold King Iam's power within you. You will receive guidance as you need it. Just follow as King Iam leads."

"No one survives Obscurity." Tims started to hyperventilate.

"That is what Peccadillo wants you to believe, but it's not the truth. The way through Obscurity isn't easy, but you can do this." Essince didn't seem to be the least bit concerned. In fact, she seemed rather relaxed. "It doesn't matter where you enter, just that you enter. Each step will take you one step closer to reaching the goal."

"What goal? You haven't told me where I'm going?"

"Your goal is to overcome Peccadillo and his forces. He believes he owns you. You must show him your true self as King Iam sees you. Peccadillo has left you no option but to do this by traveling through Obscurity, hence breaking his rule over you. I know this is difficult, but we won't fail you. The power of King Iam will be with you. You'll find your answers along your journey."

Tims clutched the *Book of Actualities* for dear life, her knuckles turning white. "So, I just go through Obscurity. Do you really expect me to go through that horrific place and survive?"

"Not just survive but overcome." She smiled and patted Tims' knee again. "You'll see. It's going to be an amazing quest. You're a conqueror, Tims. Nothing is going to stop you."

Timorous sat quiet for a few moments. "What if I can't do it? I mean, what if I'm too afraid? What if I decide I don't want to do it?" She hated her quick shift from confidence to fear.

"We'd never ask you to do something we have not empowered you to do. Why would we set you up for failure? We believe in you, Tims. You chose King Iam, and it's up to you to continue following him." Essince sounded a little sad, as if she'd seen others who chose to stop believing in King Iam before.

As Tims considered her options, she realized she could never go back to the way things used to be. She had made her choice. But would she be able to believe in herself once Essince, Radimar, and Warder weren't right beside her? She didn't have an adventurous bone in her body. Not to mention, she often felt incapable. After all, even her name spoke of her nature, timid and afraid.

Without a plan of how to actually survive her quest, completing it seemed unlikely. This quest required her to do all the things she'd always feared.

She took a deep breath and again resolved in her heart to succeed. She didn't want to disappoint her new king or Prince Radimar. "Okay, I'm going to trust you." Her tone lacked confidence, but Essince squealed with joy. They both started laughing.

Timorous looked down at the large *Book of Actualities* in her lap. While not heavy, it was quite large. "How am I supposed to keep this hidden?"

"The plan is not to keep it hidden. But until the time it's to be revealed, I will provide a solution." Essince pulled the car over. She touched the book with her finger, and it shrank into a tiny book. She opened a small box holding a heart-shaped locket. Carefully, she placed the tiny book securely in the locket, then fastened the necklace around Tims' neck.

Tims felt a comforting sensation as the locket settled around her neck. She touched it and felt its warm, smooth shape.

"Now these Actualities are hidden in your heart, and no one can take them from you." As she spoke, Essince glowed with the power of King Iam, lighting up the inside of the car and filling Tims with reassurance.

Tims shielded her eyes. Now she understood why the car needed such dark windows.

AS HEARSAY WAITED TO be interviewed at the police station, she watched the television news sending out an emergency warning. "There seems to be an epidemic of infected residents in the city of Uncertainty." Corra Spondance from KILZ News reported on multiple infected people taken into quarantine—really more like being arrested.

Screaming people ran from the authorities and others were taken against their will. The news showed crowds gathering to watch as the police dragged away their targets. Many asked why infected people were handcuffed by police in squad cars rather than being taken by medical teams in ambulances. The media justified this by saying the hospitals could not risk bringing this deadly infection into a vulnerable population.

"Mayhem has broken out. You can hear the sirens blaring and see the people running everywhere." Corra motioned to the crowds. "Rumors have been circulating that people are being placed in internment camps near Obscurity, isolating them from the rest of civilization."

Hearsay could hear people's cries for help and see the crowds watching from the distance.

"I'm not infected," screamed one woman as officers arrested her. "He healed my daughter, I tell you. I don't care what you think. Wouldn't you want your child healed no matter how it happened?"

"Mommy!" Her daughter screamed as she was forced into another squad car.

Hearsay swallowed hard, wondering what was going to happen to her.

"As you can see, the people in the cluster of Nowhere are concerned, especially here in the town of Uncertainty. It's been reported this area has the highest rate of infection. People, please do not come out while the authorities work to quarantine this area."

Corra pointed to several different groups of people, and the cameras jumped from one location to another, all showing similar scenes. People who questioned how something that brought good could be so bad were immediately considered infected. Police apprehended them quickly. "We'll have more information on this breaking news as it comes in. This is Corra Spondance from KILZ News." She signed off, but as the camera faded out, Hearsay saw concern etched her face.

"MY PRINCE," DEAMON reported to Prince Peccadillo, "We have apprehended over one thousand humans from over all the clusters. The majority are from the cluster of Nowhere."

His hands behind his back, the Prince paced the room. "And do we have the one of interest?" He glared at Deamon.

Deamon bristled and returned the glare. "We expect to have—"

"You have failed," the Prince bellowed. Even with Miss Enchantress present, the Prince would not be soothed.

"My Prince . . ." Deamon bowed. "The plan is in motion and she is expected to be within our reach momentarily."

"How do you know?" he snapped. "The enemy may have already moved her. The enemy may use her to sway the opinion of others."

"Our guards sense a change," Deamon explained. "While they cannot identify the exact location, we know there is movement. I have put all the Obliterists on guard around each cluster. We will succeed."

Prince Peccadillo's piercing blood-red eyes stared at Deamon, who waited to be dismissed. A long moment passed. Deamon felt the sweat beading down his back. Prince Peccadillo began to transform into his leathery dragon form. He drew back his lips exposing his sharp jagged teeth.

"Get out," he screamed in rage, as fire and deadly fumes came out of his leathery snout.

Deamon didn't hesitate to leave.

HEARSAY RODE IN THE squad car with Meddling as they made their way back to Tims' apartment. Meddling leaned as far away from her as possible and commented, "Isn't this exciting? We get to be a part of something really big. We might even be interviewed on television."

Hearsay grimaced at the thought. "People still might believe I'm infected."

When they arrived and exited the car, Sergeant Lawman summarized what she needed to do. "Remember, all you have to do is turn on the kitchen light, and we'll be right there."

Chapter 39

Essince pulled into a vacant lot not far from the apartment complex. "I'm letting you out here. Enter through the back of the apartment building. The enemy will be waiting."

A shiver went down Tims' spine. "What does it mean . . . 'they'll be waiting'? Will they attack?" She imagined horrific creatures coming after her.

"Peccadillo's forces live in the unseen world but work through people and things you can see. People are not your true enemy, although it may feel that way." Essince took Tims' hand. "You're going to do great."

She sounded so confident. Tims wanted to believe her.

"Grab your things quickly and head directly for Obscurity."

Tims shuddered. "Are you sure Obscurity is the only way for me to get to where you want me to go? Can't you just drive me?"

Essince smiled compassionately. "The power of King Iam will guide you. This is your quest, no one else's. Only you can do it. And you will. It won't be easy, but I promise it will be worth it." Essince hugged her reassuringly.

The moment Essince drove away, Tims began having second thoughts. What had she gotten herself into? The longer she pondered the question, the more she felt she'd made a terrible mistake.

Is it really necessary to sneak into my apartment? She decided to follow Essince's orders. The locket warmed against her chest, reminding her of promised protection.

Heart pounding, she darted from the cover of a bush to a car, to the next bush, making her way up the back street to her apartment complex in short sprints from one place to another. Just a little farther and she'd be at the back door.

"MY COMMANDER." USHER ran to tell Deamon the good news, while still keeping a safe distance from him. "The one of interest is back on the grid."

Utterly composed, Deceit entered right on his heels. "Commander Deamon, the one of interest is now off the grid." He smiled devilishly at Usher.

"What the Abyss is going on, Usher?" Deamon loomed over him.

Usher stood briefly confused but then glared at Deceit. "What are you up to? I have it right here." He referred to his tablet, which held all the up-to-date information and searched frantically. "She was just here. I swear it." He held the tablet out to Deamon as far as he dared to reach. "Look, Commander Deamon, you can see for yourself. She was on the grid."

Deamon took one large step in Usher's direction and grabbed the tablet. Usher ducked and dashed few steps away.

Deamon's clawed finger passed over the tablet a couple of times.

Usher held his breath, hoping he wouldn't break it.

Red crept up the Commander's black neck. "This is the enemy's work. They are hiding her. Send reinforcements to that area right now. I am sure she is still there."

"Yes, my Lord." Usher bowed and ran for the door.

Deceit followed.

In the hall, Usher looked sideways at Deceit who grinned smugly. "You'd better not have anything to do with this."

"If you fail," Deceit crooned, "it will be entirely your fault. I am only responsible for obeying my own lowly orders."

HEART POUNDING, TIMOROUS made it through the back-alley door and ran straight into Radimar. It took her a moment to collect herself. "What are you doing here?"

Smiling as he usually did, he took her in his arms. "I came to see you."

Tims blushed, and her heart raced faster.

"Me? Now?" she squeaked, her face pressed against his warm chest. "But it's not safe. You shouldn't be here. Essince said the enemy would be here." Tims felt Radimar's peace and love melt away her anxiety.

"We are safe. The enemy has no power over me." He held her shoulders back to look at her. "I just wanted to tell you I love you and encourage you."

"Thank you." It felt good to be cherished and cared for like this.

"You might not see us, but trust me, we are always near. No matter what you feel, remember this truth." He kissed the top of her head and held her steady as a rush of King Iam's power swept through her from head to toe. As he let her go, he vanished.

Dazed, she stood there for a moment. Heat radiated from within her, and Tims focused on her mission. She headed down the hall as the neighbor's television blared.

"It's madness out here, people. More than five hundred have been quarantined in Uncertainty alone. The government has declared Radimar an enemy of the clusters. Anyone who's had contact with him needs to report to the authorities immediately. We don't want this infection to spread throughout our community."

Infection? Radimar an enemy? What happened today?

Tims came to a turn and peeked around the corner. Seeing no one, she quietly crept to her apartment and turned the doorknob. It was locked. Maybe Hearsay had gone home. Tims unlocked the door and slipped into her dark apartment. After she carefully locked all the locks again, she turned around with a sigh.

"So where have you been all day?" Hearsay's voice sounded in the darkness.

Tims jolted in surprise. Blinking until her eyes adjusted to the light, she saw the outline of Hearsay sitting on her couch.

"I've been waiting all day. You said you'd be home after dinner and it's well past that. It's not like you to come sneaking in . . . into your own apartment."

Something seemed terribly wrong. "I-I'm sorry, Hearsay. I really am. I'm not sure what's happened today, but I didn't mean to worry you."

Hearsay sat silently.

"I know my behavior has been confusing lately. I never meant to hurt you, and I'll answer any questions you have. My life has changed in the last few days."

Hearsay's eyes gleamed from the little shaft of light coming from a street light outside. "That's an understatement. I thought we were best friends, but it appears you keep all kinds of secrets from me. I'm not sure what to believe. There's an outbreak, an infection threatening our way of life. Tims, you're in a lot of trouble."

Tims sat on the couch next to her. "What have I done? Please tell me, why I'm in trouble?"

Hearsay scooted to the far side of the couch. "You didn't tell me the truth about Radimar and your relationship with him. Prince Peccadillo announced on the television today—all day—that our enemy found a way to infect people. Radimar is the enemy, and you've spent every day with him." She crossed her arms, but she sounded slightly unconvinced about what she'd just said.

"Hearsay, I never lied to you about Radimar. I just didn't tell you who drove me home or who gave me a hug."

"And a *kiss*," Hearsay snorted.

"On the cheek. Hearsay, I haven't spent all day with him. I've seen him only a few times. I've been with the old man the last few days."

"Oh, yeah?" Hearsay scowled.

"He's been nothing but kind to me. With his age comes a lot of knowledge that our clusters have forgotten. He's taught me about our true history." Tims took a deep breath, wondering why she was about to take such a risk. "Radimar isn't the enemy. Prince Peccadillo is."

Hearsay gasped and jumped up and crossed the room. "You must be infected to talk like that. That's crazy. Life has been great with Prince Peccadillo. He created laws and . . . and peace in the clusters."

"Before the Prince, there were no clusters. People were allowed to travel and communicate with one another. People have forgotten the truth."

The Toadies screamed, and their rods crackled in Hearsay's direction. They were unable to reach Tims, for she shone almost as brightly as the king of Bliss. They covered their eyes trying to shield themselves from the light.

Tims walked to Hearsay and reached for her hand. When she touched it, Hearsay jerked. "Sorry Hearsay, I'm guessing you just felt the surge of King Iam's power rush through you." Hearsay stumbled back, wide-eyed and afraid.

One of the largest and ugliest Toadies stood right next to her, his Amplifier full-on and surging fear into her.

She ran to the kitchen. "You really are infected, and now you've infected me." She began crying uncontrollably.

Tims rushed to her. "It's okay, Hearsay. It's going to be okay. It's just the power of King Iam." She reached toward her again. "I know it feels—"

"Don't touch me. There is something not right with you."

They stared at each other for a moment.

"I'm sorry, Tims. This is for your own good." Hearsay flicked on the kitchen light.

For a brief second, Tims' eyes were open to the unseen. She saw the enemy, a dozen or so toad-like beings with pointy weapons, leering and jeering at Hearsay. She felt their presence. It happened so quickly, she wondered if she had actually seen them, but the feeling of their presence remained.

Wide-eyed, she looked at Hearsay. "Come with me. It's not safe here. King Iam is the true King, and he is good and kind."

For a second, Hearsay leaned her direction.

But the enemy creatures herded her back.

Tims watched sadly as Hearsay's expression became suspicious and resentful.

"You're the enemy," Hearsay hissed. "You're the enemy," she screamed again and again.

Tims remembered what Essince said about how the enemy worked through people. With tears in her eyes and no time to grab anything, Tims turned and ran.

A BRIGHT LIGHT FLASHED at that moment. In the chaos, the Toadies screamed and ran into each other, blinded by the light of King Iam.

Sergeant Lawman ran into the apartment with five other deputies. He quickly scanned the room. "Where is she? Did you just give us a false alarm?"

Hearsay crumpled to the floor. "She's infected. She's infected."

"Where did she go?" the sergeant demanded.

Unable to speak, Hearsay pointed toward the door.

The officer gave orders to the men to search the building, then fan out through the neighborhood.

Hearsay continued to whimper.

"What did she do to you, Miss Blather?"

Hearsay noticed out of the corner of her eye how he kept his distance. Tears streaming down her face, she stared at the floor from her crumpled position. "I don't know. She touched me and i-it-it felt like . . . *love*."

"Love?" he questioned.

She glanced up and saw him eyeing her skeptically.

Hearsay realized she probably sounded delusional. Frantic to make sense, she added, "I mean it felt like electricity went through me."

Officer Lawman stepped even farther away from her and called to another officer. "Call in the quarantine squad. I think we have another infected individual."

Chapter 40

Tims rushed out the back door from the place she considered home as the pounding of heavy boots echoed in the halls. Obviously, Hearsay had been part of a plan to capture Tims. There was no turning back now. Her quest had begun.

Timorous ran frantically, unsure of which direction to go. Her path zigzagged in no particular direction. Essince had told her to go through Obscurity, but where to find it? She'd never sought it out before. What she really wanted to do was run back to Warder, but they'd warned her it might put him in great danger.

She heard sirens all over the town of Uncertainty, as if the world were coming to an end and she had caused it all. Had she been spending time with the enemy? She remembered how she felt in Radimar's arms. No, he wasn't the enemy. He was the solution. Somehow, she just knew it to be true.

She ran, hiding behind a building, a car, or whatever would conceal her. At one point she ran past a store window with televisions displayed. A live newscast showed a picture of her. She stopped abruptly. The caption read, "Person of interest. Severely infected. Contact authorities if you see her, but keep your distance."

For a few minutes, Tims stood motionless, her hand over her mouth as she watched the caption play over and over. Infected? Infected with what?

Someone screamed, jolting Tims back to the present. She ran and hid for what seemed like hours. She stopped behind a large garbage bin to collect herself. Wiping the sweat off her brow, she peeked around the corner. The streets didn't look like the town of Uncertainty. She must be in a neighboring town of Nowhere. Feeling lost and disoriented, Tims slumped down to catch her breath.

Tims felt a sharp bite on her leg. She inspected it but saw nothing.

A very small Sprite named Doubt, dug its small claws into her right heel and hung on for dear life, determined to cause as much havoc as possible.

Late in the night, Tims found a broken-down building. The windows were boarded up and a condemned sign hung on its blocked front door. On one side, she found a short concrete ramp leading to a partially opened door. Trash littered the area. She used her foot to clear a path and pushed hard enough to make a space to squeeze through. Inside, the pitch-black darkness felt almost suffocating. But too exhausted to care, she felt along the wall and found a bench.

Maybe a little rest might help. She definitely didn't want to enter Obscurity at night. She shuddered at the thought.

Timorous fell into a fitful sleep, dreaming of the evil creatures. They were chasing her, screaming accusations and threats. They reached out to grab her but were never able to quite reach her. In her dream, she chanted, "King Iam, King Iam, King Iam." It comforted her.

WHILE TIMOROUS SLEPT, Captain Valiant stayed in the background with his mightiest Legionnaires. Although any movement on their part would immediately be detected by the enemy, he snuck a few Messengers through to comfort Tims.

Two Messengers came and went. Now two more whizzed past Doubt.

"Hey, not fair. Stay away." The little Sprite tried to warn the Messengers off. "Reinforcements are on the way."

Messenger Vigor heard the snarky comment and stopped. He stared intently at Doubt. Messengers were always moving, so this was quite rare.

"Liar. You make one move to call out to your kind, and that will be the end of you."

Doubt grimaced but didn't reply. She just looked away, refusing to let go of Tims' ankle.

AS DAWN BEGAN TO LIGHTEN the sky, Timorous awoke. The events of the yesterday came rushing back to mind. With the morning light, she could at last see her surroundings. It was mostly empty, possibly an ancient meeting place. The scant amount of furniture was broken or rotting. The whole place looked as if it would fall down in a windstorm.

Above her was a row of partially intact windows. Metal framework held bits of colored glass as though they'd once formed pictures. A podium stood at the front of the room, reminding her of something she'd read in the *Book of Actualities* about places people used go to honor King Iam.

She cautiously made her way to the podium. On the floor near it, she saw a dark red stain. It took her a few moments to realize it was dried blood. She felt her stomach churn. Something terrible had happened here. Before she ran from it, she saw something scratched on the floor near the bloody stain.

"King Iam is the beginning and the end. He loves—"

Whoever had died here had scratched a message of truth into the floor. Tears welled up in Tims' eyes.

"Could Prince Peccadillo be so cruel?" Tims whispered.

Doubt climbed waist high and jabbed her hard in her stomach.

Tims winced, thinking of it as nothing more than hunger pains.

USHER CAREFULLY DOGGED Deamon's reach now while keeping track of Tims' whereabouts on his tablet. "Why does she keep disappearing from our view?" he moaned more to himself than anyone else.

"How did an idiot like you make it to be Prince Peccadillo's assistant?" Deamon gave him a contemptuous glare. "You should know what's going on. The enemy is providing her with cover. Where was she seen last?"

"Her movements don't seem to have any clear direction. Her pattern looks more like she's running a maze. But she did seem to stop for a time last night on Cathedral Street, just outside of the town of Uncertainty."

"Why have we not changed the name of that street?" Deamon bellowed. "Didn't we have one of our greatest victories there?"

"Yes, my Lord," he said just as Prince Peccadillo entered the room. Usher and Deamon bowed.

"Have you two apprehended the one of interest?" the Prince asked calmly, taunting them.

"We are following her, my Prince," Deamon said. "We are holding back only because we feel she will show us to the enemy's plan. Her erratic movement is meant to confuse us, but we will discover her true destination. We have our forces in every corner of the area and beyond."

The corners of Usher's mouth tugged upward, impressed with Deamon's deception. He'd remember that maneuver to use himself someday.

Prince Peccadillo looked from Deamon to Usher, then back to Deamon. "Sooo, you want me to believe you have not apprehended the one of interest because there is a more important purpose in following her?" His statement sounded like an accusation.

The Commander took a step closer. "Yes, my Prince. We believe to apprehend her at this point will slow our progress of gaining access to the plan of the enemy. As long as we allow her to run, she will lead us to the greater prize."

It sounded good to Usher.

Prince Peccadillo, the father of lies, looked unconvinced.

Without taking his eyes off Deamon, he said, "Usher, what do you have to say about this? Do we know the location of the one of interest?"

Deamon nervously glanced Usher's way for the briefest moment before regaining his confident stance.

Usher worked to steady his voice and hoped the tremor in his body didn't show. "My Prince, I agree with Commander Deamon." Careful not to look his way, he added, "Not only has the one of interest's movements been erratic, it also seems the enemy intermittently shields her from our view."

Before the Prince had a chance to bellow, he hurried on. "She is always within our reach, even when she is out of sight. The Commander considers this a strategic move, as it will allow the enemy to think they are in control while we surround them and advance when the moment is right."

Prince Peccadillo stood in front of Deamon and increased his height so he could stare down at him. He then leaned down to be nose to nose with him. His gray eyes flashed a brilliant blood-red. In a low growl, he said, "Commander Deamon, your plan better work, or we may all be locked in the Abyss. Would you like that?"

Breathing out acid, Prince Peccadillo transformed into his leathery dragon form and filled the room.

Deamon edged toward the door. "No need for concern, my Prince. Our victory is certain."

Chapter 41

Tims reluctantly left the safety of her hiding place. She needed to keep moving, but how could she leave in broad daylight now that her face had been broadcast everywhere?

Having never agreed to have her picture taken, she wondered how they got it. Had she been smiling in the photo? Then it hit her. The only one who owned a photo of her was Hearsay. She'd brought over a small cake to wish Timorous a happy birthday. As Tim picked up her fork to enjoy a piece of cake, Hearsay had cracked a joke and snapped a picture of Tims. They'd argued about it until Hearsay promised never to show it to anyone.

A wave of betrayal washed over Tims. "How could she do this to me?" The one person Tims trusted most had divulged personal information so the public could find her.

Tims wept. "King Iam, I can't trust anyone. How can I trust you? You seem so far away. I need a sign—something that will help me believe." She felt silly about crying out like this, but after wiping her eyes she felt a little better.

She decided to explore the building for anything useful. At the top of some stairs leading downward, she hesitated and wondered if she had the courage to go down into the darkness.

The little Sprite, Doubt, made it past her waist and screamed all kinds of lies, hoping she'd latch on to one or two of them.

Tims argued with herself. Should she try? What if the stairs were broken? Taking tentative steps down into the inky darkness, she kept her hands on the wall to guide her. She tested each step to make sure it would hold. On the fifth step down, she heard a creaking sound. Adrenaline rushed through her and she trembled. Maybe this wasn't a good idea.

Just then, her hand felt something on the wall. Running her hands over it, she realized it was a light switch! She flipped it up and light illuminated the area. She couldn't believe her luck. Wait. Didn't Warder tell her things like this weren't luck? They were King Iam's blessings, even for those who didn't know or believe in him.

"Thank you, King Iam."

The little Messenger Vigor, who helped her find the switch, found himself in a fight with the little Sprite who'd sprung up to turn it off. Messenger Vigor and Doubt fought back and forth for a moment before a Legionnaire swatted the Sprite and sent it spinning through the air.

From Tims' perspective, the light just flickered. Once the light remained steady, she cautiously continued down the stairs, still carefully testing each step. She coughed on the dusty air and swung her arm in front of her to remove the cobwebs, hoping the spiders were long gone.

To her relief, she found another switch at the bottom of the stairs. One single bulb hung from the ceiling in the middle of the musty old storage room. Shelves lined the walls, most empty and some broken. Bins sat in the center holding what looked like old clothes.

She rummaged through them looking for a disguise. The dust made her sneeze. Several items of clothing were moth-eaten and unusable. She tossed them to the floor and continued to dig.

Finally, she found garments that showed some promise: an old, brown trench coat—several sizes too large—a black scarf, a dark green zipper sweater, an old pair of gray stockings, and even a pair of brown shoes that looked like something she imagined Warder's wife might have worn. She completed the outfit with a tan calf-length skirt. "This should work." Pleased with her choices, she sat down to consider how she might use them.

Rummaging through one last time, she grabbed some pants, a baseball cap, a small box of matches, and a few other items she thought might come in handy.

She changed into her new outfit, trying not to think about bugs that might be in them. Balling up her own clothes and the extra items she'd collected, she pushed them into the back of the coat, giving herself the appearance of a hunched over old woman. Another blessing from King Iam. She thanked him again. Finally, she tied the scarf around her head, making sure it hid her hair and pulled it over her forehead.

She practiced walking like an old woman. Just as she felt ready to leave, she spotted some canned goods on the back of one shelf: peaches, corn, broth, and chili. Who knew how old they were, but her stomach growled.

She opened every drawer and cupboard and searched through all the shelves but found nothing that could open the cans. In despair, she shoved her hands in the coat pocket. Something poked her.

"Ow." She checked to make sure her finger wasn't bleeding. Carefully, she put her hand back in the pocket and found a metal object with a point. A can opener—the kind that would puncture tiny triangles in the top of a can. She wanted to cry at this kindness from King Iam.

A can of fruit was her first choice. She needed the liquid as much as she needed the sustenance. Greedily, she drank the sweet juices and ate the fruit. Feeling refreshed and thankful, she slipped several more cans into the two large pockets of the coat. It actually improved the old woman look.

Timorous peeked out the side door, summoning her courage to move forward.

DOUBT RETURNED AND latched onto her ankle.

Captain Valiant put his strong arm out just in time to stop one of his Legionnaires from intercepting the small Sprite. "Stand back. This is not the time to cause a commotion. Tims will need to fight this Sprite with the power of King Iam. We will await King Iam's order."

"Yes, Captain." The Legionnaire nodded respectfully.

They all watched Tims struggle and sent their own silent requests to King Iam.

A SENSE OF FOREBODING enveloped Timorous. Soon the authorities would find her. Trying not to focus on this, she continued. Her orders were to trust King Iam and go through Obscurity. Could she do it? She had to try.

She took her first cautious steps into the neighborhood, keeping a wary eye out for anything suspicious. She pondered what Obscurity might be like, which just caused more anxiety and caused her to slightly tremble.

Sirens sounded in the distance, yet she seemed to be alone. She forced herself to walk slowly like an old woman and keep her head down. She'd pulled the scarf forward to hide as much of her face as possible.

Doubt whispered more lies into her mind. "What are you doing? This is insane. You'll never make it. They are going to find you."

Her thoughts were almost paralyzing

USHER RUSHED OVER TO Deamon, almost running into him as he looked down at his tablet. "Excuse me, my Lord." He moved swiftly out of reach. "The one of most interest has resurfaced. She is in the town of Confusion, just outside of Uncertainty."

Deamon grabbed the tablet from Usher with his claw-like hands. Deep in thought, he tapped the light bleeping on the screen.

Usher watched nervously, sure Deamon would destroy his precious instrument.

Deamon pushed it back in his direction. "Good. Inform the Lead Guard in Confusion to find her immediately, but let's not move on her too quickly. She may lead us to a bigger prize, just as I said."

"Yes, my Lord." Usher walked out shaking his head in disagreement. They should move immediately on the one of interest. Peccadillo wouldn't be happy. The delay had been dangerous enough last time. Usher thought Deamon was beginning to believe his own lies.

DOUBT WAVED HER HANDS to draw the attention of other Sprites. They assembled around her, squealing and jumping up and down with excitement.

"Is this the one, the one they are looking for?"

"Yes. Send for reinforcements and tell them she has her own personal Guard from Bliss watching her."

A few drew back at the mention of the Legionnaires, but others wanted to get in on the action. "You can't have all the fun."

"I don't care who joins me. Just send word to our leaders," Doubt said. "We are no match for our enemy's Legionnaires."

TIMOROUS BEGAN TO FEEL heavy, as if the weight of the canned goods dragged her down. *The evil unseen world worked to slow her progress.*

"Why did I agree to this? Is this really what they wanted me to do? I wish Warder were with me or Essince or Radimar." She spoke to herself.

The locket around her neck tapped lightly on her skin as she walked. It felt warm. It reminded her they were still with her.

"Ouch." The group of Sprites yelped as they fell off of Tims. "What was that?" They looked around for the enemy. "It felt like fire. The enemy can't be far." They continued to follow her but didn't dare touch her again.

Timorous wrapped her hand around the locket. For some reason, she felt better, more hopeful. She continued to rub its warm, smooth surface as she caught sight of the tall foliage of Obscurity in the distance. At least now she knew she was heading in the right direction.

Chapter 42

Still fixated on his tablet, Usher reported to Deamon. "A small group of Sprites gained access to the one of interest."

"Well—" Deamon put his fists at his waist. "Are they still on her?" He stared at the tablet with far too much interest.

Usher hugged it to his chest, afraid Deamon might rip it from his hand again. "They report they had to stand back."

Deamon snorted. "They are small and weak. What do you expect from underlings?"

"Why, my Lord," Usher gasped, "They were the first to find her. That must count for something."

"Ahh, are my small associate's feelings hurt?" Deamon taunted in a high-pitched baby voice.

Usher sneered at him, but the Commander laughed.

"They did not see the enemy when this happened?"

"No, my Lord. They mentioned only that she became too *hot* to touch. They sent word as quickly as they found her. Should I report this to Prince Peccadillo?"

"No," Deamon shouted. "We apparently need more than the word of a few Sprites regarding her position—especially since you can't seem to track her successfully."

BY LATE AFTERNOON, Timorous felt exhausted, hungry, and frustrated over her lack of progress. After taking a few turns to avoid being seen, she'd lost sight of Obscurity's tree line.

This town of Confusion had many hills and valleys. She felt lost again with no idea of which way to go. The last building she passed looked familiar. Was she walking in circles?

"Help me, King Iam. I don't know where to go or what I'm supposed to do." Tears ran down her face as she continued walking.

Noticing a park ahead, she decided to find a quiet spot to rest for a bit. The place appeared unoccupied. She walked to the back of the park and ducked behind a clump of thick bushes. Not a usual place to picnic, but she needed to hide.

Being hot and sweaty under her disguise, she took off her scarf, then laid her coat on the ground to sit on. The hunch on her back needed repositioning anyway. She pulled a can of peaches out of her pocket.

"How could I be so stupid and get lost again?" Again, she felt the warmth of the locket on her chest. She wrapped her hand around it, feeling its comfort.

A soft whisper, or maybe just a thought, came to her, something about how King Iam would direct her steps and supply what she needed. She decided to not dwell on the negatives and just enjoy her short break.

After making two triangular holes to release the juice, she drank every drop of liquid. Then she quickly went to work, cutting triangle by triangle until the can was completely opened. She relaxed a little bit and closed her eyes. She even felt thankful. "How strange to find peace in the midst of a difficult situation."

She dozed off until a commotion woke her. Peeking through the bushes, she barely made out several police officers a block away. They were talking with some kids.

Towering over the boys, one of the officers questioned, "Have you seen anyone unfamiliar around this area?" He held up a portrait-sized photo.

From this distance, she couldn't quite tell if it was her. She leaned forward, trying to catch the boys' answer.

While the police officer's voice carried easily, the boys stood facing away from her, making it impossible to hear them. She saw them pointing in her direction.

She quickly ducked down. Had they seen her? Had she seen them earlier? She felt exposed. Tims' heart raced as she put on her costume.

She realized the old lady disguise wasn't a good idea. They had already seen that. She needed to figure out something else.

Essince perched as a butterfly high on a branch above her. She shook her wings, and a light gold dust of wisdom fell down on Tims.

An idea suddenly came to Tims. She searched through the clothes and changed into baggy pants and an oversized shirt a homeless young man might wear. Good thing she'd grabbed a baseball cap from the clothes bins. Although it didn't fully hide her hair, maybe the scarf around her neck would help. She hastily packed the other clothes into a bundle to carry over her shoulder. She hoped it would be enough. Staying as still as possible, she waited to make her escape.

She watched as the officer gave direction to his team. It seemed odd they all wore rubber gloves. Was she truly infected? Remembering how it felt to be with Radimar and Essince, Tims decided, infected or not, she wanted more.

"STUPID HUMANS, SHE'S over here," the little Sprites waved their arms, jumping up and down.

The Toadies hadn't made much progress prodding the officers in their direction. The Sprites continued whistling, screaming, and making a scene until their unseen colleagues finally moved the officers in the right direction.

The officers spread out, but all were heading in Tims' general direction. The closer they got, the faster her heart beat.

A very large Toady prodded one officer directly to her hiding spot.

Two others came circling around her, one from the left and the other from the right. They were getting seriously close.

Tims trembled. "King Iam," she whispered over and over, remembering what Essince said about being open to King Iam's ways not always matching her expectations. Surely this was the end. But just maybe King Iam had another plan. At least, that's what she hoped.

IN THE UNSEEN WORLD, every time she called out King Iam's name, the Legionnaires became brighter and brighter. Filled with King Iam's power, Captain Valiant and the Legionnaires repositioned themselves behind Timorous. King Iam gave the orders and with ease, they blew out the power built up in them.

A sudden powerful wind blew through the unseen realm in this particular part of the town. The little Sprites shrieked as they were carried away by the gust. They looked like leaves blown on a blustery autumn day. The Toadies grunted as they put their ugly brown-green heads down to fight against the wind with all their might, their three-toed feet leaving skid marks as they were pushed backward. Before long, their rods were ripped out of their slimy hands. They screamed in anger, unable to fight against the power of their enemy. They reached for whatever they could grab onto, but against the mighty wind, each one tumbled away.

THE OFFICERS WHO'D been confidently moving in Tims' direction suddenly seemed confused. They stopped and looked around, as if questioning what they were doing. They actually looked embarrassed when they headed back to their cars, got in, and drove away. The kids seem to lose interest too and took off on their skateboards.

Tims watched in amazement. *They just left.*

Something had changed. There were no words to describe the sensation that came over her nor a reasonable explanation of what had just happened. She saw the look of confusion on their faces as they left. Still in awe, she whispered, "Thank you, King Iam."

Chapter 43

"Shouldn't I be at a hospital or something?" Hearsay asked a guard but got no response. She sat in a small white room furnished with a small cot, a toilet, a sink, and a door with a tiny window.

She'd been questioned relentlessly and kept up all night. She answered their questions over and over, telling them everything except for the part about Timorous mentioning King Iam and Prince Peccadillo being the enemy. She'd surprised herself by being able to withhold information while in such a distraught state.

The officer who had ushered her into the interrogation room wore a full body protective covering, including a mask, as if she were radioactive or something. He sat her down on the only furniture in the room, a single chair facing a mirror. She knew they could see her from the other side, which meant she was being treated more like a criminal than someone who might be sick.

"Don't I get to call an attorney?"

"You are not being charged with a crime, Miss Blather," a deep voice boomed through a speaker, making her jump. "We just need to ask some questions to better assess the nature of this infection and what level it has reached."

"What level is that? How do you even know I'm infected?" This whole thing seemed ridiculous to Hearsay, but as angry as she was, she didn't show it. Any unusual behavior right now might actually look a little crazy to them.

Several moments of silence passed.

"Miss Blather, can you tell us how you have spent the last few days?" They went on and on, asking about every detail they could think of.

Her agitation only seemed to further confirm her infectious state. Hours later, she whined, "I've answered all your questions three times over."

Then they switched their line of questioning toward Timorous. They wanted to know every detail about her from childhood on.

"Are all these questions necessary? After all, if she is infected—as you seem to think—what does her childhood have to do with it?" Hearsay was beyond feeling cooperative. Maybe Tims had been telling the truth about Prince Peccadillo being the enemy.

"Just answer the questions, Miss Blather," the authoritative voice commanded.

Hearsay leaned forward and put her head in her hands. "I can't. I'm exhausted." She began to cry.

They finally relented. Now she sat in this cool, sterile jail cell, where sleep eluded her. She spent a couple of hours crying softly and thinking and rethinking her situation.

If King Iam is for real— No, that's just a fairy tale. But what if it's not? Maybe he could help. I guess there is no harm in trying to talk to him."

She'd once heard people used to communicate with this invisible person by just talking out loud. It sounded crazy, but what did she have to lose. Sitting on her cot with her face in her hands, she whispered, "King Iam, if you are out there, please help my friend Timorous. And if you wouldn't mind, please help me too." She felt silly, but the moment she spoke the words, she heard her cell door being unlocked and female officer walked in.

Terrified someone had heard her talk to King Iam, she shrieked, "No, no! I've already told you everything over and over. Please just let me sleep."

AFTER THE PARK HAD remained empty for awhile, just before dusk, Tims emerged from the bushes and headed through a forest. She felt a little more confident with each step.

When she saw the white powder barrier that divided the clusters from Obscurity, she came to an abrupt halt. At this point, the white powder measured about four feet wide. Absolutely nothing grew in it. The thick forest on the other side looked ominously dark.

Standing still, Tims debated whether starting now, just as the sun was setting, would be the right time to enter Obscurity. It seemed strange that her usual fear of Obscurity was somehow absent now that she was so close to it. Maybe this was a good sign, even a sign from King Iam.

She took another step closer, stopping when her toes were just outside the white barrier. "King Iam, Prince Radimar, Princess Essince, I choose you."

For the first time, without letting fear hold her back, she took a step of faith.

A FEMALE POLICE OFFICER stood at Hearsay's cell door and motioned for her to come close.

Hearsay continued to cry. "I'm not infected."

"Miss Blather, we are relocating you. You need to come with me *now*."

Hearsay started toward the door. "To where?"

"I'm sorry. I can't say. It's for your own protection and the protection of the good citizens of Uncertainty. Please turn around. I need to handcuff you."

"What? Why? I'm not a criminal." Nevertheless, Hearsay complied.

As the officer secured the handcuffs, another thought came to Hearsay. "You're not in protective gear. Aren't you afraid you'll get infected?"

"I'm immune," the officer said.

Out of the corner of her eye, Hearsay thought she saw the officer smirk.

"The handcuffs are just a precaution, I assure you. You will be uncuffed shortly."

With her hand on Hearsay's shoulder, she led her through the very busy police station. No one seemed to notice them . . . as if they were invisible. No one seemed concerned an infected person walked right through their midst. Even Sergeant Lawman seemed oblivious.

They exited the station and walked to a patrol car. The officer placed her carefully in the back seat of the car and shut the door.

TIMOROUS' MOMENT OF fearlessness didn't last long. The instant she set both feet in Obscurity, she heard the sounds she'd heard near Warder's place.

"I need to continue this quest, even if I don't understand the full plan. I have my orders to go through Obscurity." She spoke out loud to encourage herself.

Essince promised to be near, always ready to help. Tims looked around to see her, but she saw only the dense forest before her. Doubt nagged in the back of her mind.

Tims ducked under and climbed over branches. The forest grew darker. She felt cold even though she'd broken a sweat making her way through the jungle-like forest. An eeriness surrounded her, strange yet somehow familiar.

PRINCE PECCADILLO PACED around the conference room while regular reports came in. Usher stood by nervously. He thought Deamon was putting off the inevitable, which meant the person of interest still had not been apprehended. He considered saying something but feared for his safety.

"Usher," the Prince growled, "If you have something to report, say it and be gone."

Usher moved forward and bowed deeply. "Your Greatness, I believe you should be informed, I mean, I feel I should tell you."

"Spit it out, Usher," Peccadillo roared.

"Yes, my Prince. I don't believe Commander Deamon has been completely upfront with you about some of the details of the investigation." He paused a moment to see Peccadillo's response.

"How so, Usher? Tell me."

Usher was more than happy to oblige until he noticed the Prince looking over him. Slowly, Usher looked behind him and there stood Deamon with simmering rage barely under control. How had he gotten there so quickly?

Usher knew his facts were solid, so he stood as tall as possible and addressed Peccadillo. "I have repeatedly spoken to the Commander about the breaches in the contact with the one of most interest. There have been multiple missed opportunities to apprehend her. He seems unconcerned the one of interest keeps disappearing and reappearing on the grid. I felt it my duty to inform you we are unaware of her location at this time. All traces of her have disappeared, hampering our ability to search for her. Do you not think this a good reason for me to come to you directly?" He stood rigidly in place.

The Prince waved Deamon closer.

Usher watched carefully as Deamon prowled around him, knowing how dangerously close he stood.

Deamon bowed. "My Prince." He glared at Usher.

"Is this true? Have you been withholding information from me?" The Prince did not sound concerned.

"I only waited to gather the facts before I came with my full report. Why should I bother you with trivial pursuits when the true prize is near at hand, your Majesty?"

"With all due respect, my Prince," Usher interrupted, "Deamon's information about trivial pursuits comes from me and my team. If a prize was about to be had, I would also know of it." He bowed again, keeping a wary eye on Deamon.

"Explain yourself, Deamon," the Prince demanded.

Deamon growled. "Usher may be of some help in the clusters, but he does not know all. There is no reason to doubt me. Things are under control."

Usher felt Deamon's intense desire to inflict great pain on him.

"Then where is she?" Usher moved farther from him, just in case.

Prince Peccadillo grew tired of these games. "Deamon, do you know where the girl is or not?"

Standing with confidence, he refocused on the Prince. "Yes."

Usher shook with rage. "He's lying. We have no indication of—"

Deamon held up his hand to tell Usher to shut up. "Prince Peccadillo, Usher does not know the whereabouts of the one of interest, but I do." He looked straight at Usher. "She has entered Obscurity."

Chapter 44

Hearsay sat silent and trembling in the back seat of the patrol car. She had asked a few questions, but the officer remained mute, which caused her to feel even more anxious. They'd been driving for approximately thirty minutes when the patrol car rolled to a stop just outside of town near an abandoned building.

The officer opened the door to help Hearsay out.

"What are we doing here?" She shrank back. "Am I going to die? Is this how they plan to stop the infection?"

The officer said nothing but removed the handcuffs.

Hearsay was on the verge of hysteria.

A black car with dark windows pulled up.

Hearsay's knees buckled and she sank to the ground. "No, no, this can't be happening. I'm not infected."

The officer firmly pulled Hearsay up on her feet as if she weighed nothing. Was that compassion in her eyes? The officer walked Hearsay around to the passenger side front door of the black vehicle and opened it. "Get in."

Hearsay trembled. "Is this the end for me?"

The officer gave her a gentle shove, pushing her head down so she wouldn't hit it on the way in, and closed the door.

Hearsay frantically searched for the door handle . . . until a strange sensation of peace came over her. She slowly turned to see her driver.

There sat a pretty young woman with golden eyes and a smile that felt like the sun had just risen. "This isn't the end, Hearsay. It's the beginning."

TIMOROUS KNEW SHE REALLY hadn't gone far into Obscurity, but it felt like she'd been walking all night. The darkness enveloped her. Actually, it was more than the absence of light and it had an almost palpable feel, like trying to walk through water. She could barely see. The noises were getting worse. She heard moans like someone being tortured. A shrill screech came from her other side, and she jumped. At first, the noises seemed to be in the distance, but now they seemed only a few feet away. She felt surrounded.

Unseen to her were a large group from Obscurity surrounding her. They had all rushed to see her. They varied in size, but the intensity of their presence felt overpowering.

Something cracked, like a window about to shatter. She froze. She told herself it was nothing, but that didn't calm her trembling.

A branch fell in front of her, barely missing her. Her heart raced still more. She took a step back. Another branch fell right behind her. No more encouragement was needed, she turned and ran for her life. More quickly than she expected, she found herself once again outside the boundary line of Obscurity.

DEAMON SMILED WICKEDLY at Usher.

"Good work, Deamon," the Prince smirked. "You should easily finish this now. Maybe now you can have a chat with the one of interest to discover our enemy's plans."

"Exactly, my Prince. I will no longer need the services of Usher. And, might I add, you may not either, seeing he is so inept at completing his duties." An evil grin spread across his ugly face.

Usher's gray skin quickly turned red. "Why, you double-crossing—" His tablet began to vibrate in his hand. He looked down, first shocked, then pleased. He made eye contact with Deamon. "My Prince, Deamon speaks too quickly. The one of interest is back on the grid."

Deamon dropped his crossed arms to his sides and took a step in Usher's direction.

"I guess he and his Guard are a little too enthusiastic about their job. They've scared her right back out again." He gave the Commander a sideways glance. "The enemy is able to keep her hidden outside of Obscurity, which is why she has continued to appear and disappear on and off the grid, as I mentioned before. He has failed you once again."

Prince Peccadillo raged at this, growing larger and larger while screaming a string of obscenities. All in the Netherworld heard his rage. As Peccadillo allowed himself the full range of the ugliness inside of him, his black leather suit began to change into leathery scales. His body contorted and shifted. He stood on his now bulky legs, with six deadly claws on each foot. He hadn't reached his full height yet, but everyone ran, even Deamon.

"Deamon," the Prince screamed.

As Deamon and Usher ran to escape the Prince's wrath, Deamon grabbed Usher by the throat and held him high. "When this is done, my little comrade, I will finish you myself." He released Usher, throwing him to the ground, and turned to reenter the meeting room as Prince Peccadillo had commanded him.

HEARSAY SAT STUNNED. "How, why? . . . Aren't you Tims' new neighbor?"

Essince put the car into gear and began driving. "Yep, that's right. Nice to meet you again, too."

Hearsay leaned away from Essince. "Why are you here? Why am I here? Who was the officer who dropped me off?" She looked out the window and noticed the officer and squad car had both disappeared.

Essince looked over at Hearsay's hands and smiled. "You might want to let go of the door handle. It would probably be safer."

Hearsay immediately let go.

"I'll explain in a little bit. First, let's get some food in you. And you seriously need a nap."

Hearsay watched in stunned silence as Essince grabbed a bag of fast food from the back seat and giggled. "Eat up. We have a long way to go."

Hearsay obeyed without another word. It was the best tasting burger and fries she'd ever eaten. And, *oh*, a chocolate milkshake. Her favorite. She finished up and suddenly felt exhaustion overtake her. She gave Essince a suspicious look. “Did you drug me?”

Essince shook her head and placed her hand on Hearsay’s arm. A sense of peace spread through her and something else. She wasn’t sure, but it felt a little like the last time Tims had touched her. She’d never felt anything so intensely wonderful. Within moments, she fell fast asleep.

DEAMON REENTERED THE room tentatively, standing just at the edge of the doorway. Peccadillo stood in his large dragon form but no longer spewed acid flames. He breathed heavily.

Deamon waited patiently for Peccadillo to regain control and transform into his human shape. When he had shurnk to about seventeen feet tall, claws still protruding from his large leathery hands and feet, he shouted again. “What the Abyss do you think you are doing, Deamon? You had her right in your hands. Your incompetence is beyond me. Did you not prepare your Guard?”

Peccadillo’s tail swung across Deamon’s feet, leaving a gash across his ankle, which quickly oozed with something like blood. Its putrid smell sent the Prince into a frenzy, much like a shark drawn to blood. He rushed toward Deamon, teeth bared.

Although shaken, Deamon refused to move. The Prince made a move toward Deamon’s neck but stopped, his hot breath burning Deamon’s skin. After several long moments,

Peccadillo stepped away and turned his back to him. "What do you have to say for yourself and your moronic plans?"

Deamon ignored the throbbing pain on his ankle. "My apologies, Mighty Prince Peccadillo, for the failings of those under me. I will deal harshly with them. I will send Terror to encourage her back into Obscurity. She is on the run, with nowhere to go, and no one to turn to. We will wait until she is deep enough in Obscurity before we begin the process of interrogation."

"And just how will Terror encourage her back into Obscurity now that she fled from there?"

"Trust me, my Prince. Terror will convince her she is safer in Obscurity than outside of it." Deamon gave a sinister laugh.

The Prince took a sip from a goblet, leaving a small line of red blood on his upper lip before licking it away with his forked tongue. "Do what you must but Do. Not. Fail. Me." I am sending Miss Enchantress back with you. She is especially skilled in these matters. I expect you to follow her lead on this."

LOOKING BACK TOWARD Obscurity, Timorous tripped and fell to the ground. Trembling, she sat there feeling like a failure. She was supposed to go through Obscurity, not in and out.

"What was I thinking? I can't do this. It's impossible. Why would they even ask me to?"

Messengers quickly came to her aid: Encouragement, Comfort, Faith.

Tims felt a little dizzy when she stood. For a moment she thought she saw little stars. Or was it a brief look into the unseen?

Quite a commotion swirled around her. A great host of beings were sent to assist her. It looked a little like fireworks in the unseen realm.

Tims felt more hopeful. She remembered the stories of the battles fought in the *Book of Actualities*. At times, the people felt like failures, but they still overcame.

"Well, maybe I can count that as a test run," she whispered to herself. "King Iam, please help me find the strength and courage I need." She found a spot in the woods right outside of Obscurity. It seemed a good place to remain hidden.

Although she still heard the strange sounds, somehow she knew she was safe for now. She gathered a few twigs and built a small fire with the matches she'd found. Using her small can opener, she opened a can of chili and heated it in the fire.

She settled in for the night, thankful for the fire, food, and layers of clothing that kept her warm. She never thought it possible to feel safe lying outside in the open, alone, and so near to Obscurity. Maybe she wasn't really alone. Didn't Essince say they would always be near? Yawning and too tired to look around, she shut her eyes and fell asleep.

OBLITERISTS ALMOST never ventured out of Obscurity. It was seen as an act of war, just as it was for the Legionnaires to enter the clusters. But Terror had his orders, and he planned to enjoy himself. He strutted out of Obscurity and rounded the corner, catching sight of Timorous a hundred feet away.

"Stand back," came a booming voice.

Terror slid to a halt. He didn't know who spoke, but he did know *what* it was.

"Show yourself. Or are you too afraid to face me?" Being blind to the location of the Legionnaires, he was at a disadvantage.

"You have no right to be here," he continued. "This is Prince Peccadillo's domain." Terror set his hand on the hilt of his sword and crouched like a tiger set to spring. He heard no reply, but that didn't mean his enemy wasn't near. His eyes shifted from here to there and back again. "Show yourself, you coward."

Right behind him and very close, a voice said, "Really? You think insults will work?"

Shaken, Terror jumped and stumbled away. He hadn't expected to see this Legionnaire. Captain Valiant's reputation preceded him, and even as he casually leaned against a tree, his powerful, intimidating size reminded Terror he'd better be especially careful.

They stood staring at one another for several moments as tension rose. Putting on his best façade, Terror partially unsheathed and re-sheathed his sword as a warning.

"You really don't want to do that." Valiant spoke with authority. "But do as you please. This one is ours. She is no longer in your power."

"No," Terror hissed. "She belongs to us, as do all the humans. We are the rulers of this world." He shook with indignation and fully unsheathed his sword as he bared his pointed yellow teeth.

Captain Valiant slowly walked toward him.

Terror backed up, sword held high in the air.

"Have you forgotten?" the Captain of the Legionnaires said. "A wager was made, and your Prince lost. This is no longer your world to rule."

Terror's eye bulged in anger, and he shook with rage. "Lies! Our Prince was tricked. The victory is rightfully ours."

Valiant calmly took another step toward Terror, who stepped back again. "Say what you want, but all of the unseen world knows the truth. Now you will leave. Timorous is under my care, and nothing will happen to her while she rests tonight."

The power of King Iam gripped Terror so tightly he gasped for breath.

In pain, his eyes shifted to Timorous, then back to Valiant. "I will go for now. But know this, you arrogant one, we will have our battle, and we will use the very ones you hold so dear to defeat you." He plunged immediately into Obscurity and made straight for Commander Deamon's lair.

Chapter 45

Timorous woke up feeling refreshed. She thought about her attempt to go into Obscurity the night before. It had been scarier than she'd imagined, but she reasoned it didn't help that night had fallen. She felt better now in the sunshine than in the dark of night.

"King Iam, help me. I can't see you, but they promised I would never be alone." She didn't really expect to see them. They never explained how that worked. But maybe they were already in Obscurity waiting for her. With a new resolve and her request to King Iam, she stepped through the enemy line.

TERROR RAN HASTILY into Deamon's lair. Warpt tried to stop him but Terror quickly kicked him out of the way. Breathing heavily, Terror almost stumbled right into his commander. He managed to stop just in time, almost falling over.

"Commander Deamon." He took a breath to collect himself. "Forgive me for not waiting to be announced. I have important information to report." He bowed on one knee and waited nervously for a reply.

"Terror, what the Abyss are you doing here?" Deamon put his fists on his hips. "Have you completed the simple task I gave you? Is the one of interest well within the confines of Obscurity?"

Terror stared at the ground.

"Get to your feet, you imbecile," Deamon bellowed. "And give me your report with the appropriate attitude of a Lead Guard."

Terror quickly stood. "Commander Deamon," he began again with confidence. "I entered the cluster and prepared to make contact with the one of interest when I was intercepted by the enemy. I had no choice but to back down."

Deamon took a step closer to him and growled. "And why did you not just do away with the enemy. You are a Lead Guard, are you not?"

"Yes, Commander, Sir." Terror refused to make eye contact with Deamon. "This Legionnaire was not the typical rank we deal with."

They both spat.

"This was the Captain of all Legionnaires." Terror's eyes darted between the Commander and the floor a couple of times.

Deamon stood nose to nose with Terror. "You mean to tell me Valiant, *the* Valiant, came to protect this most insignificant one?" He spat.

Terror flinched when spit hit him in the eye. The acid mucus slid over his eyelid and down his cheek, leaving open flesh in its path.

Standing at attention, he answered with less confidence. "Yes, my Lord."

Deamon walked away. With his back to Terror, he slammed his fist on the desk in front of him. "Tell me what you know, and don't leave out a single detail."

Hiding his nervousness, Terror told him how he chose not to engage the enemy in battle.

"You showed weakness. Our Prince will be displeased."

Cutting off Terror's groveling excuses, Deamon continued, "Why have they sent the top Legionnaire? This must be quite the plan to send for one so inconsequential." Irritation radiated from his large frame.

"Patience, my dear." Miss Enchantress sauntered over to Deamon.

At her distraction, Terror saw his chance to leave, but for the moment, he could not take his eyes off her. She wore a slinky white gown . . . so beautiful.

Putting his hands on her hips, Deamon pulled her tightly to his body. They kissed, almost violently. He dismissed Terror with the back of his hand.

"It's nice to have you back." Deamon stepped away, leaving her wanting more. "I hear you are to lead the interrogation."

"Yes, I suppose so." She sounded bored as she inspected her pointed black nails. "Prince Peccadillo knows I can be very persuasive when needed." She slithered back up to him.

He kissed her again. A moan escaped her, as his lips trailed down her neck.

Breathing heavily, he said, "That you are, my dear; that you are. Yet we must be careful with this one. She must be allowed deep into our territory or she may flee."

She pushed him away. "I've heard the plan. I will take over once you have her cornered. We'll play a little game of cat and mouse with her." She purred as she leaned in close again.

Deamon released her and walked to the table, which held strategic plans. "I know your abilities are beyond measure, but I think maybe a game of good cop, bad cop would be better. After all, you don't want to scare her. You want to coax her into telling us the enemy's plan."

Before Deamon took his next breath, Miss Enchantress bent toward his face, with all her flesh-dripping, skull-screaming rage. "I. Know. How. To. Do. My. Job. I do not need to be lectured by *you*. The Prince put *me* in charge." She quickly reclaimed her beautiful façade.

Deamon was unmoved. "Just my point, my dear." He waited a moment to let his meaning sink in. "I only suggest, after having watched the one of interest for the last couple weeks that you should take it slowly. But, of course, ultimately I will follow your lead."

AS TIMOROUS STEPPED into Obscurity, it seemed much quieter and calmer than the night before. Encouraged, she made her way forward. It almost felt easy, like a path had been laid for her. She felt good about the progress she made.

Then in mid-afternoon, she began hearing unusual sounds again. She hoped she had traveled more than halfway through. The jungle-like forest grew much denser, and the path was no longer clear.

Warder had told her the unseen evil forces fed on fear. Obscurity was, after all, created to scare people. A few rays of sunlight made it through here and there. In those moments, she'd remember Radimar smiling at her and how it made her feel. The evil unseen creatures all around her noticed her smile and protested.

"Ow," she yelped a moment later. She walked into a swarm of biting insects and swatted at them, running deeper into Obscurity, screaming as she went.

The Obliterist snickered behind the trees and the Sprites in the underbrush joined in. They'd been given strict orders not to do their normal fear-inducing pranks, but a little fun never hurt.

After several minutes of running while bushes tore at her clothes and skin, Tims finally was free of the horrid insects. They left V-shaped welts on her face, neck, and arms. There was a stream nearby and the bites now stung like fire. She splashed some water on her face, but it burned like acid, making the pain of the bites almost unbearable. She frantically tried rubbing some dirt on her face to soothe it. It didn't help much.

Covered in welts, red blotches, and dirt, she knew she must look a mess. She looked at her bug-bitten hands in disgust.

The water must be poisoned, but her thirst felt almost unbearable. She remembered the cans of food. Quickly opening one, she drank the broth eagerly but decided to save the actual food for later.

Obscurity was difficult but not as scary as she'd thought. That comforted her. Still, she knew she must keep moving. It wasn't safe here. The probability of her getting to the other side in one day was low.

She looked back in the direction she had entered and wondered if she could find her way out if she needed to. The thought of going back through the biting bugs was enough to keep her moving forward. "Please help me, King Iam."

"HOW IS OUR PLAN GOING for our cherished one?" King Iam asked Radimar.

"She is doing quite well. It's good to hear she's calling on you regularly. Her trust is growing."

"Captain Valiant reported he made himself known to the enemy. Peccadillo sent an Obliterist outside of the boundary of Obscurity. They will not be easy on her." The King sighed. "Sending Captain Valiant will certainly put our enemy in a tailspin."

Remembering the dismay on the enemy's face when he saw who he was dealing with, Radimar chuckled. "They will not be easy on her, but she has a heart open to the truth. And Essince is in close proximity. Tims does not yet see the strength within her, but I have confidence she will."

"Yes, the ones we love seem to either think too little of themselves or think they have the answer to life's problems. We direct their hearts only when they are willing."

"She is willing, my Father, she is willing."

THE FOLIAGE GREW THICKER. Tims struggled to press through. She pushed past bushes with all her weight and barely had the strength to climb over some of the fallen logs. It seemed the forest itself fought her.

Her bundle became harder to manage. It kept falling off her back and hitting her side. Canned goods don't make good traveling companions, she decided.

The unseen creatures on top of her bundle kept swinging it from side to side, laughing gleefully over their shenanigans.

Tims saw what looked like a patch of light pouring through the thick forest ahead. Some sunshine would help her feel more hopeful but when she got there, the sun dipped behind the trees. It wasn't a good place to rest as she had hoped.

Timorous heard a swiftly moving river ahead of her. The swarm of biting bugs had followed behind her and if she crossed the river, she might be free of them. She made her way to the sound of rushing water.

The only way across was a dead, moss-covered tree about ten feet above the water. It wouldn't have mattered if it were a hundred feet above the water. Tims had always been afraid of heights. She stared at it for a long time. Just when she'd collected the courage to cross, she noticed snapping creatures with yellow eyes in the water. A small bird flew a little too close to the water and the creatures jumped. Only one caught it, but they all bit at one another. Blood covered the creatures, and the water turned red. An acidic smell wafted upward.

She took a few hasty steps back, tripping and falling before she began to vomit. A sense of hopelessness engulfed her. How could she do this?

She felt the warmth of the locket on her chest. Wrapping her fingers around it, she remembered Warder showing her the promise in the *Book of Actualities*, how King Iam would give her strength when she had none. "When you are weak, he is strong," Warder had said.

The hopelessness seemed to fade just a bit. Even with Despair and Discouragement still nipping at her heels, she sat down on the log, took a deep breath, and began scooting across. The snapping creatures seemed to sense her fear. She pulled her feet up to keep them out of biting range. This caused them to snap even more, as though in a feeding frenzy.

"King Iam is with me," she whispered repeatedly.

When she approached the midway point, the log began to sag. She chanted louder.

The log began to crack. The snappy creatures went wild with anticipation.

She rose to her feet, still holding the log with her hands and leaped, shouting, "King Iam is with me!" She landed hard on her stomach, barely making it to the riverbank. The ground shook when she hit it, or did she imagine it? She glanced back just as the log plunged into the river.

All of Obscurity went silent.

Another piece of her heart moved into place. Somehow there was power in the name of King Iam. She sat up, bewildered and amazed.

Chapter 46

The ground trembled.

"What was that?" Commander Deamon roared.

Everything went completely silent for a moment. An Obliterist, Lieutenant Fearsome, ran in and bowed at Deamon's feet.

"My Lord, we can wait no longer. The one of interest is gaining strength and just discovered a weapon to use against us." The usually imposing Guard trembled.

"Stand up, you groveling fool." Deamon snarled. "Panic in facing the enemy will not be tolerated. She is nothing but a fearful girl."

Those in the room jeered at the Obliterist.

Lieutenant Fearsome stood. Nearly as tall as Deamon, his dark leathery skin had an orange sheen. He wiped the sweat dripping down his face with the back of his clawed fist. Taking in a deep breath, he presented the facts. "She has learned there is power in our enemy's name, Sir."

The veins in Deamon's neck pulsed. Deamon balled his fists, preparing to take out his rage on Fearsome.

"What is this I hear?" Miss Enchantress sauntered in, smiling seductively as she made her way to Deamon. As she passed Fearsome, she ran her hand along his jaw, making eye contact with him.

He barely managed to refrain from emitting a low growl.

"It seems the lieutenant here fears the enemy."

"Hmmm, here in Obscurity? With all you strong Obliterists to protect Prince Peccadillo's kingdom?"

The room erupted in raucous laughter.

She pulled away from Deamon and strode slowly among the guards and staff gathered in the room.

Deamon gritted his teeth, his jealousy obvious. "It seems the one of interest may have happened upon some misguided strength from the enemy. I doubt very much that she is even aware of what happened."

Taunting Deamon with her eyes, Miss Enchantress continued to saunter around the room, drinking in the desire emanating from the Guard. "We cannot know for certain unless she is pressed again." She stopped in front of another Obliterist and allowed him to run his hands down her torso.

Deamon was livid but kept his composure.

Miss Enchantress made her way back in his direction. "Commander Deamon, your underlings have done a fair job of making things less than pleasant for the one of interest, but I think they push her too slowly, giving her time to gain strength. Now's the time to press harder in preparation for our next step. What do you think?"

Never taking his eyes off her, Deamon breathed through clenched teeth. "Yes, I believe you are right. Let the Guard of Obscurity give her a night to remember."

Anger flickered across her face but quickly disappeared.

Deamon crossed his arms. "Then you can work your wonders as only you can."

TIMS MOVED AWAY FROM the water and the snapping creatures. The whole area smelled of blood. She stopped a few times to heave until her stomach emptied entirely. Fearing spending a night in Obscurity, she decided to keep moving through the dense forest.

Moss hung from the tree limbs. As the sun set, things began to take on an almost ghost-like appearance. No grass grew on the uneven ground, only shrubs and prickly weeds. She redirected her route multiple times as she kept finding herself near the edge of cliffs. The air smelled of decay, like the stench of dead creatures.

As the darkness crept in, she decided it best to stop rather than walk off a ledge. She found a little three-foot clearing with no prickly weeds and unrolled her bundle. Hungry, she opened her pack and found only two cans left.

"Wow, didn't I have more than that? My bundle felt a whole lot heavier earlier."

She heard laughing—or was it cackling?—from an animal of some kind.

To lighten her load, she could get rid of a few extra things but not the food. She wouldn't eat it tonight because it might be the last she had for awhile. She hoped she only had a day left of traveling. A shiver ran down her spine at the thought of being trapped in Obscurity for longer.

She tried building a fire, but the matches kept blowing out or breaking. Again, she heard cackling, sounding closer this time. Not wanting to use up all the matches, she finally gave up. But what would keep her safe from the animals? In the pitch black she barely saw her hand in front of her. She'd never experienced this kind of darkness before. It held a feeling of foreboding.

"King Iam, what should I do? Please help me," she whispered.

A slight tremor shook the ground.

She sat with her legs drawn to her chest and placed her chin on her knees. After some time, her legs began to ache, but she refused to lie down.

She almost dozed off but was abruptly awoken by what felt like a snake slithering across her feet. Shrieking, she jumped and took off running blindly through Obscurity. After a few minutes of fighting the forest, she stopped and looked around into the darkness. There was no way to find her way back to her spot, nor did she want to. An eerie cold breeze blew over her sweaty body. The bites festered and burned like fire.

A great host of evil beings had been given permission to attack. Many more came to watch the show. The Commander decided to start with the smaller Sprites. The enemy swirled about her, throwing every negative thought, doubt, and feeling they could at her.

Her resolve now gone, she shook with fear. She looked around but saw nothing. *Timorous was far from being alone. The evil hordes were very good at their job, jumping up and down on her head as if trying to pound in their lies.*

Her heart sank.

"I'm lost. I'll never get out of here. Where are you, Essince?" she quietly called out. "You said you'd always be near. I don't feel you now. I've been so foolish. Maybe this is some kind of cruel joke."

She heard loud cackling.

"It's not funny," she yelled back.

The enemy laughed more.

Something bit her backside.

"Ouch." Tims jumped. She could hear snarling nearby. What vicious creature did that come from?

The darkness hid everything. Feeling like a trapped animal, Tims ran blindly, often into thorny bushes that tore at her clothes and left bloody scratches on her arms and legs. She swung her arms from side to side trying to feel her way. The sounds drove her deeper into Obscurity. The most terrifying sound seemed to be getting closer—a screeching howl, much like a woman being tortured. Tripping and falling, tripping and falling, she ran on. She lost her sense of time. Exhaustion overtook her.

"Where are you, Essince? Was it all a lie?"

With a hiccupping sob, she fell one last time, rolled onto her back, and cried.

Rain began to fall in large drops, then in a downpour.

"Great, just what I need. Could things get any worse?" She continued to cry but noticed how the rain ran off the large leaf overhead. If she positioned herself just right, it would run into her dry mouth. She drank as much as she could until the rain stopped. It soothed her swollen, festering wounds. Entirely fatigued and lying on the muddy ground, she fell into a cold, fitful sleep.

FROM HIGH ABOVE, ESSINCE watched with a keen eye as Tims struggled. The dear girl didn't know how near Essince was, nor did she realize how this experience would be worth it in the end. In spite of Tims' doubts, Essince sent the rain as a gift, a sign that she was with her and felt everything she did. When Tims smiled, Essince smiled. When Tims cried, Essince cried with her. While Essince was never afraid, she understood Tims' fear and her struggle. She hoped Timorous would see the blessing in the rain. Growth came only through difficulties.

TIMOROUS WOKE WITH a start. Disoriented, she jumped up. Where was her pack, her food? Memories of the night before came flooding back. She was covered in mud from head to toe. Her face and neck were swollen with festering bug bites, and her hair hung in filthy strands. Her clothes were torn, and she had somehow lost a shoe. Red gashes covered her arms and legs. She couldn't go back now, but what was forward? Being lost in Obscurity was not what Tims had expected. She needed to go through it, but how did she know she wasn't circling around as she had in the neighborhood?

MISS ENCHANTRESS AND Commander Deamon received regular reports. It was pure entertainment to hear of her tortured state.

Miss Enchantress cooed in his ear. "Deamon dear, let's open her eyes so she can see who she's up against." She arched one eyebrow high. "There's no danger since she will not be making it back to the clusters, thanks to the good work of your Guard."

Deamon's yellow teeth bared as he smiled, pleased with how deeply into Obscurity his Guard had prodded this weak one, this one the enemy seemed so interested in. It would soon be time to interrogate her and find the true purpose of the enemy's plan.

"At your command," he responded, happy to oblige.

TIMOROUS WALKED ON, trying to make sense of her direction based on the sun. But most of the time, the trees blocked all the light. She continued hearing eerie sounds. "Just stop, will you?" she said to no one. Her shoulders slumped, and she limped, not only from the wounds on her unshod foot but also because of the cuts and bruises on her legs.

Tims felt a shift in the air around her, as if someone had just opened a door. She slid to a halt. Looking down at her ankles, she saw the creatures of the unseen world she'd been told about. They clung to her for dear life, digging into her skin and laughing, sounding very much like the cackling sounds she'd heard. Their beady, lifeless eyes watched her intently as their razor-sharp claws pierced her skin. She screamed, kicked, and ran, trying to get them off. She would succeed for a moment, only to have others chase her down.

Finally, she seemed to have rid herself of the vile creatures. She leaned against a tree, trying to catch her breath. The tree smelled awful. As she looked at the roots, it suddenly dawned on her. Those were not the roots of a tree. Those were very large clawed feet. Warder told her the big ones were called Obliterists.

She stepped back and slowly looked up its twisted gnarled form. She had to step back even farther to see its face. It looked down at her and gave her an evil grin. Some sort of slime dripped from its lips and made a sizzling sound as it dropped to the ground.

She stumbled backward, then took off running again.

Time and time again, no matter which way she ran, the Obliterists found her. They would block her, trip her, grasp at her, then let go as if it were some sort of game. There seemed to be many Obliterists chasing her in this never-ending nightmare. One Obliterist seemed somehow familiar, but she couldn't quite figure out why.

Her heart raced as she pumped her arms as hard as she could. Covered in sweat and debris, her hair a stringy, filthy mess that stuck to her dirty tear-stained, bug-bitten face. She had no idea how long she'd been running but knew she couldn't continue much longer.

The familiar one that chased her was the largest Obliterist of them all. The ground shook with the thump of its long heavy feet hitting the ground. It was confusing, how they seemed to appear out of nowhere. She just knew she needed to get away and fast.

A moment later, Timorous ran down a hill, gaining a little distance but tripped and landed hard on the ground, letting out a loud "oomph." Stunned, she laid breathing heavily and spitting out the dirt now crusted to her lips.

"What's the use? There's no way to outrun this thing."

She should have stayed home where she felt safe—or at least *played* it safe.

The heavy footsteps of the beast were awfully close now.

Where is Essince? Wasn't she always supposed to be near to help? Timorous felt utterly betrayed.

Chapter 47

Everything grew eerily still. Tims did not move, but her body began to tremble. This couldn't be good, not here in this horrible place of Obscurity.

As soon as Commander Deamon gave the order, Lieutenant Fearsome chased Tims. Since his fellow Oblisterists made sport of him, he was compelled to prove them wrong. His worthiness to be the Lead Guard was at stake. He stood a few feet away from Timorous, who still lay face down.

"Get up, you peon," he roared as he towered over her.

Slowly and with quivering legs, Timorous sat up and scooted away.

Like most Obliterists, Lieutenant Fearsome had large feet and hands with long sharp claws. His broad muscular chest and black leathery skin occasionally cast a light orange sheen when the light touched it just right. He must have been in many battles, for his body had multiple scars. One started at his forehead and ran down through one dead eye to his chin. The other eye also seemed empty. Still Tims felt like he could see into her very soul. On Fearsome's head something resembling hair hung in a mess down to his shoulders. Tims had never seen a scarier face in her life.

She sat as if frozen in place. Eyes unblinking, she stared at his grotesque features.

Fearsome leaned down and looked intently into her eyes. "That's more like it." He paused as a crooked smile slowly creased his face. "Fear." He prowled around her like a cat ready to pounce.

Tims couldn't take her eyes off of him. Her head turned but her body remained frozen.

"You know you were named after me." He pointed his sharp claw at his chest.

Tims didn't answer. *What does that mean?*

"That's right. It's what you do best, isn't it, Timorous?" He emphasized each syllable of her name. "That is why you can never succeed. I, FEAR, own you." He laughed wickedly.

Feeling the crushing weight of this Obliterist's words, Tims trembled almost violently. She finally realized why this particular Obliterist seemed so familiar. Fear had been her constant companion throughout her life. Now she was face to face with it as if looking into a mirror but seeing only the woundedness on the inside.

"I know all your dirty secrets," the Obliterist sneered.

Tims' body gave a hard, involuntary jerk.

Fearsome grinned. "Yes, the ones you want no one to know. Tell me, did you like it when your stepbrother—" He paused for effect. "Touched you?"

"No!" Timorous screamed, rocking back and forth. She didn't want to hear any more. When Fearsome spoke, she felt as if she were reliving every horrific event she'd ever experienced. Throwing her hands to her ears, she screamed again. "No. Stop!" All the horrible memories came flooding back. Memories she had worked so hard never to remember. Her stepmother's beatings. The humiliation and powerlessness she'd felt when her stepbrother attacked her. "No. No. No!" Eyes closed, ears covered, she tried to block it all out.

His booming voice still made its way to her heart. "You are a used filthy rag, worthless." He emitted a malicious laugh and slapped his knee as if he had just told the funniest joke.

With her eyes tightly shut, she curled up into a ball, wishing death would claim her right now. Then everything went uncomfortably quiet. What new horrors awaited her? Trembling, with tears still streaming down her face, Timorous opened one eye.

Shocked, Tims sat up. Fearsome had disappeared. But what she now saw surprised her even more.

Before her stood the most beautiful woman she'd ever seen. It wasn't the kind of beauty that Essince had, which permeated her whole being. This woman's beauty seemed to be more on the surface. Still, Tims stared in awe of her. It felt almost impossible to look away from her beauty. Tims had never seen a woman this tall. It reminded her of the Obliterists who had chased her.

This woman wore a beautiful flowing white gown. A slight breeze tousled her shiny hair. Light shone around her. Or was that the sun? It seemed she scared off the Obliterists. Even the smaller creatures who'd been biting and grabbing at Timorous were gone. This woman's appearance was quite a contrast to Timorous' small filthy body.

She spoke in a soothing voice. "There, there, my child. Don't listen to those foul creatures. I have been sent to keep you safe through your quest." She smiled, but it didn't quite reach her eyes. "I am Miss Representation. I represent the help you called out for." She held a wand and raised it in the air.

Bewildered, Tims stared at her. Did Miss Representation mean to look like she was some kind of fairy godmother? Somehow it felt off to Timorous but she was relieved to have Fearsome gone, along with all the smaller creatures. This gave her some comfort, but not the peace she felt with Essince. Still trembling, she didn't move. Miss Representation didn't seem anything like Radimar or Essince.

Miss Representation watched her carefully. She coaxed her, "Come, sit down." She sat on the ground and patted the spot next to her.

Tims hesitated, still uncertain about moving closer.

The woman patted the ground again and smiled. "Come, come."

Tims moved cautiously to her side.

"There is nothing to fear. I have been sent to help you. Haven't you been told you would be cared for?"

This promise had been given to Timorous but uncertainty weighed down her enthusiasm. But maybe she *was* the help Tims had asked for. Continuing this quest alone seemed an impossible task—more than she could endure. Maybe King Iam had sent her. "Thank you for coming. Who did you say sent you?"

For the briefest moment, an unreadable expression passed over Miss Representation's face. "It is of no matter." Miss Representation waved a hand dismissively. "I am here now. I'm sorry I was delayed. I came as quickly as commanded."

"I'm sorry; who commanded you?" Tims felt shocked at her boldness. Why couldn't she just accept this gesture of help without question?

Miss Representation gasped, letting her perfect mouth hang open and putting her hand to her heart as if Tims had offended her.

Tims felt a pinch of guilt.

"The powers that be, my dear."

The powers could be King Iam, couldn't it?

"Tell me, how is your quest going? Have you found what you are looking for?" She leaned toward her, eager for an answer.

Her sincere interest boosted Tims' hope. Looking down at herself, she thought it obvious by the way she looked that things had gone terribly wrong. Not wanting to be rude, she merely responded, "Unfortunately, not well." She tried to rub dirt off her filthy arms. "I must look a mess, and you're . . . you're so beautiful." When she looked back at the woman, she was again captivated by her glamor.

Her guardian ate up the compliment. "You're so sweet, my child. You look—" She regarded her for a moment. "You look just fine. We'll get you cleaned up when all this is over. So, tell me, have you found what you came for?"

The question confused Tims. What was she looking for? She forced herself to look down at her dirty hands. "I think I'm lost."

"Tsk, tsk. This is not good. What is your destination? I am sure I can help you find it." She waved her wand in the air as if preparing to turn a pumpkin into a carriage.

The whole waving of the wand thing made Tims question Miss Representation's promised help. But she wanted to believe her, so she pushed her misgivings away. "I don't know my destination. I wasn't told. I thought you would know. Didn't King Iam tell you?"

The ground trembled just as it had the day before. Miss Enchantress' appearance flickered like static on a television. For a split second, Tims glimpsed the ugliness of this woman's evil. She had not been sent by King Iam. Tims now knew that for sure.

Miss Representation repositioned and collected herself. "I am not always privy to all the information. It's top secret, you know." She smiled again but still not with her eyes. "How about I walk with you and keep all the nasty creatures away. Would you like that? Maybe we can find what you are looking for."

With a sense of foreboding, Tims decided it safest to play along. She stood and brushed off some of the dried dirt on her backside. Without looking at Miss Representation, she ventured to ask, "Do you know the way out of Obscurity?"

"Well, that I can help with. Which cluster are you looking for?" Miss Enchantress stood gracefully. Her captivating beauty seemed such a contrast to this evil place.

Tims again found it hard to turn her gaze from her.

Miss Representation looked pleased with Tims' wonder of her. When she stood to her full height, Tims felt very small and realized how easily Miss Representation could overpower her.

"I'm not exactly sure, just not back to the cluster of Nowhere." At least she was being honest. She couldn't go back to a place where everyone seemed to be hunting for her.

Miss Representation frowned. "My dear, if you aren't willing to give me a little more direction, I'm not sure I can be of much help." Her soothing tone turned a little snippy. She forced a smile to her face.

Tims felt her anxiety rise, like when her stepmother was about to do something mean. "Well, let's start walking, and maybe we can figure it out together," she replied, amazed at her own calm. With every step she took, her heart-shaped locket tapped against her chest. She felt its warmth. The stories she read with Warder came rushing to her mind. Stories about the ordinary people who won seemingly impossible battles. She felt secure in the truth the locket held.

They walked in circles, but at least traveling was easier. Who was this Miss Representation? Tims felt her guide had no intention of helping her find her way out of Obscurity. Instead, the woman peppered her with so many questions, it left Tims' head spinning. It felt like an inquisition.

Timorous gave vague answers or claimed not to know, which was often true. Miss Representation's agitation grew. Her kindness and patience slipped a little more every few minutes.

"Do you mind if we sit for a bit?" Tims felt exhausted, and her head hurt from all the questions. A scowl crossed her guide's face, then quickly vanished.

Miss Representation leaned her head to one side and tapped Tims' head as if she were a child. "Let's not stop quite yet. I feel we are about to have a breakthrough." She clapped her hands with glee.

Tims dragged her feet, agitating Miss Representation even more. One of her steps equaled three of Tims'.

Tims felt a little annoyed herself. She decided she wanted to ask some of her own questions. With only a causal sideways glance in Miss Representation's direction, she said, "You must have spent a lot of time in Bliss. What is it like?"

Miss Representation's graceful glide faltered.

"Are you okay?" Tims reached out a hand as if to catch her, knowing there was no way to stop her fall.

Miss Representation turned her face away for a moment, but Tims caught the look of anger she tried to hide. She looked back and smiled. "Yes, I'm fine, dear." She took a moment to carefully formulate an answer. "I have spent time in there. It is a . . . um . . . a beautiful place."

She seemed to struggle to say something positive about Bliss. For some reason, this bothered Tims greatly. People she loved and who loved her came from Bliss. That realization reminded her of why she started this quest. Radimar and Essince believed in her even though she didn't believe in herself. She found her confidence growing. "And King Iam? Have you met him?"

The ground shuddered again, but with more magnitude. Even Tims had to catch her balance.

Miss Representation faltered again, throwing her long arms out to regain her balance. She collected herself quickly but red anger climbed up her neck. She glared at Timorous, no longer smiling. "I don't think it is wise for you to say that name here in Obscurity." She leaned down and quietly hissed the last word. Her breath smelled of blood and heavy perfume.

Tims turned her face and leaned over, trying not to vomit. Miss Representation looked affronted by Tims' revulsion. When Tims stood back up, the locket patted against her chest, growing hotter. Without thinking, Tims wrapped her hand around it.

"What is that, my dear?"

Tims avoided the question but kept her hand tightly around the locket. After motioning for Miss Representation to come closer, hoping her stomach wouldn't get the best of her, she asked again in a whisper, "Why shouldn't we say King Iam's name? I was taught that King Iam was just a fairy tale."

The ground shook with great might, as if it were afraid of the King's name.

Miss Representation not only lost her balance but fell to the ground, her perfect white dress smudged with dirt. She leaped up and leaned over Tims, screaming with all her ugliness, "Shut up!"

Tims fell back in fear. What had just happened? Miss Representation's beauty had vanished, replaced by a skeleton with flesh dripping from the bones. Her white dress had morphed into black rags that hung from her bony arms. Jagged ebony nails swung at Tims, sending her reeling back and stumbling out of reach.

Miss Representation's ugliness was the mirror opposite of her beauty. Tims had never seen a viler creature in her life.

She vomited even though her stomach held nothing. When she had finished and looked back at the creature, Miss Representation had returned to her former beautiful self, yet she still snarled at Tims.

IN THE UNSEEN REALM of Bliss, shouts of victory arose. A small opening appeared in Obscurity through which Messengers were sent to help Tims. They knew this window would soon close, so the Legionnaires worked quickly. With the power of King Iam, they threw the Messengers with all their might. At this speed, the Messengers went undetected. Three made it through before the window closed. More cheers were heard.

King Iam sat on his throne, pride beaming across his face. All of Bliss rejoiced in this small victory.

Chapter 48

Suddenly, with sword drawn, a dangerous looking Oblitterist stood in the path not far from Timorous. His imposing size terrified her, and his vicious stares bore into her. He appeared only a second after Miss Representation screamed.

If looks could kill, Tims would be dead. She felt the evil rolling off of him. She stood still in apprehension. Without taking his eyes off of Tims, he spoke to Miss Enchantress. "I believe the one of interest is holding out on us. Shall we welcome her properly?"

Miss Enchantress seductively slithered over to his side and hung on his shoulder. She smiled maliciously and whispered into his ear. Almost paralyzed with fear, Tims watched their interaction.

With a quick nod to the woman, he continued. "We are Prince Peccadillo's Lead Guard of all of Obscurity. I am Commander Deamon." He spread his arms, along with his lethal sword, and never took his eyes off her, appearing both impressive and terrifying. He pointed toward the woman. "And you've already met Miss Enchantress. I'm sure you have been warned not to enter Obscurity; yet here you are."

He began stalking around her. "Why have you trespassed?"

Unable to find her voice, Tims cowered beneath him. She stared up at his large, monstrous frame.

Deamon glowered at her. "Speak now, or this will be your end." He held the hilt of the sword with both hands and slowly raised it, facing the point downward for the kill.

Tims' mind snapped to attention. "I-I was told to go th-through Obscurity."

Deamon stayed in position, sword ready. A menacing grin tugged on the corners of his lip as he watched her shaking before him. "Who told you this?"

Miss Enchantress slowly made her way around Timorous. Feeling like prey in the midst of wild animals, Tims kept a careful eye on the woman.

"Look at me!" Deamon's demand pierced her ears.

She cringed, throwing her hands to the sides of her head.

"I said, who told you to go through Obscurity?"

She knew whatever she said might end her life. Her locket felt like it was on fire against her skin. Without thought, she wrapped her hand around it and nervously fiddled with it.

Deamon watched her for a moment and glanced at Miss Enchantress.

Miss Enchantress made her way around Tims and whispered again in Deamon's ear. When she stepped away, Deamon shouted at the top of his lungs. "I command you. Who told you to go through Obscurity?"

Miss Enchantress laughed wickedly.

Tims instinctively ducked as she mumbled, "Essince."

"What did you say?" Deamon raised his sword even higher above her head, positioned to make one strong thrust to end her life.

Miss Enchantress again prowled around Tims and now stood behind her. Throwing her head back, she laughed.

Tims' nerves were raw. But to her surprise she found herself screaming back at him through her tears. "Essince of King Iam."

The ground quaked as it never had before. Miss Enchantress snatched Tims' locket from her neck before stumbling backward.

Deamon lost his balance and fell. Furious, he quickly jumped to his feet. He ran up to her with his sword in one clawed hand. He swung straight down toward her. Tims instinctively rolled to the side.

Miss Enchantress held the locket up, dangling it from the chain for Deamon to see. With a satisfied smile, she said, "Look what I found."

Tims' hands flew to her bare neck where the locket had been. "No! That's mine."

She grabbed for it, but Miss Enchantress held it out of reach, toying with Tims and laughing at her failed attempts. Timorous gave up and sat on the ground breathing heavily.

Miss Enchantress sauntered a couple of steps away. "What is this we have? Might it be a clue, Deamon?"

Deamon watched with triumphant interest as she inspected it.

She held the heart close to her face, dangling from the chain. "There is nothing inscribed on it. It seems rather ordinary." She huffed with disappointed.

"Look inside," Deamon ordered.

"Patience, my dear, patience. Maybe Timorous, our little mouse, would like to tell us what this is. Hmmm?" Miss Enchantress tried to lure Tims into jumping for the prize again, letting it hang within arm's reach.

Tims ignored her, picking at the dirt on the ground as if she'd lost all interest. "It's nothing. It was a gift from a friend."

"I imagine an important friend," Miss Enchantress cooed with one eyebrow arched high. "You seemed so intent on getting it back just a moment ago. Would you like it back?" She swung it in front of Timorous' downcast face.

Timorous desperately wanted it back, but she didn't want them to know that. It took everything in her not to attempt to grab for it. She had failed. How could she let Warder down like this? It was precious to him. Maybe they would lose interest in the locket if she acted like it was nothing. She shrugged her shoulders, "Whatever. Keep it if you want." It didn't come out with the confidence she had hoped.

"Really? Why, thank you." Miss Enchantress smirked wickedly.

Tims' heart fell.

"Let's have a little look-see." With great flare, she held it high, then laid the heart gently in her palm. It looked dwarfed in her large beautiful hand. "Ow," she screeched, dropping it to the ground.

The scream pierced Tims' eardrums. She fell to the ground and threw her hands over her ears.

"What?" Deamon roared as he ran to her, his face filled with rage. "What happened?" He glared at Tims.

Tims felt just as confused as him.

Imprinted in the middle of Miss Enchantress' palm was a nasty blood-red heart-shaped burn. "The enemy cursed this." Her eyes shot daggers at Tims. "Was this a trick to torture me?" She looked up to the sky and screamed, "It is not our time."

Tims looked up to the sky but couldn't see anything. She had no idea what the woman meant. When she looked back down, she noticed the locket lay only a few feet from her. She threw her body forward to grab it, figuring this was her only chance. With a swish of his sword, Deamon swung downward, catching the edge of Tims' finger.

She pulled back and held her hand to her chest, thankful he hadn't sliced her finger off. It bled but was only a flesh wound.

Deamon glowered at her. "What do you think you are doing?" He spat. It really wasn't a question. "This is no longer yours. You gave it to Miss Enchantress."

Tims gulped but said nothing. The locket lay open and face down on the ground. She looked at it longingly.

Deamon took the tip of his sword, not wanting to touch it, and flipped it over. "It's empty." He glared at Tims. "What tricks are you playing?"

Tims cowered.

Miss Enchantress stepped toward them, still holding her hand. She leaned down to take a closer look. "Maybe there is a message inside. It might hold the plans of the enemy," she added eagerly.

With the tip of his sword, Deamon turned it one way and then the other. "I see nothing written on the inside or the outside." He rushed at Tims. "What does this mean? What spell has been cast on this, you twit?"

When he advanced in her direction, Tims jumped but stared at the locket. She could see something they could not, an inscription meant just for her. She wondered why only she could see the message: "To my Chosen One: May the *Book of Actualities* ever be in your heart and sharper than a two-edged sword."

Deamon noticed her reaction and inspected the locket again. "What do you see? What is the purpose of this locket?" His shoulders rose and fell with his heavy breathing.

Tims scooted farther away. She needed to give him some kind of answer, but what should she say? "I-I d-don't know. I've never opened it before."

In all his terrifying evil strength, Deamon closed the distance between them. "Did it hold the enemy's plan? Speak. Where are you going and for what purpose?"

Tims didn't respond swiftly enough. Deamon picked her up by the throat. Her feet dangled in the air. She clung to his arm to keep from being strangled. With much effort, she gasped out, "I . . . don't . . . know . . . I . . . wasn't . . . told."

Deamon dropped her suddenly. Rage filled his face and he howled so loudly Tims thought she'd go deaf. He looked at the back of his wrist. There, still sizzling deep into his flesh, was a square-shaped burn mark.

Miss Enchantress rushed to him. Seeing the burn, she looked terrified and stepped farther away from Tims.

Deamon's scream was heard by all of Obscurity, sending a ripple of trepidation throughout the land. In the seen world, the clusters experienced what they thought was a mild earth-

quake. Those in Obscurity shook with fear. This was Commander Deamon, the most feared of all—other than Prince Peccadillo. But no one rushed to his aid. That kind of scream could only have come from an attack by King Iam. They had no wish to be anywhere near it.

USHER PROMPTLY RUSHED to Prince Peccadillo and bowed. He fidgeted as he waited to be acknowledged.

"What do you hear of Deamon and Miss Enchantress' progress? Have they subdued the one of interest?" The Prince looked over details of happenings in the clusters.

Usher felt a little surprised that Prince Peccadillo had not already heard of this unusual happening. Even the Netherworld felt the ground shake several times.

"I am hearing conflicting reports, my Prince, but I thought it prudent to let you know that all of Obscurity has heard Deamon, uh, screaming." Usher realized this might sound ridiculous and cause the Prince to lash out at him.

The Prince moved in Usher's direction. "Deamon can be quite loud," he responded coolly. "It is not uncommon for Obscurity to hear him from time to time."

"Of course, my Prince." Usher chuckled, remembering how true this was. He cleared his throat. "But this was no normal scream," Usher tried to emphasize again. "It seems neither the underlings nor his Guard have ever heard him scream in pain or in . . . fear."

Prince Peccadillo looked up. A hard, dark glare washed over his face. "This is the work of our enemy."

Usher saw the prince's apprehension and worked to quiet the trembling in his own legs.

The Prince began to pace. "It is not our time." He seemed to be speaking to himself. His eyes turned blood-red, darker than Usher had ever seen.

Chapter 49

Commander Deamon raged at Tims. "What do you have in your hand?"

Miss Enchantress came to his side. The heart-shaped burn in her palm looked very similar to the square-shaped burn on Deamon's arms. She bared her yellow teeth at Tims.

Timorous stood shaking and confused. She had not been able to grab the locket, but in the midst of her failed attempt, without realizing it, she had grabbed its contents. The tiny copy of the *Book of Actualities* felt comforting in her palm. She must have held it to Deamon's arms while he dangled her in the air.

"Open your hand," Deamon screamed at her again.

She could feel the warmth of the *Book of Actualities* in her hand, but it wasn't burning her like it had Deamon. Slowly she opened her hand.

Both Miss Enchantress and Deamon leaned down to see this tiny object. As she unwrapped her fingers all the way, a bright light shot out without warning, shining as brightly as the sun. Deamon and Miss Enchantress were both thrown back twenty feet, temporarily blinded by its light. Even Tims had to look away.

The evil ones were groping around, screaming obscenities.

Tims closed her fist and started running as fast as her legs would take her. She jumped over logs and dodged bushes like there was no tomorrow, which might very well be. The underlings kept out of her way. The jungle canopy seemed to have been split open, and the sun shone down to become her guiding light. Tims followed it.

IN BLISS, MORE ROARS of victory erupted. "She's doing it. She is overcoming!"

As soon as Captain Valiant received the signal, he and his team of Leading Legionnaires swooped down with blazing swords of light, clearing the path for Timorous.

REPORTS FROM THE OBLITERISTS all over Obscurity rolled in, all conflicting with one another.

"What the Abyss is happening?" Peccadillo raged.

The Netherworld was in an uproar. Everyone and everything had been thrown into confusion. Their instruments weren't working correctly.

"Prepare for battle," the Prince ordered.

The inhabitants of the Netherworld panicked. Fights broke out everywhere. Everyone screamed orders or blamed each other for the problems. Obscenities were heard throughout the dark halls.

TO THE SEEN WORLD, a thunder and lightning storm raged over part of Obscurity. The people in the clusters didn't really pay too much attention.

Down on the edge of the town of Uncertainty, Warder stood outside watching the storm. He smiled broadly, not caring that it had begun to rain. Cozy, his cat, meowed. "Just a minute, Cozy. This is a sight to be seen. You go, Tims. You're almost there."

TIMS KNEW SHE MUST be getting closer to the edge of Obscurity. The underbrush was thinning. As she rounded a corner, she slid to a halt, breathing heavily. Commander Deamon, along with several other large Obliterists, appeared before her, swords readied. "You thought your little trick would stop us."

Tims didn't know anything about what tricks he thought she'd played, but she did know she couldn't outrun these creatures.

Not sure what to do, she leaned forward and thrust out her arm, with her hand tightly around the *Book of Actualities*. The Guard took a step back, all except for Deamon. Were they afraid of this? "Don't come a step closer, or—"

"Or what?" Deamon mocked. "We are ready for you this time."

They now wore dark, protective eye gear.

"What would our enemy want with one so timid, so useless?" He prowled around her.

She kept her arm extended and hand ready, trying to keep an eye on Deamon as the rest of the evil Guard fanned out around of her. Moving her hand back and forth between them, she stepped back, trying to create more distance from them.

"Why would our enemy choose you?" Deamon continued to prowl. "You have no value."

Tims' mind flashed back to Radimar. He'd held her hand and told her she was of great value. Another piece of her heart moved into place. "I am of great value." She opened her hand.

White light shot from her palm and transformed into a powerful three-foot-long, two-edged sword she now held in her hand. Lions were engraved on the pure-golden hilt. Seven precious stones encircled the pommel. The blade curved perfectly to the middle ridge. It ended with a point true to its straight form. When she waved it through the air, it gave off waves of light and music.

Surprised shown on everyone's face. The Guard hesitated and stood still for a moment as if trying to decide how to proceed.

"She knows nothing. Attack, Sergeant Terror," the Commander shouted.

Terror took a step toward her. Grinning, he gnashed his crooked yellowed teeth at her.

She flinched. His deep evil laugh left her shaken.

He swung his sword.

Never having wielded a sword, Tims grabbed the hilt with both hands, closed her eyes, and swung back with all her might. Opening one eye, Tims was shocked to see that the clash had knocked the Obliterist down.

Timorous let the tip of her sword fall to the ground, accidently touching Terror's foot. There was a *whishing* sound, and a little wisp of black smoke hung in the air where Terror had stood. *What just happened?*

Everyone froze in place. The other Obliterists were alarmed. One Obliterist whispered, "She sent him to the Abyss." They all turned and ran. All except Deamon.

His voice boomed, "Get back here right now and fight for our Prince, you cowards." When they didn't obey him, he roared with rage.

Tims took advantage of the moment by running in the opposite direction. She felt tingling in the hand that held the sword. She looked down as the sword shrunk back into the tiny *Book of Actualities*. She closed her hand around it, not wanting to lose this special gift.

Finally, she made it to the edge of Obscurity. She stopped abruptly. Her heart sank as she teetered on the edge of a great chasm that separated her from safety.

Behind her, Deamon was fast approaching.

"King Iam, I need you. Have you brought me this far to die?" She felt the crushing weight of hopelessness.

As Deamon closed the gap, she turned to face him and opened her hand, sword ready. Could she hold him off? For how long? Her heart raced.

"Timorous," someone faintly called to her.

Maybe it was one of Obscurity's tricks to distract her. With her back to the edge of the cliff, she stood ready to fight, feet spread apart, both hands holding tightly to the hilt of her sword.

"Timorous." There it was again, someone calling her name.

Deamon stood twenty feet away. Holding his sword with his large clawed hands and his face filled with rage, he towered over her even from this distance.

"Tims, down here," someone called from the below the cliff.

Should she take a quick look?

Deamon watched her carefully. As quickly as possible, she looked over her shoulder. The chasm looked bottomless, and she almost fainted from the sight.

Deamon took advantage of the situation and made one large step toward her.

She noticed his bold move.

"Tims, down here."

This time Deamon seemed to have heard it too. Hatred filled his face, and he ground his teeth.

"Tims."

She had to see who called for her. Taking a step back, she looked again. There, fifty feet below, standing on a rope strung tightly across the chasm was Radimar.

"Jump!" Radimar shouted.

"What?" She couldn't believe her eyes or ears. This had to be some kind of trick. There was no way anyone—not even Radimar—would be tightrope-walking across what looked like a bottomless chasm. Would he?

She glanced back at Deamon. His eyes were pinned on her. A low growl built in his throat, and he bared his teeth like a wild animal ready to pounce on its prey. Taking another step, he could easily reach her now.

Tims gripped and re-gripped the sword's hilt nervously, willing herself to stay focused on who stood in front of her. It didn't help to be distracted by Radimar's voice calling to her.

Deamon prowled around Timorous in a semi-circle. He moved close enough to look over the cliff. She didn't think he could look angrier than he already did, but there was no denying the deep abhorrence on his face. He looked back at Timorous and laughed mockingly, now realizing her dilemma. His menacing glare sent a chill down her spine. He was going to kill her.

Louder than before, she heard Radimar's voice. "Jump, Tims. Trust me. Jump, I'll catch you."

Tims' mind raced. That's crazy. That couldn't be Radimar. Even if it was, there was no way she could jump off a cliff and expect someone on a tightrope to catch her.

"So, here we are," Deamon sneered. "Just your tiny nothingness against the mighty Deamon. I will cut you down. Or maybe I'll just push you off." He took a quick short step toward her.

She flinched, taking a small step closer to the edge.

Deamon laughed as he continued to make half-circles back and forth around her, keeping her pinned against the edge of the cliff.

Holding the *Sword of Actualities* at full arm's length in front of her, she waved it around. Yet to her surprise, her arms didn't grow weary. Now she understood, *Actualities* was full of all that is true and right. And the truth was light.

Deamon swung his sword at her in what seemed like slow motion. When it struck her sword, a great clash split the air. From her blade, a bright light burst forth. She almost lost her balance, stumbling but not falling. Closing her eyes probably didn't help either.

Deamon seemed shaken too. Tims saw the confusion on his face, but he regained his composure quickly.

"You don't even know what you are doing, your smallness." He bowed mockingly, spreading his arms wide as he did so, never taking his eyes from her.

Tims was even closer to the edge of the cliff. Again, she heard Radimar. "Jump, Tims. I'll catch you. You can trust me." She looked back for a split second, feeling dizzy.

Taking advantage of her shakiness, Deamon thrust his sword at her. She ducked to the right. This time she did lose her balance, falling back just inches from the cliff edge. She jumped to her feet and tried to run away from the edge. He blocked her with a large arm on one side and the sword on the other. He kept her pinned to the edge, forcing her to fight him.

This is your answer, King Iam? Die by the sword or jump to my death? How could she know for sure it really was Radimar down there? Maybe it was the enemy tricking her.

When Deamon's sword came down with a swish, barely missing her, she leaned to the left and ran a few feet away.

Deamon's last swing had brought him close to the cliff himself. He looked over the edge and spit.

It must be Radimar. Only he would bring such a response. She readied her sword.

Deamon advanced. "So, you have a little rescuer?"

Slash. Slash. Clash!

Tims danced around, swinging her sword with very little proficiency.

Deamon kept her pinned to the cliff's edge as he mocked her. "Really, is that the best he can do for you?"

Clash, clash, clang.

Tims had no strength to speak but could only hold onto the sword when Deamon swung.

"He must care very little for you to ask you to risk so much." He breathed heavily. His strength seemed to be fading, even though he was four times her size. Every time his sword hit hers, she saw his brief pained expression. As the moments passed, she realized he worked to avoid hitting the *Sword of Actualities*, aiming instead directly for her.

With a battle cry, he screamed and swung his sword with one mighty motion. The blow threw her to the ground and knocked the *Sword of Actualities* out of her hand. She reached for the sword just as it fell into the nothingness below.

Deamon laughed. "You're next."

Chapter 50

Dread filled Timorous as she lay on the ground near the cliff edge. How could she fight the Obliterist with no weapon?

Deamon salivated over killing her, acid literally dripping from his ugly mouth. It sizzled as it hit the ground.

She heard Radimar's voice and turned her head to listen.

"Trust me. I have already overcome the enemy. His only true weapon is deception. Take the leap of faith."

On her belly, where she now lay, Tims noticed a small patch of white flowers with red centers and a splash of red on each of their four petals. Promise Flowers, she remembered Radimar telling her. She argued within herself. What good promise can come of this? But Radimar never hurt her. He only tried to help her. She heard Deamon snarl behind her but couldn't stop staring at the Promise Flowers, trying to focus on what was true.

"Giving up so easily." He tried to pull her attention back to him. When she didn't look his way, he unexpectedly screamed in pain.

Startled, Timorous jumped up and looked at him. Deamon was on the ground, his hands over his ears and his sword useless on the ground.

Teetering on the very edge of the cliff, Tims heard Radimar call to her.

"Jump. Trust me. You are safe with me."

She briefly glanced toward the cliff. Is that really *him*? Or is it a trick?

Deamon let out another cry as if severely wounded.

Tims' attention flew back in his direction. Deamon laid on his back, struggling to get enough air into his lungs. Tims tried to see where he'd been wounded but saw nothing.

Deamon exhaled loudly and went very still. "You win," he weakly conceded. "I have no strength left. You are free to go." Deamon appeared completely paralyzed. His sword had fallen several feet away. His eyes were mostly closed and he labored to breathe.

She hesitated to move.

"Don't you see? You've won. The power of my enemy has overtaken me. You have completed your quest. I have no strength to fight." He coughed a couple of times as spit dribbled from the corner of his mouth. He peeked in her direction and continued to lie there unmoving.

Tims felt torn, yet a bit of hope began to grow. Maybe there was no need to jump. King Iam had opened another way. This pleased her very much. She'd taken more risks in the last day than she had in a lifetime. She took a tentative step away from the cliff.

"Don't buy into his lies, Tims," Radimar's voice sounded from below. "There is no life except through me."

Or was that voice a lie, too? Her body gave an involuntary shake at the thought of jumping off the cliff.

Deamon growled and coughed but didn't move.

Tims took another step away from the cliff, watching Deamon but listening for Radimar. Out of the corner of her eye, something moved. She stared into the dense jungle-like forest but saw nothing.

Deamon groaned louder, as if in pain, jerking her attention back to him. "I am powerless against you."

Relieved to see he still hadn't moved, Tim's eye caught another movement, some kind of motion to the right of her. Was that the gleam of a sword?

"Tims, I have chosen you. Choose me." Radimar's calm, confident voice reached her.

She looked back toward the cliff. *What is right? Who should I believe?*

Just then, Miss Enchantress ran screaming out of the dense forest toward Tims, a sword raised above her head. Her appearance kept shifting again like static on a television, flickering between her ugly skeletal, flesh-dripping self and her façade of beauty.

Fear filled Tims to the core. She took two steps back.

"We still own you." Deamon was still on the ground but shifted to his side, leaning on his elbow to watch the show. "You see, insignificant one, once we persuaded you to fear, you took over the job for us. You chose us." He laughed maliciously. "Sure, we kept our underling of Fear on you, but you fed him, you nurtured him."

Miss Enchantress was rushing in her direction while Deamon worked to crush her spirit.

Tims' eyes filled with tears.

"Don't be so hard on yourself. You were one of the best at feeding fear." He laughed again.

For the first time, Timorous could see it clearly. Throughout her life, almost all of her decisions were based on fear. She worried herself sick over things that might be but rarely ever were. She couldn't imagine living without fear. She began to weep. There was no hope for her. Deamon was right. They owned her because fear owned her.

Even Miss Enchantress stopped to watch her misery.

Tims fell to the ground with soul-twisting grief and sobbed.

"Tims . . . Tims . . . Tims . . . Listen to me." Radimar broke through her heartache.

She sucked in shallow breaths, trying to stop wailing long enough to hear.

"Tims, I can take your greatest fears and turn them into your greatest strengths." Radimar's words were a salve to her soul.

Hearing their enemy's words, Miss Enchantress and Deamon became enraged. Deamon roared like a hungry lion and stood. Miss Enchantress took up her screaming and ran straight for Timorous, sword ready in her bony, bloody hand.

Tims stood to face her future.

Miss Enchantress was just seconds away from reaching her.

As Tims looked straight into her opponent's blood-thirsty eyes, she felt another shift in her heart. Taking one last step back, Tims now stood on the very edge of the cliff. "I choose Radimar." With that, she spread her arms out wide and let herself fall backward into the bottomless chasm.

She could hear her enemies screaming in defeat fade away as she fell.

ALL OF BLISS REJOICED as another tear in Obscurity was ripped open, creating another hidden path to further the Gathering until the time of the great war. Each new tear weakened Peccadillo's kingdom.

THE GROUND SHOOK IN Obscurity. Deamon and Miss Enchantress' swords fell from their hands and their bodies jerked as if they had been struck with a force that sucked a piece of strength from them.

THROUGHOUT THE NETHERWORLD, Peccadillo's screams could be heard,"Nooo!"

All those in his kingdom experienced a spasm of weakened strength. Usher gasped for breath. "My Prince, our enemy uses the insignificant to continue weakening our power."

"We. Must. Stop. Them!" In a blink, Peccadillo transformed into his dragon-like self but his temporary loss of power kept him pinned to the floor and incapable of taking his wrath out on Usher.

Chapter 51

Tims felt the wind rushing past her and wondered how long it would take to reach the bottom of the chasm. This would be her end. She had failed. Closing her eyes, she cried.

Moments later, the wind became gentler and she felt as if she were floating. She took a deep breath. It smelled like a fragrant garden. Peace and comfort wrapped around her. She'd never felt so relaxed in all her life. If this is what death felt like, wow, she didn't want this feeling to go away.

"Timorous." The voice kind of sounded like Radimar.

"Tims . . ." *Or was that Essince?*

"Tims, open your eyes."

She smiled but shook her head. She didn't want this feeling to stop and felt certain opening her eyes would end it all.

"Tims, you're safe."

She sighed happily. "I can tell."

She heard a familiar gentle chuckle. Her eyes snapped open.

Radimar held her in his arms and gave her another sunrise smile.

"You caught me?"

He chuckled again and placed her on her feet, but they weren't on a tightrope. They were in a wide-open meadow. It was bright and so green. Flowers lined several pathways to the bluest, most peaceful stream one could ever imagine.

"Where are we?"

"We are in Green Meadows. It's a place of rest." Radimar watched her look around.

When she made eye contact with him again, he spoke with excitement. "I have so many things to share with you." He took her into his arms.

Tims felt power pass through her and warm her hands. The scratches and wounds there disappeared before her eyes. In fact, every one of her wounds had healed. "How did you do that?"

When he released her, he held on to her shoulders, making sure his power had not left her on shaky legs. She inspected her still filthy body. For some reason, she didn't feel embarrassed about her appearance.

"All good things come from King Iam—even the power to heal."

Tims looked up at him with her usual guppy-face pose. He put his finger under her chin, closing her mouth, and looked deep into her eyes. She felt as if she would melt.

"I'm so proud of you, Tims. You didn't let fear hold you back," Radimar beamed.

Essince instantly appeared. "Correction. *We* are proud of you. Now that you've completed your quest, we must change this name of yours. It no longer suits you. What do you think, Radimar?"

Radimar didn't hesitate. "We will call you Audacious." He held her hand as she processed this new name.

"What does Audacious mean?"

"It means fearless—just like you."

She liked it. She didn't want to be identified with fear any longer. He continued to look at her with loving pride. She felt almost embarrassed, but not quite. Her heart sang with his praise.

"Is that how you see me?"

Radimar's eyes shone bright gold. "I've always known you as Audacious. You just haven't been able to see it until now. We've planned for you long ago. You are capable, kind, and brave."

Warmth filled her cheeks. She wasn't used to being complimented. "Audacious. I like it." She needed more time to believe it, but she decided to work on it. Audacious felt overwhelmed by Radimar's love for and belief in her.

She looked around, taking in the beauty of this place of rest. "How did we get here? I remember falling. I saw the chasm."

"It was all an illusion. Remember how I told you the only tool left to the enemy is deception? He's quite skilled at it."

"You mean it was really a lie?" Audacious thought back over the last couple of days and wished she'd been able to figure it out. But it had all felt so real.

"Yes. They were trying to deceive you into believing you had no choice, that you were trapped. But you overcame." Radimar smiled proudly.

The brightness and power of Radimar and Essince's presence together was overwhelming. Audacious almost lost her balance being so close to them, but Essince caught her. Her whole body was relaxed. She wanted to lie down in the presence of peace that enveloped her.

"You two need to . . . . um . . . tone down whatever that is." She twirled her index finger around in the air as if trying to explain. "But I like it. It feels amazing."

They all laughed again.

"I have something of yours, Audacious." Essince handed her the chain with the heart-shaped locket. Her eyes grew wide. "Yes, the *Book of Actualities* is in it."

Audacious held it reverently in her hand while tears blurred her vision. "But how? I lost the sword, I mean the *Book of Actualities,* over the cliff. How did you find the locket?"

"You may have felt like you lost the truth, but you can never lose King Iam's *Actualities* once it's been given to you. The time you spent with Warder reading the *Book of Actualities* helped to hide its truth in your heart of hearts. And the locket was easy. We have our ways." Essince winked at her. "The enemy has no real power over us."

"Many people have been deceived and think they no longer need the *Book of Actualities,*" Radimar sadly explained. "But the truth is still buried deep in their hearts. They have only to choose to open their hearts again." He touched her shoulder. "Now, I need to take care of a few things. Essince will show you around."

Audacious watched him walk away, then turned to ask Essince her burning question. "Why would they close their hearts to the truth? Can't people see you are the answer?"

"The enemy is cunning. He convinces people they have all the answers and have no need of King Iam. People begin to rely on their own knowledge and strength. It's not so strange and can happen quite easily. This is why you must always guard your heart. Read the *Book of Actualities* so you can remember the truth."

A few paces away, a group of people were gathering around Radimar. They appeared to be of all ages and cluster origins. Audacious wanted to ask who they were but didn't want to interrupt the meeting, which had apparently just started.

Radimar stood on a rock and called them to attention. "You are an important part of the Gathering and have been specifically chosen for this work. Each of you proved yourself through your quest and your choice to follow King Iam. The time is short to complete our mission, and we don't want to lose anyone to our foe. We will soon be in full battle with the enemy, but we already have the victory."

Everyone cheered enthusiastically.

"Your job will be to awaken the *Truth of Actualities* in others who have not yet heard or have been deceived by the enemy. We must gather as many as possible before the end. You will be sent in small groups of two or three to draw the least amount of attention. Each quest will be difficult, but you will grow stronger and stronger."

Essince held up the *Sword of Actualities*. "To King Iam."

Everyone quickly followed, including Audacious.

"To King Iam."

The power of that moment sent a ripple effect across all the clusters. While the seen world felt a mighty gust of wind, the unseen Netherworld trembled in fear, and Bliss shouted with joy.

Epilogue

Audacious spent a few days resting along with the others who had gathered in Green Meadow. They ate together and got to know each other. They roomed in groups of ten. Audacious liked every one of them and loved hearing their stories of how they had overcome Peccadillo's hold on them.

Essince and Radimar where constantly in their midst, teaching, encouraging, and warning them about the enemy's deception. Even the chosen could still be led astray.

Several teams of people were sent out every couple of days. Audacious wondered who she would be partnered with. After seeing the number of people in Green Meadows dwindle, she became more concerned. When their numbers had dwindled to a dozen or so, Audacious decided to just ask rather than to worry about it.

"Essince, I haven't heard who I'm being sent with. When will I know?"

Essince just smiled and pointed toward Radimar. Turning to look, Radimar had his back to her, talking with someone. She noticed a blond head nodding. Then he hugged her.

"No, it couldn't be." Audacious ran to them.

Radimar stepped out of the way as Audacious hugged her friend. "Hearsay, I can't believe my eyes. *How* did this happen?"

"It's great to see you, um, Audacious, right?"

Audacious confirmed with a quick nod.

"You can call me Genuine now. You helped plant the seeds for me to see the way." She smiled shyly at Radimar. "Essince and Radimar helped with the rest."

The girls hugged and laughed. Both had transformed in many ways since they'd last seen each other. They had so many things to catch up on.

"I'm sorry to interrupt this happy reunion," Radimar said. "But we have little time to prepare you two."

Over the remaining days, Essince and Radimar worked closely with Audacious and Genuine, preparing them for their next quest. The day finally arrived when they were ready.

Audacious and Genuine stood on the edge of Green Meadows and clasped the other's hand. They looked to Essince for her send-off.

"I will always be with you." She smiled as she shown brighter than the sun.

The two young conquerors shielded their eyes.

Then they looked forward, giggling with joy, and took one step closer to the edge.

"To King Iam!"

Into Obscurity they went, heading to the cluster of Hopelessness.

About the Author

Stacey Womack is the founder and executive director of Abuse Recovery Ministry Services. She wrote their recovery curriculum, which has been translated into four languages. She is a 2020 Cascade Award Winner and has been published in various magazines. Stacey is married to Jerry Womack and has six children.

Read more at https://www.stacey-womack.com.